ISBN 978-0-9812724-2-9

Near As I Can Recall.....

Short stories

by

Jim Prebble

James Prebble

The Brandon Press

ACKNOWLEDGEMENTS

For being a patient first reader, my wife Elaine.

For word processing and invaluable reaction to the stories, my thanks to Wendy and Richard Haime of Carleton Place, Ontario and Mission, Texas.

For encouragement and expert technical assistance in all stages of producing this anthology, most sincere thanks to Marguerite Boyer, publisher, and David Shanahan, editor, of the Brandon Press,
Oxford Mills, Ontario

CONTENTS

Turnarounds

THE SWIVEL CHAIR

Looking back, I have two striking recollections of that time. And while they're not necessarily connected, they came together in a way that moves me as strongly now, thirty years later, as it did then, that summer of thirty-four on the Black Sturgeon River, just west of Nipigon and thirty miles north of the Lakehead.

My first powerful impression was of tobacco. More specifically, the effects of tobacco and tobacco juice. Bentley Loomis chewed, hawked, and spat from wake-up to lights-out, and his presence and passings were marked by a tarry black trail outside, and a pungent coffee can forever at his side indoors. And while I may revile the habit today, then it assumed for me an aura of dashing glamour and bravado. Think of Sherlock Holmes and his deerslayer cap, or D'Artagnan and his sword. Bentley Loomis cannot be conjured up without the image of his chaw and the mighty expectoration it produced. Even after I'd sickened myself ingloriously trying to emulate our camp boss, and had dragged my weak and shaky body supperless to my cot, my admiration for his stylish expellations remained undiminished. Tobacco juice was an ever-present and overpowering factor in all our waking hours. However, as strong and pervasive as it was, there was another feature of that summer, something so compelling that it brought Ben's mastication at least temporarily to a halt. It all had to do with an old swivel chair and two little boys from the backwoods of north-western Ontario.

We were working out of an old abandoned farm house on the edge of a tamarack stand on a stream running into Black Sturgeon Lake. I use the word 'house' charitably; the dilapidated structure was little more than a shack, tumbled down and caving in after a decade or more of abandonment. The building consisted of a parlour and a kitchen-dining area, with two cramped bedrooms, hardly more than closets, completing the downstairs. We never did ascend the broken ladder to the loft. A sagging front porch, greying board-and-batten siding and three broken-framed windows admitting more weather than light completed our home away from home. Ben had given his blessing to the derelict structure as we drove into the yard on our first day.

8

"Well, Judas Priest, boys. She's no palace, but lemme tell ya' . . . it beats tentin' 'er!" Splat!

He punctuated nearly every utterance with that grand stream of black juicy sludge, only the smallest trickle of which appeared as a sticky line oozing like treacle down the stubbled creases on either side of his mouth. I'd never seen anyone like this voluble paunchy red-faced bear of a man. Elwood had worked for Ben the summer before, and had given me some idea of what to expect, but nothing could have fully prepared me for this grizzled old-timer who was to oversee our labours through ten weeks of cutting a survey line for Abitibi from Black Sturgeon Lake to the English River.

I think Ben wore the same red-checked flannel. shirt the whole summer, though maybe he had more than one. The long-johns threw me at first, but Elwood said the old-timers did that, wore long underwear the year 'round, to soak up the sweat. It was his arms and hands that established Ben physically ... massive untanned forearms and chunky weathered paws the size of shovels, with seven sausage fingers still intact. And could he talk! His stories, drawn from over forty years in the bush and rendered with raspy gusts and coloured by that magnificent spit, were endless. As long as he could regale us with tales of life in the camps, Ben was content to oversee our labours with minimal exertion on his part. Not that we over-extended ourselves; much of our work time was taken up just getting to and from the site, bumping and rattling along in Ben's wheezy old International, then hiking in to the line for three or four hours cutting and piling, then hiking out again and bumping back to the base.

"Judas Priest, boys. Let's not break our backs here, now. We'll get 'er done b'fore she snows." Splat!

Ben worked the compass and transit while Elwood and I held the rod, did the pacing, and wielded the axes. There was little heavy cutting; most of it was through alder swamp and across blueberry bog and over miles of old burn. We could have cut a mile a day. In the first week, before I'd twigged to the rhythm, Ben had put the brakes on me a couple of times.

"Whoa ... whoa ... Judas Priest, boy, slow'er down there, lad." Splat! "Elwood, you gotta show young Walter here the proper pace. He's gonna have us back at the Lakehead next week if he don't slow down. We got all summer, lads." Splat!

It was a summer job most of my classmates would have killed for.

The two youngsters showed up one day just after supper in our third week there. Elwood saw them first and called me to the rear of the old house. There, a path diverged around the wood pile, one branch leading fifty yards into a poplar stand and a three-sided privy, while the other swung down to a brook that ran fast and cold over moss-covered rocks and served as our refrigerator. Two boys, probably six and eight, and indisputably brothers, were at the woodpile, watching the old shack with a mixture of curiosity and trepidation. They seemed poised for instant flight.

"Hey, guys, what's up?" At my greeting, they edged back to the corner of the woodpile. "Hey . . . I lowered my voice, "it's okay ... nobody here's gonna hurt you."

The younger boy pushed his brother forward and then fitted himself in behind and peered around at us. I saw two frightened, curious little under-nourished monkeys, at once captivated by and wary of this human contact. Certainly neither I nor Elwood should have posed any serious threat. Elwood spoke then.

"You guys live around here? Where's your house?"

Surely they couldn't be far from home, boys that young. But our old farmhouse was, as far as we knew, the only habitation for some miles.

"C'mon over here, guys," Elwood offered. "I'll bet there's some cookies left. Bet you guys like ginger snaps ... ?"

Reluctant to meet our eyes, they edged timidly forward to a safe distance of twenty feet or so. They stood and gently kicked at the ground in front of them. The younger boy wore oversized black sneakers that must have been passed down the line more than once. The laces were butcher's twine. The older boy had scuffed worn workboots, also oversized, with soles adhering only patchily to their uppers. He too sported twine laces. They were less tense now, their fear no doubt subsiding at the prospect of Elwood's treats. Each sported a recently-trimmed bowl cut. They wore bibbed overalls, the same size, I'd say, with the older popping out of his while the younger was dwarfed by his ill-fitting garment.

Elwood turned to fetch the cookies. They followed him with wide eyes. I sat on the chopping block.

"So ... are you guys just out for a walk, or what? Where do you live, anyway?"

The older one indicated the tamarack bush. "Back there up t'other side a'that bush." It was a start. Elwood reappeared with the five-pound bag of ginger snaps. Ben was with him.

"Well, lads . . ." Splat! "And who've we got here? A couple a' woods-men, eh, boys?"

They were transfixed and wide-eyed now, torn between the brown bag in Elwood's hand and the stubbled bear-like man with the booming voice and the magnificent spit.

10

"What's yer name, fella?" Ben addressed the older boy. "And this big guy's yer brother, right?" Splat!

"He's Douglas ... an I'm Angus." His eyes went back to the cookie bag as Elwood unrolled the top and held it out. The older boy reached in, seeming at first to be maneuvering for a handful, and extracted two ginger snaps. He handed one to his brother. They turned the cookies over in their hands, eyes once more cast down.

"Go on, boys, go ahead ... eat up. There's lots. Here, Elwood, gimme one a' them cookies." Ben reached in, grabbed a ginger snap and popped it in his mouth. "Ummm, boy, that's good stuff. . . the very best, yessir!" Ben's lead did the trick. The boys attacked their cookies.

"C'mon up to th' house, lads we'll see if there's any milk. Ginger snaps are the very best with milk, y' know. Give 'em some more a them cookies, Elwood."

Ben had won them over. This time they reached individually into the bag and then scampered after him up to the house.

On this first occasion, the boys stayed long enough to devour another dozen cookies while Ben mixed some condensed milk and water and tried to learn more about our visitors. Between bites and sips they offered sketchy information. Home was indeed on the other side of the tamarack bush, where their father cut pulp, hunted, and grew a few vegetables, and had some goats and cows. There were, apparently, a mother (about whom neither boy seemed willing to say much) and two siblings. The more we tried to learn, the less they seemed willing to divulge, preferring to look around the decrepit old building we called home.

For some reason we'd never figured out, there was an old swivel chair in the farmhouse, the kind commonly found in any office in the country. It boasted a contoured well-worn seat and arms giving off a dull oaken shine, and had only one back slat missing. This chair, still in good swivelling order, was an immediate object of wonder and fascination to Angus and Douglas. While Ben plied them with cookies, milk, and questions, their eyes kept shifting to the chair. It was obvious they'd like to try it out, but for now at least lacked the courage. Ben saw the flash of excitement in their eyes when Elwood sat and swivelled the chair.

"Say, boys ... betcha'd like a turn in the chair, eh?" Splatunk. Indoors, the gob landing in the coffee can gave a sodden glutinous sound. "Wanta give'er a try?" And he gave Elwood a mighty twirl

It was enough to interrupt their voracious snacking. The boys watched Elwood's whirling spin as if it must be the adventure of a lifetime. It was obvious they'd like nothing better. But it wouldn't happen this time.

11

"We better go now," Angus announced. "Thank you for the cookies." He nudged his little brother, who repeated, "Thank you for the cookies." Then he took his brother's hand and led him out and across the yard and into the tamaracks.

For the rest of the evening we had a change in routine. Ben's stories were put on hold, and replaced by speculation regarding our visitors.

"Imagine them little buggers comin' up here, alone, through them woods." He cut off a chunk of Red Man and made room for it in his left cheek, oblivious to the still-sizable wad in the right one. "Wonder if they'll be back ... Judas Priest, if they was my kids, I'd tan their little backsides ... wanderin' off like that." Spulunk! "Kinda cute little buggers, though ... Don't suppose we'll see 'em again.

That Saturday, Ben drove into Red Rock to Earl McMahon's General Store. He wanted to know more about the family beyond the tamaracks. He learned that Harland MacWhirter lived with a young Indian woman on ten or twelve acres of windfall and rock-strewn land bordering a small branch of the Gull River. There he and his brood subsisted on his hunting and trapping, and God knew what else. His wife had died delivering their fifth child, leaving father with four surviving children all under the age of seven. In the three years since her death, he'd taken in the native woman (McMahon knew nothing about her, except that she was from somewhere up on the Gull River where Harland hunted and ran a trapline with two of the girl's brothers). The kids were pretty well left to fend for themselves, though McMahon guessed the Indian woman must have given them some attention. She and MacWhirter would show up with the four kids every six weeks or so to buy and barter for flour and salt and the like.

"Yep ... the whole lot a' them. Not much to look at, none a' them." McMahon ran his stubby fingers over Ben's purchases: kerosene, two dishtowels, six plugs of Red Man . "Quiet little fellers ... looked okay to me. But I'd rather see a bit more meat on their bones, if y' know what I mean."

"Well, Judas Priest, we prob'ly won't see the little buggers again. Just in case, though, gimme another bag a' them ginger snaps, Earl. An' half a dozen cans a' Eagle Brand. Just in case. An' a couple a' them chewy bars. No ... them big ones."

"Yer gonna spoil them kids, Ben."

"Yeah? Well ... we'll see. Prob'ly won't see 'em again anyway." He prepared a juicy gob and then remembered he'd left the Maxwell House can in the truck. His mastications continued. "How far you figure they had to walk to git to our camp?"

"Oh, must be a couple a' miles anyway."

12

"Judas Priest! Them little monkeys! Th' older one couldn't a' been more than seven or eight!"

They'd come first on a Thursday. We saw them next on the following Sunday afternoon, the day after Ben's trip to Red Rock. I was splitting cedar slabs when they appeared around the wood pile. Cedar kindling was strewn all around the block and the two boys began gathering the pieces, piling them under the tarpaper lean-to. They kept close watch on the house as they worked. I gave a whistle.

Ben came to the screen door, saw the boys, and hollered, "Hey, you two! When yer through helpin' with the wood pile, c'mon up here and give me a hand, will ya?!"

I finished splitting and stacking the kindling and walked up to the house. Angus, flushed with excitement, sat on the swivel chair, hands clamped to the seat and cheeks bulging with ginger snaps. Little Douglas was squealing with glee as he scampered and wound his brother in a twirling spiral of sheer delight.

"Just give'er a fling there, young lad ... let'er go . . . she'll turn by herself. That's the ticket. . . atta boy!" Ben, also flushed, shouted encouragement and direction to the happily gyrating celebrants. The spinning chair slowed.

"My turn ... my turn ... " Douglas hopped from foot to foot waiting for it to stop. "C'mon, Angus. You turn me now." He clambered up and assumed the same vise-grip on either side of the seat as Angus, heeding Ben's direction, grabbed the back of the chair and gave it a mighty spin. The little boy's eyes widened in terrified delight, and as the chair spun through its orbit he thrust his legs straight out and shrieked his joy.

"More ... more ... do it again, Angus. Whee!" And then, as if remembering where he was, he cut off his shrill scream and said, quietly but still with urgency, "Again, Angus. Push me again!"

Ben put his coffee can on the counter and approached the chair. "Here, you lads. Both a'you git on up there. Go on, Angus, git up there with yer brother. I'll give y'both a spin."

It could have gone on for hours, probably. The boys were transported, and quite immune to dizziness or vertigo. Ben, on the other hand, was good for only a minute or two, and then lurched woozily back to the table where he sat rasping and happily surveying their antics.

It was just past mid-afternoon. Elwood was peeling potatoes and when, finally, the boys had tired enough to pause in their scampering play, he said, "Hey, you guys wanta have supper with us?"

I thought that was dumb. Here they were, hardly more than babies, two miles from home at a place and with people unknown to their parents. They ought to be at home, safe and accounted for, at dinnertime. I don't know why these feelings assailed me at that moment. I looked over at Ben. He dropped a slow, reflective gob into his Maxwell House can and cleared his throat.

"That'd be real nice, boys, supper here with us. But maybe yer folks'd worry if you was late." He watched their faces. In this more solemn moment, after the wild chair rides, Angus had again taken hold of his little brother's hand. "Tell you what," Ben continued, "you prob'ly should ask yer folks first. Say, how 'bout next Sunday. Whaddya think?"

It was hard to say just what they thought. Their recent exuberance gave way to downcast eyes and a barely-audible whisper as Angus said, "Okay. Thank you for the chair rides." And out they went.

Elwood turned back to the potatoes; I found my book; and Ben cut a corner off his plug before busying himself with a worn deck of cards. No one spoke. An hour dragged slowly by, the only sounds the turning of pages, the desultory snap of playing cards, and the regular but now somehow lugubrious moist deposits in the coffee can.

Finally Elwood spoke. "Well, hell. I shoulda thought first. Shoulda kept my mouth shut. But, you know ...

"I know," I tried to help him explain away the solemnity that had descended upon us. "It was only natural ... you know, they were having so much fun with that damn' old chair, and..."

Splurt! "Yep. Well, Judas Priest, they're gone now. Funny how quiet this place gets without them little monkeys around." You'd think they'd been a fixture, to listen to Ben. He was becoming mawkish, I thought, as he mournfully sighed and regarded the sludge in his can. "Don't suppose they even got to finish their cookies, runnin' aroun' that old chair. Did ya see 'em hangin' on fer dear life ... like a coupl' a' little squirrels!" Splurt!

"Wonder if they'll tell their ol' man? D'ya suppose they'll ask about next Sunday? Course, they git to be a nuisance, always under yer feet, y' know ..."

I was setting out plates and Elwood was wrapping a dish rag around the pot handle when we heard the scampering up onto the porch and the knock at the screen door. Ben, in the act of lowering himself onto the bench seat, straightened and turned so violently that the bench went over backwards.

"Judas Priest! What's that ... who's that? Git that door, Walter ... see who's there. Well, I be ... Judas Priest, it's our woodsmen! Come in, lads ... come in. Yer just in time." He turned to give directions, but Elwood was already putting down two more plates and reaching for tumblers and cutlery.

It was hard to believe that in that time they'd been home and back. But there they were, out of breath, flushed and monumentally pleased with the circumstances, and with themselves. Each boy's hair had been carefully

14

brushed and parted, much more precisely, by the look of it, than either of them was capable of.

The stew and condensed milk, followed by limitless ginger snaps, were to us a feast - as I suspect our visitors did in fact regard the meal. Then Ben dragged out a new story, about the time he'd chased a bear out of the cook-house when he'd been cooking for a railroad crew in Algoma. The boys' eyes grew wide as the tale progressed. Their awe spurred Ben to great embellishments. He was in excellent form and high spirits, and gave every indication of just getting warmed up.

Elwood seized an opening when Ben paused to cut another wedge of Red Man.

"Say, Ben. These guys'll prob'ly want another go-round on the chair before they head for home. Whaddya think?"

"Oh ... oh, by Judas Priest, right you are, Elwood. Yessir, you guys better get a spin before ya have to leave. Hop to it, men!"

They attacked the chair, pushing and riding in pure uninhibited joy. Ben beamed like a grandfather. He turned to me at one point and said, "Gotta get that old chair lubricated. Remind me t'git some light oil next time I'm in t'McMahon's."

And then, their playful instincts satisfied for the moment, and without bidding from any of us, they climbed down to go again through their simple departure ritual: little Douglas's hand taken by his older brother, the solemn 'thank you for the supper and the chair rides', and out the door and on their way.

Ben shuffled to the screen door and called after them, "So long, fellas. Git on home now, before dark. And remember, tell yer folks yer invited next Sunday. Bye now, lads."

He turned and found both of us regarding him with some bemusement. There was something inexplicable about the situation. We all, I think, wanted to articulate our feelings, yet somehow we felt restrained. Ben made a gruff attempt. "Judas Priest," he rasped, "those little buggers ... more trouble than they're worth, eh?" Splurt.

It became routine, after that. Our work continued. Ben knew what the company expected as far as the quality of work, straightness of line, amount of clean-up, and rate of progress were concerned. I don't think we missed more than half a day for rain. And the boys became more and more a part of our life that summer. Usually twice and sometimes three times a week we'd drive in after work to find them sitting on the back steps or playing by the wood pile. Despite their fascination with the swivel chair, and with neither door locked - Ben's theory being that locked doors only invited damage -

they never went into the house if we weren't around. But once we arrived and issued the standard invitation, `want't' give'er a spin, boys?', they'd be on that chair before we'd finished speaking. Sometimes they'd stay for the evening meal, usually a couple of cans of corned beef and Elwood's biscuits, and the inevitable ginger snaps, all washed down with diluted Eagle Brand condensed milk. Then a quick spin or two before they hit the trail through the tamaracks.

But Sundays became special, taking on a more formal air, for want of a better term. No fine china and cutlery, no one dressed up. The menu might vary, to include stew rather than corned beef But somehow the three of us, and, I hope the same was true of the boys themselves, came to look upon those Sunday meals as rare and - dare I use the word - privileged occasions.

Early on in our association with the MacWhirter boys, when it became clear that we'd be seeing them more or less regularly around the place, Ben went in to Red Rock for some one- inch rope and a piece of two-by-eight pine. He got us to tie one end of the rope to an oak branch over by the woodpile, and then he fixed an old tire to the other end. And with the ten-foot plank he rigged up a teeter-totter just off the end of the back porch. Strangely, he was almost sheepish in explaining why he'd done this.

"Well, chances are they don't have too much back home, back in the bush an' all." Splat! "Least this'll give 'em somethin' to do if we're not around when they git here." And just to be sure Elwood and I didn't get the idea he was going soft, or crazy, "Course, they're gittin' to be a nuisance, always under yer feet." Splat! "Judas Priest, just what we need, bunch a' kids gittin' in yer way all th'time!"

Right on schedule, according to the Bentley Loomis timetable, the job came to an end the first day of September. We ran the final sighting in the morning, and that afternoon began packing for our departure the next day.

The boys showed up as Elwood and I were loading the truck. For seven weeks they'd been part of our lives, and during that time I don't suppose we'd even thought about, let alone discussed, the end of the job and the severing of this relationship.

Elwood hitched up on the tailgate and regarded the boys. "So, gents," he said, "guess you'll be gettin' yourselves ready for school in a couple a' days. An' you know what? Walter and I are goin' back to school too. In the big city."

The seven weeks had wrought change in the MacWhirters. Initially shy, cautious, and reserved, they'd become scampering chattering squirrels. But today, seeing the gear packed under a tarp in the back of the pickup, and hearing Elwood's words, they became shy and withdrawn. Douglas sought his brother's hand, and edged away from the truck, sheltering behind Angus,

16

who lowered his eyes and said nothing.

We should have anticipated it. . . should have been easing up to it, gradually severing the ties that now seemed perdurable. And then Ben appeared on the porch with the box of surveying instruments. He stopped at the top of the steps and put down the box. He too was caught off guard and unprepared.

"Hullo. . . well ... hey, lads . . ." He sat on the transit box and reached for his plug. "So ... I `spect y've come to say goodbye.." He was flummoxed. "Well ... yep, we're off. . . First thing in th' mornin'. Gotta move on, lads." No response, other than the closing in on each other. Elwood slid off the tailgate and walked over to the woodpile. I wanted to fade away too, but I couldn't. Not with them just standing there. And Ben, old garrulous grandfatherly Ben, never at a loss for words, especially when it came to our boys, was simply buffaloed. He just sat there with the plug of Red Man in his hand and looked beseechingly from me, to the retreating Elwood, to the stoney-faced boys huddled at the rear of the truck. He looked down at the plug as if unsure what it was. He tried again.

"Tell ya what, lads. Me `n Walter and Elwood ... we gotta go to another job. Way t'other side a' th'country. We don't wanta, but th'company's movin' us. . we gotta go. ."

No response. I could see sweat on his forehead. I could think of nothing to say. He tried again.

"Maybe we'll git sent back here to this ol' house, next summer. We'll see you fellas then, ever' day."

It was no good. He was not drawing them out; rather, they were withdrawing more as he stumbled on, desperate now.

"Y' know, lads, I could use some good workers on my next crew ... couple a' men like you fellas. Walt and Elwood are goin' back t' school pretty soon." Still they refused to look up. "An' I guess you two'll be heading off t' school, too ... otherwise, I'd take ya with me ... yessir, you'd be comin' t'work fer me at th' Lakehead."

"We gotta get back now," Angus said then. "C'mon, Douglas." And simple as that the boys slipped around the truck, past the woodpile and into the tamaracks.

We played euchre for an hour after supper that night. It was a dismal game, a dismal last night in the old farmhouse. Not much was said, either about the game, or the job just finished, or the year ahead. At one point Ben snapped at me.

"Cryin' out loud, Walter, you gonna play that card or not? Judas Priest, you guys are more dam' trouble than yer worth! Sometimes wonder why I bother with y'at all." Splurt! We turned in earlier than usual that night.

17

An urgency to get away overtook us in the morning. We all felt it, the need to put the place behind us and out of sight.

"Throw them things in behind th'seat, Elwood. Leave the rest here. Just coffee, and let's git goin'. Walt, you put the levellin' rod in?"

Ben backed the truck up to the steps and turned to drive out of the yard. And there they were, right in front of the truck. Angus held his brother's hand, and in his free hand each boy carried a small cloth bag with a draw-string fashioned from butcher's twine. Even through the dusty windshield I could see that their faces had been scrubbed and their hair trimmed, brushed, and carefully parted. Ben jammed on the brake, and leaned out the window. Angus beamed up at him.

"Our dad says we kin go with you. To work with you."

Ben leaned his head on his hand on the wheel. "Oh dear sweet suffering Jesus," he groaned. Elwood reached over and turned off the ignition. No one spoke; the smiling faces, freshly scrubbed and eager, were more than any of us could bear to look at. Ben croaked to the floorboards, "Oh God ... oh, sweet jumpin' Judas Priest! I never thought . . . I didn't mean that they ... oh, God, what'm I gonna say t'these little boys? What kin I tell 'em."

Elwood nudged me and opened the door. We slid out of the truck. He stuck his head back in and said softly, "Ben, you just take a couple a' minutes with the boys. Me 'n Walt are gonna start down the road. Just tell em it's a misunderstanding. . . you were only foolin' around ... you know. They'll be okay, Ben. You just talk to 'em and then pick us up down th' road."

We were at least an hour, Elwood and 1, hoofing it down the road before we heard the old International growling up behind us. I looked at Ben as he slowed and stopped. He held the wheel in a death grip and stared straight ahead. We climbed in and Elwood pulled the door shut.

The silent trip to town seemed endless.

18

A FEW CHOICE WORDS

The first three years of Jeremy Buckle's life were almost normal. He responded with happy smiles to the loving warmth of beaming parents and doting grandparents. All seemed well, and even when his mother Stella voiced her concern about his slow development, specifically with respect to verbal skills, his father Tom was unperturbed.

"No worry, Stell. Give him time. He'll be talking soon enough, an' then you won't be able to shut him up!"

But all the other two-or three-year olds she knew, or heard about through her knitting club, were talking, some in complete sentences. Jeremy had no vocabulary. He had attempted some sounds, sibilant, sometimes guttural, but nothing that anyone could describe as words.

"I was reading the other day that Robbie Burns didn't talk until he was three," Tom said, on an afternoon when he'd come home to find Stella in tears. "And then, when he did talk, he came out with sentences. Probably rhyming."

Stella was not comforted. "Tina Ramsey was here today, with Colin. He's not even two yet. And he knows dozens of words. And he can count to 20..." And the tears continued.

"Stell, he'll talk soon enough. He's bright. You see the way he plays. And he loves the National Geographics. He's taking it all in. An' when he's ready, he'll surprise us all!"

The surprise did come, soon after that, on an afternoon when Stella had exhausted herself with the efforts to coax a word from the reluctant child. Nothing she did with word or action could elicit a response, and she sank back on the sofa in desperation. Jeremy looked in bemused silence at his mother as she lay there with an arm flung over her tired eyes. And then he got down on his knees and tugged at her arm, and said, "M...m...mu...mu....mu...."

Stella sat up and stared at her son. "What's that, Jeremy? What did you say?" She reached to hug him. "Tell Mummy again, sweetie. What did you say?"

Jeremy tried. "M..m..m...mu..."

19

Stella hugged him to her. "I know, sweetie. I heard you." And this time the tears were tears of joy. "Try again," she said, "nice an' slow...mummy....I know you can do it. Try again, mummy; that's th' boy...."

But nothing came, just the strangled "m...m...mu...mu...." And Jeremy buried his head in his mother's lap. And nothing she could say or do that day could change anything. She knew then that there was something seriously, frighteningly wrong. At the very best, she knew, their son was a stutterer. At worst, he might never speak.

"Well, at least we know the problem now, Stell. And now we'll find the solution. Lots of kids stutter, and they can fix that. It's the1970's, not the 1920's....Don't worry."

Within a week they had an appointment with a children's speech thera-pist. They went with renewed optimism once a week for two months, at the end of which time Dr. Spalding told them their son's case was unique to his experience and beyond his capacity to treat.

"But you've done wonders with kids," Tom protested. "We read about your work, about your successes. Surely Jeremy's no worse than many other kids you've treated. Can't you say there's some improvement? It's been two months."

"I'm sorry. I've put Jeremy through every test I know. After a couple of sessions, you know, we get a pretty good idea...With Jeremy, I'm not sure....I can't find any physiological cause for his inability to speak."

"What does that mean? Is he....is there some brain damage?"

"Not that we can see. But...ah...well, we can see nothing to explain it, except that he has chosen not to speak. It's as if he's made this decision, and---."

"---Doctor, he's three years old!"

"I know. As I told you, this case is unique. And baffling. Consciously or not, I can't say, this boy has chosen not to talk. Now, is it permanent? I can't say. At this point, it's wait and see..."

They tried other specialists, including psychologists. But the diagnoses differed very little, wherever they turned. All the experts agreed: the boy could speak if he chose to. It appeared that he had chosen not to.

The Buckles were determined to provide a normal life for their nearly-normal child. Birthday parties, tee-ball, Little League–all elements which they hoped might spur Jeremy to verbal utterance. And he played well and hard, proving to be a good little athlete, enjoying more successes on the play-ing field than Tom and Stella might have hoped for. Except in the matter of speech. He followed directions, knew the rules, and played his heart out. In school, he did very well, handing in clear and coherent writing assignments,

20

and scoring well in all his tests.

Inevitably, Jeremy became the target for those who loved to find and exploit weakness in others. He was the butt of jokes and pranks. It was almost as if his tormentors assumed his muteness was matched by deafness, and often he was openly mocked.

"Dummy", "Belt Buckle", "Suckle"...he heard them all, some much worse than others, and he responded as the bullies no doubt intended, with his fists. It wasn't long before he gained a certain reputation, and notoriety might better describe his stature after he broke the nose of a particularly obnoxious cretin two years his senior.

"I don't want him fighting," his mother said.

"He's gotta fight, Stell. It's the only way he can make his point," his father said.

"You have to stop this fighting, Jeremy. Somebody's going to get hurt badly," his principal said.

It was worse with the girls. By age twelve, Jeremy was, like every other twelve-year-old boy, aware of girls. Their mockery was especially painful. Would verbal response have spared him the mortification and hurt? If so, he never took the step.

In high school, his reputation either preceded him, or was established very early on. He was not one to torment or challenge. In his sophomore year he played varsity football. As a fearsome middle linebacker he led his team to successive city championships and was touted for athletic scholarship. Half-a-dozen big name colleges had him on their lists.

"He's the best high school player I've seen in twenty years," his coach said. "He'd be captain of the defensive squad, if he could talk. But y' know, y' need someone out there who can call the defensive numbers. He can't do it. But just th' same....I'm tellin' yuh, when he hits, he brings a load!"

Academically, he brought a load as well. "This guy is amazing," his teachers would say, adding, "It's as if he's on the very edge of talking, y' know, and then he just seems to pull back. I swear, it's as if he could talk if he wanted to."

It was an accurate observation. While his communication at that time was achieved through action and the occasional nod or shake of the head, in both elementary and early high school years he had gone so far as to mouth a 'y...y...y...yeah' or a 'n...n...n...no'. But the attempts had seemed so forced and painful and each attempt had caused a further withdrawal. Besides, without the awkward attempts, the real and imagined taunts came less frequently. Even worse than the mockery, as far as he was concerned, was the pity he was sure he could see in the eyes of those who witnessed but did not participate in his mortification. He could fight the spoken taunts; pity hurt much more.

And so the self-imposed exile by silence seemed to be his lot in life. And then, near the end of his senior year, he met Adrian Franklin.

It was in the school cafeteria where a new student, smiling nervously, bespectacled, and reed-thin, was causing a hold-up among the dozens of students in line for lunch. He was trying to make his requests, the serving lady couldn't understand him, and those behind were becoming noisily impatient.

"G...g...gi....give me a b...b...." And he couldn't get it out. There were titters and curses, mild at first, but as precious time passed ,their amusement turned mean.

"Try singin' it, loser..."

"Spit it out, four-eyes..."

"Ain't got all day, marble-mouth."

And then Jeremy, all six foot two and two hundred twenty pounds of him, was in front of the tormentors, and they fell silent. He needed no words to convey his menace. Turning his back on them, dismissing them with a contemptuous shrug, he moved up to the new boy and handed him a pen and a page torn from one of his notebooks. He nodded to the selections displayed behind the glass. The boy took the pen and paper, smiled, and wrote 'muffin', 'yogurt', and 'iced tea'. The order was promptly filled, and Jeremy nodded the newcomer to a table near the exit. He took the paper from the boy's tray and wrote his name on it. The boy read the name, scribbled 'Adrian' below it, and extended his hand.

"Hi, J...J...Jer...Jeremy. Th....th....thanks..."

So began a firm friendship between the two afflicted boys. They got by through the exchange of nods, gestures, and short notes. Adrian was keen to attempt verbalization, but it was halting and incomplete, and not much beyond Jeremy's self-imposed muteness. The exchange of information via short notes became their chief form of communication. Adrian, unlike his new friend, was by nature, docile. He never did display the anger that characterized much of Jeremy's behavior. Although continually frustrated by his inability to communicate, he showed an unfailing determination to succeed, taking every opportunity to try to force the words out.

A month or so into the friendship, Adrian suggested Jeremy accompany him on a Friday evening to meet some friends at his church. By this time in Jeremy's life, social outings were rare to non-existent, as he refused to expose himself to more failure and humiliation. Adrian would not be put off, though, and finally Jeremy agreed to go.

It turned out to be a group of five young men and the minister meeting in the minister's study every Friday night to confront their shared speech

22

impediments. All were stutterers, and all had struggled with the problem from birth. The minister, Dwight Mosley, was himself a stutterer. When Adrian and Jeremy entered the room, Mosley rose to greet the newcomer. He extended a hand to Jeremy, and spoke slowly and deliberately. "Wel.... come, Jer-e-my. Ad...rian....told...us...about...you...We're...glad...you... came...Please ...take...a...seat."

Jeremy's skepticism was not dispelled that evening, nor in the next half-dozen Friday nights. He saw the two-hour sessions as exercises in frustration and futility, painful attempts by the boys to verbalize individual words, strings of words, fractured sentences. But he continued to attend, to observe if not to participate, to witness the laborious slow encouragement of Minister Mosley as he prompted and prodded and applauded the halting attempts of speech. Adrian, with his skinny shoulders hunched, his pinched face flushed in concentrated effort, was probably the least accomplished among the boys, but the most determined, the most focused on the task. On those rare occasions when he was able to get through a whole sentence, even though it was usually a mix of strangled grunts and staccato bursts, his face lit up in triumph as he and Mosley exchanged high-fives.

As the weeks went by, and Jeremy's reluctance to participate solidified, he became aware of two things. Here in Mosley's office, he saw something in Adrian, saw a brightness in the skinny boy's eyes, saw a pallor that hadn't been obvious when they'd first met, and saw a tremor that accompanied his most strenuous exertions. And he realized with shock that he was seeing his friend regressing, physically, slipping even as he urged the others around him onward and upward, determined, it seemed, to extract success from the others if he himself could not make progress. Jeremy was witnessing, by slow but sure increments, the physical deterioration of his friend.

And the other thing Jeremy was becoming more attuned to was the special attention Adrian was receiving from the reverend Mosley.. While the minister spread his efforts among all the boys, there was no doubting that Adrian got the lion's share, as if the minister's great goal in life was the restoration of speech in this particular boy.

It was almost enough to spur Jeremy, to convince him to make the effort that he saw all around him. But his anger was stronger than his will to succeed. The very few times he made an attempt, the outcome was predictable—barely controlled fury, clenched fists banging down on his knees. The hopeful expectant eyes of the group would focus elsewhere, choosing not to see the internal struggle evident in the rigid body, the flushed face. And Jeremy would sink back in a few seconds, scowling, beaten again, and inwardly vowing never to repeat the humiliating exercise.

'Easy...does...it Jeremy," the minister would caution at the end of the mini-rage fueled display. "No...s...sense...in b....beating.....yourself up. N... nothing....gained..."

And of course he was right. The exertions, rare as they were, and the predictable failures, were doing no one any good. Failure was almost the team emblem here, and how the boys handled their failures was the key to any successes they might achieve. No more, Jeremy promised himself, no more attempts.

In Jeremy's third month of the weekly sessions, after another of Adrian's unproductive performances, and Jeremy's flat refusal to make any more attempts to get words out, everyone present was struck by the condition of his friend. Adrian's attempts that night had been weaker than any Jeremy had witnessed over their time together. And even more unsettling, rather than offering smiles of encouragement and high-fives to anyone showing even the slightest progress, Adrian barely looked up, and had no smiles for anyone. The reverend Mosley was obviously attuned to the change in demeanor, and kept a watchful eye on him throughout the evening.

At the end of the session, the minister had an announcement. "B...boys, we....have ....a special....g...guest...next...week." The boys paused in their departure. "You'll...meet....H....H...Harley....G.....Gaines..."

Jeremy's head snapped up. All the boys responded, none with more alacrity than Adrian. Harley Gaines!! An N.F.L. legend...the 'Undertaker'.... Coming to next week's meeting! The boys came back into the room pounding each other on the back, high-fiving and smiling their excitement. Adrian, snapped out of his funk, seemed fit to burst. Harley Gaines!

'Well', thought Jeremy, 'maybe I won't quit 'til after I see Harley Gaines.'

They all arrived early for their next meeting. Reverend Mosley was already there, at the desk, standing and talking in carefully modulated conversation with the great man himself. Harley Gaines, still fit and menacing at six-foot-four and a shade under three hundred pounds, looked at the expectant faces and waited for the reverend Mosley to speak.

"B..boys, this...man...n...needs...no...intro....duction. Har...ley...Gaines."

"Thank...you....Dwight. You boys...never...saw...me...play...I'm...sure.... my.....last game...was...in...nineteen...seven...ty..."

The boys were shocked. The great Harley Gaines was a stutterer!! How many people, anywhere, knew that, Jeremy wondered. Gaines continued, "D...Dwight...asked...me...t...to speak...to you...b...be...cause...he....knew...I... sh...share...s...some...of your...problems. And I want...ed...t...to..speak...to... you...t..to...t..tell...you...there's...hope..for...us...all. Th...this...p...problem.... can...be....beat."

24

A revelation, and inspiration. If this great athlete had achieved success, had been able to perform so mightily,....the boys hung on every forced word. Jeremy scarcely heard the words, lost in his images of the great middle-linebacker, images from the past, from news reels, from excited tales of gridiron excellence recounted by his father, taken from magazines and post-ers. No, he'd never seen Harley Gaines play, but the image of the great man had inspired his own play over the past four years. He knew the statistics of the ferocious Cleveland defensive corps, and of Gaines in particular, the scourge of halfbacks and quarterbacks, nine-time All-Star, already in the Hall of Fame. And here he was in the same room, admitting to the affliction that plagued them all.

Gaines spoke, haltingly but confidently, for twenty minutes or so, cau-tioning them against defeatism or self-pity, and giving them some simple exercises for word and phrase formations. At the end, he dropped another bombshell on them.

"I d...don't suppose Dwight ever t...told you, but.....he...was....one...hell of a p...player....himself. At...P...Penn...State...w...wide...re...ceiver. And... he was....the...the...b...best, boys. W..we...p...played...t'...together...but he... wrecked...his knee and..th...that was...the..the end of it....f...for...him."

The boys looked at Mosley. He waved off their admiring questioning glances, and Gaines continued.

"Any...way...b...boys. It's...been great...m...meeting...all of you....and...I... hope...you...all keep up....the fight."

That visit, that speech, lifted the spirits of all the boys, none more so than Adrian. In the next few sessions, his efforts were redoubled, both in his own attempts and in his encouragement of the efforts of others. While he'd been impressed, even awed, by the appearance and the slow but effective speak-ing voice of the great footballer, Jeremy showed no willingness to meet the challenges they'd been given. In fact, another sign of his discontent was now beginning to manifest itself. The signs were subtle, and probably not obvi-ous to the other boys, but reverend Mosley was aware of the change. The suppressed rage had been evident to all. The self-pity was new, and it wor-ried Mosley. The angry Jeremy Buckle was one thing: but an angry Jeremy Buckle feeling sorry for himself was something more serious, he thought.

He decided to try dealing with it from an oblique angle. "B..boys", he said, as they shuffled their notes together and prepared to leave, "y...y'know... there's...always...hope. Y..you...must b...believe that. And...th...that's ...s...so so ....im...portant. B..be..lieve..it;..b..be..lieve in your...selves. Re..mem... ber what H...Harl..ey said. W..work hard; b..believe in...your...selves, and n... never...g...give up. Never...g...give up. When I...f....first..met...Har..ley...he...

couldn't say...t...ten words. B...but he never...asked for..p...pity...or...help. He worked...an...he..ne...never gave up."

The speech tired him. He looked at Adrian, saw the exhaustion in the boy's pinched face, in the sunken eyes behind the thick lenses. A tiredness that no amount of optimism could conceal. And he looked at Jeremy, strong hulking Jeremy, whose sullen eyes and down-turned mouth bespoke a resentment of everything and everyone that conspired against him. He couldn't recall a time, in their brief association, where Jeremy had ever made a genuine attempt at speech. Rather, the boy exuded surrender and capitulation.

Rather than circulate among the boys the next night, Mosley sat at his desk and watched the progress, or lack of it, as the boys struggled to put Gaines's exercises into practice. Adrian was animated, sweating with the efforts of himself and those he tried to push to greater lengths. And there were some recognizable sounds, each of which elicited Adrian's unfailing laugh of delight accompanied by a congratulatory high-five.

Jeremy, as usual, chose to sit morosely by himself. At 8:45, fifteen minutes earlier than usual, Mosley addressed the group. "Okay..boys...enough.. for...t....to..night...Great...work...I'm...p..proud...of..you..all....Jeremy...c...can I...see you..f...for a minute?"

As the boys filed out, Adrian gave Jeremy a slap on the back and a nod to convey that he'd wait outside. Jeremy slouched lower in his seat.

Mosley came and sat beside him. He had a notebook and pen with him. He opened the notebook to show Jeremy a page with four vertical lines, top to bottom, forming five columns. At the top of each column was the name of one of the boys. Jeremy looked at the page, and at the minister, and shrugged.

Mosley began to talk, "Y...you've...been..here..a...about...three months." Jeremy nodded.

"Adrian...brought you...here." And he put a check mark under Adrian's name. "Most of...the...b...boys are....m....making some progress...wouldn't... you say?"

Jeremy nodded, and Mosley put check marks in every column except his.

"S...Scott and d...Dan did...well...this week...d..don't you...th....think?" And he gave them each a check mark. "And..h..have you....n...noticed, Adrian is...the.....f..first...to....give..help..t..to...th...other boys?"

Jeremy tried to look away, but felt compelled to watch as Mosley added another couple of checks to Adrian's column.

"R...Roger...g...got a whole...s....sentence out to..night. Not..p...pretty... but..c..complete."

A check mark for Roger. "And who...s...seemed...happiest..about it?" Another check for Adrian.

26

"Y...y'know, Jer...emy...this...class...was...Adrian's idea in...the...f... first..p...place." He put the pen down. No need to demonstrate any further. Jeremy wanted to leave, but he stayed there...stayed to take whatever more the minister had to unload. He wondered if Adrian would still be waiting.

"When we..st..started..he was...com..completely...m...mute. Had..to ...write...every..thing. L..like you...L...look at him...now. B...but....the... real..p...point is..how..he...wants...t..to..help others."

Mosley was tired. He took up the pen and wrote across the bottom of the page, and passed it to Jeremy. There were three separate notations.

(i) meninigitis - age 14 months

(ii) rheumatic fever - age 4 years

(iii) occular degeneration - age 9 years.

"S..some of..the...p...problems..your..f..friend..has..f..faced. Oh...I... forgot...severe headaches...al...almost every...d...day. I'm...g...guessing... you...d...didn't know...these things, Jeremy. And...this....b...boy...has more s...spirit and c..courage...than..anyone..I...know. And he wants...success for...every....one...you..especially. No...you...Jeremy. In...t...twenty-one...c... classes, what...have...you...done? What...have..you...a..a..attempted, even?"

Jeremy looked at the clock, and hung his head.

"Y..you..c.can..quit. You..can..stay. I just w...wish you'd give some.. thing...p...positive...to..the...c.class...s...some...effort..or even..a...smile..now.. and..then." He tore the sheet from the notebook and placed it on Jeremy's desk before he rose to leave.

Jeremy stayed away from class for two weeks. In that time, he went over the minister's words and decided there was nothing to be gained from return-ing. Graduation was a week away, and he had to think about his immediate future, whether to go to one of the colleges that had sought him out or to give up on school and football and find employment.

His mother came to his room on the Wednesday. "Jeremy, did you hear about your friend Adrian?" She handed him the paper. The obituary notice was circled. He sank to the bed to read the notice through tear-blurred eyes. Death attributed to congestive heart problems and complications from pneu-monia...he skipped to the bottom...the funeral was two days hence.

The Reverend Dwight Mosley conducted the service. The church was nearly full. Jeremy found a seat in a pew four rows from the back. He saw Harley Gaines and the other boys half-way back. All the others were strang-ers to him.

The service began, and Jeremy let his thoughts wander, thoughts of the past five months, back to his first encounter with Adrian Franklin. The closeness they'd found from the outset, a bond based on shared afflictions.

He recalled the eagerness of Adrian to bring him to meet Dwight Mosley, his confidence that their impediments could be overcome, their working together under Mosley's direction and encouragement. The dominant image was one of Adrian's eager smile, a smile that split his pale face at every instance of success, whether his own or someone else's. An infectious smile, with everyone in the room gaining from it in confidence and joy—everyone except himself, Jeremy realized painfully, as he imagined himself, sullen and pouting in the shadow of his departed friend. And the height of Adrian's joy—the visit of the great Harley Gaines, now sitting among the mourners. Adrian's efforts to succeed and to help others seemed to have doubled after that visit. Jeremy wondered now if part of the reason for that might have been the boy's knowledge of his own frailty, of a weakening body, driving him to make more and more progress before his weaknesses took over completely. With ever-increasing shame Jeremy recalled his own unwillingness to put forth the effort, and the scorn heaped upon him by the minister, and so richly deserved, the last time he'd been in class. And then he realized that had been the last time he'd seen Adrian.

His thoughts were interrupted by remarks now being made by Adrian's grieving father.

"Adrian had few close friends. He made, and treasured, a few acquaintances in his brief life. Some of those, like Adrian, have difficulty with speaking. But there might be some here today who could, or would, give us a brief comment, to recall some aspect of Adrian's life. Adrian's mother and I would welcome any thoughts or reflections along those lines..."

And as Adrian's father sat down, Jeremy rose and made his way to the front of the church and up the three steps to the pulpit. He cleared his throat.

"I was privileged to call Adrian my friend," he began, the words springing easily to his lips.

WORTH

In 1998 the University of Maine awarded a sabbatical to sociology professor Quincy Lott. The stated purpose of the year off was to research the customs and mores of the backwoods mountain communities in five Appalachian states. After twenty years at Orono, Quincy was delighted, and figured the months ahead would provide sufficient fodder for a text book, a comprehensive study of the unique lifestyle of this largely ignored segment of American society.

His wife Mona was somewhat less enthusiastic at the prospect of Quincy being underfoot for a whole year. That is, until he mentioned the $75,000 grant that went with the year off.

"Mone," he said (he'd called her Mone from the outset of the marriage, recognizing the unfortunate blend of her first and their married names), "here's what I'm thinking. We load the van and head out, all four of us, as soon as the kids are out of school. We travel the back roads, we stop at all kinds of places...houses, general stores, garages, whatever....I talk to people, get a feel for them and how they live."

"This'll take us through the summer. I collect all this first-hand material..you know, observations...From what I know about them, the way they speak and think and live, it's a fascinating sub-culture. They're so different from...uh...you know, they're like nothing you've ever seen. Backward, an' clannish, an' suspicious..."

"You think this'll be good for the kids?" she asked.

"Tell you what. You and the kids don't have to get involved. Most times, you can stay in the van, or walk around. With the kids. Or how about you take pictures? That could be really important...pictures. An' I'll be getting a handle on the big picture..."

"What do you say? And then, in the Fall, I'll write it all up, put it all together. You could really contribute, with pictures. And right after Christmas, we'll go someplace, just you and me, someplace special. Maybe Spain, or Hawaii, for a month or so. What do you say?"

Mona's eyes had glazed over as he described the summer routine. Now they lit up. "Well, yeah, I suppose. A month away....What about the kids?"

"What about your mother?"

"Maybe...I'll ask her. Kid's might not be too thrilled, but I'll ask her."

Then, the Lott children were told of their summer plan. Fourteen-year-old Louisa Jane was to enter high school in the Fall. Twelve-year-old Bendix, named after an uncle who'd left Mona a small inheritance, and known, sometimes affectionately, as Bennie, was finishing grade seven. Their reactions were predictable.

"Yeah, Okay. Can we stay in motels with pools an' video games?" asked Bennie.

Lulu was less given to displays of enthusiasm. "Whatever," she said.

They left Orono on the twenty-sixth of June, heading for Bowling Green, Kentucky, from which point Quincy's odyssey would take them through the Virginias, Tennessee, and on south-eastward to the Carolinas and the Sandhills State Forest, near Cheraw.

The kids had been primed, as well as Quincy was able to prepare the two who seemed jaded even before the trip began. Now, as they headed out on I-95 South, he tried again. "Well, guys, here we go. This should be a real adventure for you two...for all of us. And, a real eye-opener. You'll see new country. Wait 'til you see the mountains! And you'll see people like you've never seen before. They may shock you, at first...the way they talk, and dress, and live. They have a language all their own. Probably you won't understand a word they're saying."

They took two leisurely days to get to Quincy's starting point, the Mammoth Cave National Park, and took a motel just outside Bowling Green. Quincy got his maps and schedule organized, and tried once more to prepare them for what the next eight or nine weeks would offer.

"Now remember, kids, these people are different. They'll probably seem backward to you...maybe shy, or standoffish. Try not to stare too long...we don't know how they'll feel about that, or about Mummy taking pictures. Remember, it's a whole new culture you'll be seeing."

Lulu looked up from her Screen Gems magazine long enough to roll her eyes, and Bennie continued flipping through the T.V. offerings. Mona put down her Harlequin romance novel and attempted to help her husband. "Kids...listen to your father. This is very important to him. It should be to you, too. To all of us, if this book sells. Like Daddy says, we're gonna see a whole different..uh..a different side of life here. And you can learn a lot... we can all learn something here. Kids?"

"Whatever."

For the first few days, as Quincy made his first tentative forays into the

30

new and strange world, they were caught up in the novelty of the project.

"Lookit that dumb hick, Bennie," his sister sniggered, twisting around to get a better look. "Get a picture of him, Mom."

"Where, which one?"

"She means the one Daddy's talkin' to now. I heard him tryin' to tell Dad something, but holy cow, I couldn't understand a word!"

Mona fumbled excitedly with her new Minolta, but by the time she was ready to shoot, Quince was back at the van.

"What was that dumb bunny tryin' to say, Dad? Could you make it out? Don't they know anything, these hillbillies? Do they even have schools out here?"

"Now, Bennie, that's not fair. They seem backward to you, but don't forget, they..." Quincy's admonition faded as the kids continued their backseat mockery and mimicry.

Mona, too, tried at first to counsel them. "Lulu...Bennie...you know better than that. You shouldn't poke fun at people for being different. They're probably very nice people. An' they probably haven't had the upbringing you kids have had. Just watch and you'll learn lots this summer. And give me more warning, all of you, when there's a chance for me to get a picture."

Most times, Mona stayed in the van with her Harlequin and the air conditioner running while the kids ran off their boredom cavorting over the rock strewn yards of the 'hicks 'n hillbillies' being interviewed by their father. Occasionally Quincy would beckon to Mona to bring the camera, to record some side of this 'new and different' world he was examining. And these moments seemed to provide Bennie and Lulu with their greatest amusement, as the subjects, unused to such attention, posed stiffly and seriously for Mona's shots.

"What a bunch of morons. You can't understand them, they live in dumps, an' they let you take their pictures, like they're proud to be such hicks!"

"Oh, Lulu, that's not fair, Honey."

"Well, I never saw such dumps, why don't they fix 'em up? An' why do they just leave everything lying around, like those old trucks, an' washin' machines?"

"That's enough, you two. Let's not be so critical, okay. I think those pictures should be good, Mone."

The scenery was sometimes majestic, and, more often than not, gloomy and depressing. Mona read her romance novels and waited for the mountains to get another picture, and the kids continued to gawk and derive their pleasures from what they saw to be the misfortunes of the mountain people. Quincy drove and stopped and made notes, and the tasteless mockery continued.

"Hey, lookit. There's a whole family of them goin' down that lane. Holy cow, must be about ten kids. Prob'ly all sharin' one brain!"

"Bennie! What did we tell you!"

"Geez, what a bunch of losers. Look at the clothes, on all of them. Yuck!"

Lulu, with her nose ring and purple hair and fourteen years of fashion sense, was amused and appalled by the strangeness of it all. Bennie was simply amused.

"Yeah, what a bunch of freaks. Do we ever get to see any, like, normal people?"

Mona put her book down. "Now look, you two. Your father has to be here. I have to be here. And you...you don't. We can send you both to stay with Gramma Millie for the rest of the summer. No? Alright then. Just be glad you don't have to live and dress and talk like these people, and quit makin' fun of them. That doesn't make it any easier for your father and me."

"But don't they ever wash? Don't they have clean clothes? An' what about those dumps they live in. Ugh. I wouldn't even go in one of them!"

"No," Mona agreed, "we don't live like that; we wouldn't live like that. But we know better. They don't. It's all they want, all they've ever had."

"But lookit," Bennie persisted, "They got outdoor pumps. Don't they have water inside? Who uses pumps anymore? An' lookit the dirty windows, an' a lot of 'em are broken. An' the porches, an' steps...all broken or falling down. Why don't they fix them?"

"I know it's hard for you to understand. We don't live like that, and we don't expect anyone else to, either. But it's all they know. They probably could live better, because they get lots of help, from the government and all. But they just keep on living like....like what you see."

"Waddya mean, help. You mean money?"

"Oh, yes. Government gives 'em all kinds of help...money. Isn't that right, Quin? But what do they do with it? Who knows. I'd guess it goes to booze and lottery tickets..."

"But–."

"–Bennie, Honey, let Mummy read, would you. You and Lulu go walk around, run around a bit. Just while Daddy goes inside here. Go on, now. You don't have to talk to anyone. Just stay together. Quin, should I get a shot of that yard?"

"Okay, C'mon, Lu. Bring th' skateboard. Oh, never mind. I forgot. They don't have any pavement."

Quincy's notes filled three binders. Mona had five dozen pictures of general stores, garages, churches and gaunt and hollow-eyed 'hill people', as she called them. She was into her sixth Harlequin, and the children were,

32

by her admission, just short of insufferable by the time they hit Cherokee National Forest in mid-August.

They had crossed the Appalachian Trail a number of times during their wanderings, sometimes seeing hikers resting at the crossing points.

"They don't look like hillbillies, Dad," Lulu had remarked. "Look at their clothes. An' look at their cool boots."

"You're right, Sweetie. These are people just like you and me. They're active people. They're hiking. It's a sport, a hobby, y'know. They hike this trail through the mountains...through a whole lotta states. That trail goes all the way to northern Maine.....about a hundred miles from our place."

Bendix was suitably impressed. "Holy cow! They walk from here to Maine!"

"It's more than that, Bennie. The trail runs from down in Georgia all the way to Maine. More than a thousand miles...maybe twelve hundred miles. Course, not everyone does the whole thing. Most of 'em do bits an' pieces. But some do. They get some kind of award for that."

"Not for me, thanks," sniffed Lulu. "I'll ride. But at least they look normal, not like the losers we've been seein' all summer."

"Well, you're right there. They aren't much like the mountain people, are they? These hikers–."

"These hikers are normal, decent, healthy people," Mona claimed, perhaps more emphatically than she'd intended. "They have jobs, or they're retired, or on vacation. They have some purpose in life. They dress decently. They speak properly. They don't live like hermits or cavemen; they don't take government handouts; they contribute something to society....they're normal!"

"Hmmmm....well, your mother's pretty well covered it there, kids. But you know, we really can't criticize these...uh....mountain folks too much. Remember, they haven't had it easy...haven't had all the advantages you guys enjoy. But I must say, you're learning some great lessons this summer. Learning that it takes all kinds. Right?"

"I suppose," Lulu conceded. "But you'd think at least they could...like...wash, try to clean up. Get some clean clothes, or paint their dumpy shacks."

"You mean spend money on paint, instead of booze," sniffed Mona.

It was nearing the end of August. Quincy decided he had enough of observation, anecdote, and reflection. Mona had long since lost her enthusiasm for portraiture. She was exhausted and longed for her own bed, her own home, her own kind of people. And neither Quin nor Mona could be sure of another week on the road without killing one or both of the kids.

"Tell you what, guys," Quincy said after breakfast. "We can wrap this up and head home. There's just one more stop I want to make. We can get there before noon. I'll spend an hour or so, and then we're done."

"What is it, another grubby store, or what?"

"Wait and see, Lulu. You never know. You might like this one, though... might see something completely different."

"Whatever."

The Bickerton Mill, built by Josiah Bickerton shortly after the Civil War, was still in operation as it had been when it opened in 1870. Quincy had read about the mill in his North Carolina Tour Book, and decided this might be their last and best examination of hill country industry.

"And get that camera ready, Mone. I've got a good feeling about this one!"

He pulled into the Conoco station in Ramseur, seeking directions and some information regarding the mill.

"Yup....you bet she's still goin', still grindin'," the stubbled and toothless attendant replied. He cleared his throat and hawked an impressive gob, most of which missed the front fender. His whiskery chin bore testament to many such spewings. "Yuh go on up this here road t'th' overpass." Splat! "Then yuh turn right on number 22, keep goin' fer about, oh, I dunno, five miles er so, 'til yuh come t'Foster Cromarty's old wood silo." Splat! "Red silo... least it usta be red. Yuh go on t' th' bridge over Deeley's Creek, an' then yuh turn onta Birchall Road. An' there y'are. Should find ol' Worth hisself. He's there most ever' day." Splat!

"Didja hear that, Dad! 'Old Worth.' Bet he'll be a winner. An' did y' see that guy spit! Wow!" Bendix had come alive, captivated by the gas jockey's appearance and treacly gobs punctuating his utterances. "You shoulda got a picture of that guy, Mom."

"This mill guy," whined Lulu, "is he really gonna be the last hick loser we gotta see?"

"What did we say about judging people, you kids? You keep those thoughts to yourself."

"Well, I'm afraid I agree with Lulu, Quin. I've just had it with these lowlifes. And that little scene at the gas station...disgusting! Absolutely disgusting. Why would they have someone like that working there, serving the public. That man was totally repulsive. We should write to the company, Quin." Mona's irritability had increased since she'd finished her last Harlequin. "Do we really need to see more of these dumps, and these dirty people? I sure don't want to waste any more film on them."

"It won't take long, Mone. I really think I can get something worthwhile from seeing this mill, and talking to the guy who runs it. Sure hope he's there. Shouldn't take long."

34

"Well, I've had enough, Quin. Didn't feel this way when we started. And at first I thought the kids were being too hard on these people, mocking them and all. But I tell you, I've had a bellyful of ignorant dirty hillbillies who don't know enough to come in out of the rain. Or wash their hands...or stop having kids...or...oh, I don't know. I just want to get back to normal life and normal people. People who do normal things and live in normal houses and know how to use a hanky, and change their socks....Instead of taking government handouts an' all that. Our hard-earned tax money, for God's sake!"

"Yeah, for God's sake!" echoed Lulu, emboldened by her mother's outburst.

Quincy found the mill and drove down to a small parking lot at the water's edge. The stone building was obviously sound from foundation to roof. Stone and concrete and heavy squared timbers bespoke superior workmanship producing a structure that had weathered so well for so many decades.

"Daddy, lookit," Lulu whispered, "there's a creepy old man starin' at us. Lookit, by the door. He looks like he must be a hundred!"

"Okay, okay. Last one. Mone, why not come on in with me. This is no dump. You can see that. Why not bring your camera. You kids can come in if you want to. But you have to be really careful. This is a working mill, with heavy machinery and all."

"Yuck, I don't wanta even touch anything in there," Lulu whispered. "This place is creepy. An so's that old man."

"Lulu, you stay near me. You, too, Bennie. You never know. Quin, let's not stay long, please." Mona put a protective arm around her daughter. "I'll be so glad to see the end of these people!"

"Me, too, Mom."

The man standing just inside the open door was indeed elderly. Quince guessed he had to be well into his eighties. He wore baggy denims and a heavy flannel shirt with sleeves rolled up to reveal long underwear. His work-roughened hands trembled slightly as he took a piece of shop cloth from a hip pocket and wiped clean a nicked and oily spanner.

"How do," he said, extending his hand to Quincy. "I expect y'all want to look around a bit. Grand Tour ain't scheduled for another hour or so." And he smiled at his little joke, the humour of which seemed to have escaped the family in front of him. He turned to Mona and the kids and continued, "Just don't get too close to that ol' wheel." He pointed to the slowly-rotating stone wheel in the middle of the high ceilinged room. "That ol' wheel just loves t' gobble youngsters....grabs 'em an' gobbles 'em up an' turns 'em into flour an' meal."

The 'younguns' met his smile and words with blank expressions.

"I'm with the university," Quincy said, neglecting to say which one. "And I'm preparing a book on working mills in the Carolinas. I wonder if I could ask you a few questions about this operation. Or maybe I would talk to the owner."

"Hell, I'm th' owner. I'm Worth Bickerton. Shoulda introduced myself right away, but I was kinda concerned yer younguns might get too close to my wheel."

"Mr. Bickerton....a pleasure to meet you. So....it's your mill, and it's been in operation for quite some time, I understand."

"Yep...a hundred and twenty-seven years. Been workin' it myself over sixty years. With some time off, now an' then. Been in our family all that time...."

Lulu and Bennie, tired of the trip, the stops, the yokels, and now this tiresome old coot and his grubby mill, had wandered outside.

'Stay close by, you two." Mona watched them head down to the edge of the stream.

"Best keep an eye on' em, Ma'am....keep 'em away from th' sluice. Water's quick there, an' them rocks is slipp'ry."

"They'll be fine. They're careful, and they're well-behaved." Mona moved into the mill then, leaving Quincy with the old man. "So, 1870,"she heard him say, "long time to be in business, Sir. I don't suppose...." And then she was around the massive stone wheel, and the conversation was lost to her. No matter, she wasn't the least bit interested.

In one of the dark corners at the back of the mill she came upon a small protruding enclosure, a walled-off room, possibly an office or small storeroom. One projecting wall had a window allowing a view of the mill's interior from inside the room. But it was curtained on the inside, and Mona could not see in. There was a closed door marked 'Private'. Idly, she gave the doorknob a tentative twist. The door swung open on well-oiled hinges to reveal a small neat office containing a desk behind which hung a current calendar from Hanley's John Deere in Ramseur. A nearly-bare notice board hung beside the calendar, and a four-drawer filing cabinet sat in the corner by the desk. But what caught Mona's attention was a series of four framed documents on the wall beside the door. She looked back into the main mill, and decided it was safe to enter for a closer look. She went up to the wall.

The first frame held a Master's degree in Civil Engineering awarded by the University of North Carolina to Calder Worth Bickerton. It was dated 1947. She moved to the next frame, a Doctoral degree in Chemical Engineering from Yale University, dated 1950, and again in the name of Calder Worth Bickerton.

36

The third document was a certificate edged in black and gold, and bearing at the top a seal embossed in gold. Mona caught her breath–it was the Seal of the President of the United States! She read the inscription:

To Worth Bickerton, in recognition
of dedicated service to mankind characterized by
his tireless efforts in the rebuilding of Post-War
Europe. He has earned the gratitude of nations,
and that of his close friend,

And Mona gasped aloud. The signature was of Dwight D. Eisenhower.

The fourth frame contained another letter, this one plain and unembellished. It was on the letterhead of the Gilead Baptist Church of Ramseur, North Carolina, and was dated 1974, and commended Worth Bickerton for forty years of service to the church, as choir member, Sunday School director, and lay preacher.

Mona let the words and actions of the past seven weeks flood over her as she stood, transfixed, before the wall of tribute. She heard again the cruel jibes and taunts of the children, the mockery of 'worthless bums', 'losers', 'dirty faces and funny clothes', 'dumps and shacks'. And though it pained her, she brought back the equally cruel and mean-spirited words she and Quincy had used: 'we know better', 'we're normal and decent', and 'they live on handouts'. And on and on. And Mona knew she was most to blame, abetting and encouraging the thoughtless cruelty of her whole family.

She stood silently before the four framed pieces, the degrees, the presidential encomium, the simple church letter. Then, slowly, almost reverentially, she backed out of the room, closing the door quietly behind her. She looked around the old mill, at the great beams, the complicated workings of rods and gears and wheel, the barrels and crates stacked along the far wall. She heard the gentle murmur of the water as it sluiced by one side of the mill, gently, inexorably, and evenly turning the huge stone wheel. She heard, too, faint and persistent, the shrieks of her children running aimlessly somewhere outside. Quincy, she knew, would still be out front, learning all he could from the old man. The old man named now as indelibly on her mind as it was on the documents behind her. She continued to stand there, unwilling and maybe unable to break the spell that had settled over and around her....a spell at once humbling, painful, and uplifting. She stayed there, alone. Stayed there so long that finally her husband came looking for her, came to take her back to the car.

GLOSSY BROCHURE

Much as she hated to admit it, Gord had been right, and they had enjoyed the week at Myrtle Beach. It wasn't that Myrtle Beach did not appeal to her, quite the contrary. But the idea of spending a week in an R.V. had not been the least bit attractive. Add to that the prospect of sharing the accommodations with another couple, and Judy had flat-out refused to consider it.

"No way, no how, Gord. You should have known how I'd feel about it before you even started. You know me well enough, surely? One week in a trailer...no way!"

"It's not a trailer, it's an R.V. you know...a motor home, an -."

"I don't care if it's the Taj Mahal on wheels. I won't do it. And share this V. R., or whatever you call it, with someone else? You must think I'm completely crazy!"

"Judy, for Pete's sake. You've never even been in one. They're roomy, an' comfortable. They've got everything a house has. You've gotta see it."

And after a week or so of relentless selling, Gord got Judy to drive up to the Bongard's place to see the new R.V.

"I'll come and look, if that'll make you happy. But that's it, that's all I'm doing – looking. Don't for a minute think I'd actually stay in a trailer. For a week. With another couple. No way."

"It's not a trailer, Jude."

"Close enough. And you've seen those dreadful trailer camps. We've driven by them. You know what they look like - you wouldn't leave a dog in one overnight."

"It's not like that, Jude. You've only seen the dumpy -."

"- yes, dumps," she insisted. "And the people who live in them. You know what they're called. Trailer trash!"

"You have no idea how they set up these R.V. resorts, Jude. These are high-end places...they have huge lots, an' rec centers, an ...."

"Well, "she sniffed, "that may be, but not for me, thanks. Not for us."

Richard and Wendy Bongard had been good friends for nearly twenty years, and Richard had only recently purchased his dream vehicle, a thirty-eight foot Holiday Rambler. It featured every convenience that Gord had promised, bathroom with tub and shower, slide-outs, and full kitchen and laundry facilities. Reluctantly, Judy examined the rig and, grudgingly, gave it a qualified approval.

"It's nice," she said, on the way home, "but for four people? For a week? We'd be in each other's way the whole time. I couldn't imagine anything worse. It would be the end of our friendship for sure."

"No...you don't spend all your time inside, for one thing. We'd be on the golf course, or out on the beach. We'd even be eating the meals outside, y' know, under the awning. It's a whole new way of doing things..."

"Well...."

"And think of what you save. No hotel, no restaurant meals..."

"Hmmm.....I don't know..."

But her resistance was visibly weakening, and Gord knew another few weeks of subtle suggestion might just bring success. By the time winter had secured its icy hold, Judy was openly discussing the prospect and he'd caught her on more than one occasion looking through the R.V. magazines that Richard had sent home with them.

They drove down to join the Bongards in Myrtle Beach in mid-March. Judy had drawn the line at driving down with them in the R.V.

"We have to have our own car. God help us if we get sick of each other after the first day and we have no way to get away, to get a place of our own."

Gord had not argued. He'd won the main battle.

"I just pray this works, an' doesn't change our friendship. Wendy loves her soaps and I'm not gonna sit around and watch T.V. for a solid week!"

"We'll be fine. You'll see."

The six days were just as Gord had promised. Judy's main fear, the single bathroom, did not pose a problem at all: Gord and Richard went each morning to shave and shower in the rec. center a hundred yards away, leaving the girls the run of the cubicle in the R. V. Most of each day they were out, either on the beach – the R.V. park was on the ocean – or on the golf course, and then it was back to the R.V. to relax under the canopy at the water's edge. They ate in the rig, or at the table outside. With two tip-outs, room inside was ample, and sleeping arrangements were ideal.

"I don't think I've ever slept better," Judy confessed. "That bed is so comfy. Who'd have guessed they'd have beds that big! And the sound of the waves!"

Their nearest neighbor was fifty feet away, the camp was just over half-full, and there was never any feeling of being hemmed in, either inside or out.

"You know." Judy said on their last night, "I was so wrong. This is nothing like what I expected. I really didn't think it would work, with four of us."

"So, a convert." Richard laughed. "Whadd'ya know! We knew you'd love it, Jude."

"It's been a great week," Gord agreed. "Would you do it again, Jude?"

"In a heartbeat!"

They left the next morning, heading back for whatever cruel jabs late winter had in store.

"It was a great week, Gord. You were right....as usual."

"Well, you were right to be skeptical. But really, I knew it would work. Why wouldn't it – a new rig, all the bells an' whistles, and with good friends...."

"Well, I'd do it again." She paused. "Just one thing...."

"I can guess: it would be even better with just the two of us?"

"Yep. Don't get me wrong. I really like Richard and Wendy. We're lucky to have friends like that. But let's face it, four people in a trailer...."

"It's not a trailer, Jude. It's a motor home."

"I know, I know. But even in something that...uh....fancy, after a week... you know. It's really meant for two."

Gord smiled, and said nothing. She was hooked. And so the research began. They picked up folders and ads at the camp office. They looked for information on lot rentals, rig rentals, daily, weekly, and monthly fees.

"Maybe we could rent one back home, and drive it down..."

"But you really need a car..."

They knew they wanted to repeat the experience, and on the way home they stopped at the Welcome Centers to pick up what they could on R.V. resorts and motor home rentals.

"I'll call some of these places when we get home." he said. "Might get better rates, booking early."

Some of the flyers they ditched immediately. If they were shoddy in presentation, how could the places themselves be any better?

"Look at this", he said, "coarse-grained paper, black and white. No pictures. What's with that? What are they expecting, putting out a brochure like that?"

And at this stage, Judy's interest was at a peak. "Keep looking", she said. "See if there's anything like what Richard and Wendy have. That was super!"

"We've gotta assume some of these are two-bit operations," he replied. "Usually y'can expect the better the ad, the better the product. Look at some of these. *Gold Crest Park*. They don't even have a picture, just a drawing. Or this one...*Sandhills Ranch*. No picture, either. And only black and white

40

lettering. And a ranch in the Carolinas? I don't think so."

Judy held up a glossy brochure. "Look here, Gord. What about this one?"

"Hey, not bad." He took the colorful three-fold pamphlet. *Red Pine R.V.Resort.* "This is better." The front panel featured a gently-sloping hillside leading down to a small lake. "Listen to this: a two hundred acre gated Motor Home Community. Year 'round and seasonal occupancy. Seventy lots set among towering pines on the banks of a small private lake. Close to Pinehurst and the Sandhills, featuring all the modern facilities demanded by today's knowledgeable R.V.'ers'."

Things were looking up. "And look at the pictures." He spread the brochure open to show smiling campers relaxing in front of gleaming rigs and happy children paddling about at the shore of a small lake. "This is more like it, Jude. How many have we seen like this, on glossy good quality paper, with pictures and all...?"

"Could be pricey," she cautioned.

"Maybe. But what the hell, I'll call. Can't hurt to call."

He dialed the 1- 800 number.

"Red Pine Resorts."

"Ah, yes....we have your brochure and I was wondering –."

"Which resort, Sir?"

"Pardon?"

"Which resort...Scottsdale, El Paso, Sandhills, or Charleston?"

"Oh. This one says Sandhills, near Pinehurst."

"One moment. I'll connect you."

He looked over at Judy. "They're connecting me," he said. "Looks like they have three or four with the same name. Same company...." And after a wait of a minute or so, he heard a woman's voice, as if from some great distance.

"Red Pine."

"Uh, yes...I'd like some information, please. We're interested in spending some vacation time in the Pinehurst area. And we have your brochure. It looks very good. Can you tell me a bit about your resort, and your fees?"

The lady now sounded angelic. "Well, darlin', I surely can. I'm Carla Blatchley. We run the resort, my husband and me. We surely would be proud t'have y'all stay with us."

Briefly, Gord told Mrs. Blatchley about their Myrtle Beach experience, and explained what they were looking for, something along the same lines.

"Oh, yes," she purred, "we have rigs like that, to be sure. Y' all can get somethin' here that'll suit your purpose....mebbe even a little better than what y'all had."

"Well, we think we'd like to get your fee schedule...maybe get a price on the whole package. You know, a rental...a lot near the water..." Judy rolled her eyes as he plunged ahead. "We don't have our own rig, yet, so we're looking to rent one. Something maybe thirty-five or thirty-eight feet, you know, with tip-outs." As if I knew what I'm talking about, he thought.

"Well, darlin', we have just what y'all are lookin' for. How about our new Citation? It's a thirty-six footer with ever'thin' y'all could ever want."

He gulped and looked over at Judy, and took the critical step. "How much would that be, Mrs. Blatchley, say for a week? We're thinking of the first week in November. I'm guessing that's still off-season?"

"Well, darlin', seein' as how y'all are callin' so early to book, I'll let y'all have it for $450.00."

He repeated the figure, and Judy nodded.

"That's sound good, Mrs. Blatchley. Uh, your brochure shows a main gate. It sounds very secure."

"Why, darlin', y'all are as safe here as in the heavenly pastures, sure enough. We're gated. An' wait'll y'all see our beautiful lake. I know y'all will love this place just as much as me an' Earl do."

Gord nodded to Judy to indicate he'd made a deal, and a good one. Just as he went to say they'd take the one-week booking, Mr. Blatchley added, "An' right now we're offerin' a discount on a two-week stay. It's only $800 for two weeks."

"We'll take it."

"That's fine an' dandy, darlin'. I'm puttin' y' all down for lot number 9, right on the lake. An' I'm gonna set y'all up in our new Citation. It's a beautiful unit. Me an' Earl stay in one all year 'round. 'Course, ours ain't new...."

"Sure, sounds good," he said. "'I've gotta tell you, Mrs. Blatchley, your brochure pretty well sold us, even before we called."

"That's so good to hear, darlin'. Yes, it's a piece of heaven on earth here. I'm so happy for y' all. Now, I've got y' all down for November, then, the 2nd to th' 16th. An' of course, we need a deposit. That'll be four hundred. Y' all send that along to me right away, an' I'll mark y' all down 'reserved'. I'm so glad y' all signed up early, 'fore all the good spots get filled. Can't wait t' meet y' all!"

"I told Richard how to get there. They may drive over to see us while we're there. Maybe the four of us can play Legacy or Talamore, an' then come back to 'our rig' for a nice meal. They could stay over..."

42

"Oh, Gord, I'm really getting excited about this!"

"Three more days. And pack light, Jude. Looks like they've got a super laundry room. I'm telling you, I can't wait. Everything looks so good an' clean there!" And for the hundredth time, he looked through the glossy brochure.

"Red Pine Resort", she read as Gord drove slowly through Aberdeen, "nestled in the piney woods of the Pinehurst-Aberdeen Sandhills, a short five miles off Hwy 501."

They found the turn-off, a sign for Red Pine Resort pointing down a gravel road with stunted pines and small sand hummocks on either side.

"Looks good so far. I can see the pines getting a lot taller up ahead."

"Uh huh...doesn't look too hilly, though, does it? The brochure says 'set in rolling hills'. Looks pretty flat so far..."

"Jude...we've got five miles to go. Don't worry. It'll get hilly soon enough."

At the three-mile mark , Gord pointed ahead. "Look there...I'd say we're coming up to come pretty good-sized hills." And sure enough, a mile or so ahead they could see the landscape changing as they approached more hilly terrain. However, at that moment they came upon the second Red Pine sign, much smaller than the first and pointing left off the gravel road and onto a sandy track that appeared hardly traveled as it wound through a field of scruffy dwarf pines and sumacs and what seemed to be an old burn whose vegetation struggled for a foothold. And still the terrain stretched flat before them. Gord's optimism was fading and Judy stared glumly ahead.

"You don't suppose we missed a turn," Judy ventured after a minute or two of heavy silence. "You don't suppose someone moved the sign...y' know, a joke or something. This sure doesn't look much like resort country."

Gord didn't want to agree, but she was right. This was not promising, and he was just about to suggest going back to the main highway when they came upon the third sign, a weathered piece of barn board urged them onward with a barely-discernible "Resort – 1/2 mile". And in the field where the sign was posted there was proof of life: an old wringer washing machine, three or four broken plastic milk crates, a derelict pick-up with headlights and windshield shot out, a jumble of pieces of asbestos and vinyl and aluminum siding, a broken lawn chair, and a cracked commode with missing scat.

"This does not look good, Gord!"

"I know. But what do we do we sent the money...four hundred bucks. We've gotta have a look."

"I don't like this...I've got a bad feeling."

"Just a little farther. We'll prob'ly turn a corner an' find everything just

43

like we want it. You can't tell by this junk. It's prob'ly just junk from the farmer who owns the field. Y'know, the Augusta Golf Course....where they play the Masters...that course is just off a real junky road. Remember the pictures....look at the brochure..."

The sandy road turned sharply right at the edge of the junk-strewn field. And there it was. The entrance to Red Pine Resort was a grand arch formed by two upright cedar poles topped by a reedy horizontal pole on which a slab of barn-board announced the resort. At least, they assumed the words were there: time and weather had obliterated most of the letters. And stretching almost the entire width of the opening, at a height of three feet or so, was another reedy pole with a white plastic jug wired to its free end. On the jug, in bold red lettering, was the command STOP. The other end of the pole was run into a box of some sort, a black piece of machinery that Gord thought looked familiar. This mechanical device was set atop a forty-five gallon drum wired to one of the upright poles. And on this pole, another hand-lettered sign ordered visitors to report to the office.

Judy was in no mood to report to anyone. "This cannot be the place. They said it was a gated resort. Where's the gate – this pole?! Where's the guard? This is some kind of joke and I'm not laughing!"

He felt the same hollow dread, but Gord thought of the kindly Mrs. Blatchley, and the Citation, and the four-hundred dollar deposit. "Hell. But we've gotta see what's up. Let me park here....I'll go check it out." He got out of the car. "You wait here, and keep the doors locked."

A faded green board-and-batten shack sat beside the sandy track inside the gate. It was low-slung, with a tin roof over-hanging a screened verandah running across the front end. To all appearances, deserted and abandoned..... could this be their office, he wondered? It was certainly nothing like the office pictured in their fold-out pamphlet.

A dog of indeterminate breed, and even less-clear intentions, slunk around the corner and regarded him with rheumy eyes. He saw another sign, this one nailed to one of the two-by-fours supporting the overhanging roof: "USE PHONE FOR MGR", and sure enough, on a small shelf just inside the screen door sat a black rotary phone, and another small sign which directed "DIAL '0'".

He dialed, keeping one wary eye on the dog which had taken up position just outside the door.

"Yes."

"It's Gord McComb. We have a reservation. Is this Mrs. Blatchley?"

"Gimme a min, hon!"

In less than a minute an old green golf cart wheezed and bumped across

44

the field behind the office, and he was face to face with the genial Carla Blatchley. "Mr. McComb. So good t' meet y 'all. I'm Mrs. Blatchley. Y'all can call me Carly...."

She could have been fifty, or seventy. On the phone, she had sounded so young and vibrant, and Gord had pictured some vivacious southern belle with sparkling eyes and beautiful skin. He was having trouble reconciling that image with the wraith before him. Carla Blatchley was thin and ropey, with skin the color (and texture, he guessed) of nugahyde, speckled with darker brown splotches the size of quarters. She squinted through the smoke of a cigarillo curling around her hawk-bill nose. Some sort of scarf or bandana hid most of her hair except for those strands escaping at the nape of her skinny neck.

"Well," she said, expertly maneuvering the cigarillo from one side of her mouth to the other, "I expect y'all want t'see yer lot."

"Well...uh....we weren't' really sure we had the right place," Gord said, trying to marshall his thoughts in order to make their disappointment clear, and to convince the manager that: one, they could not accept this situation, and two, they must have their deposit refunded. No question about it, Judy would never stay in this shambles of a place. Nor would he. But how best to go about it, to demand their money back? "We weren't sure," he repeated, " and then, we, uh, saw the sign, and, uh...how do the cars get in...and out?"

"Easy. It's a garage door opener, operatin' the pole with th' stop sign. Earl rigged it up. My husband. An' each camper gets a remote t' come an' go."

"Uh....the brochure said you have a gated resort. We thought there'd be something a little more...uh...official." He knew the word sounded out of place, but everything was out of place...nothing seemed right, or as it should be.

"Well, that's the gate. Not like all th' fancy resorts. But it works. An' that's why we kin offer reasonable rates." Gord thought he detected the first hint of an edge to her voice. "Yep, y' come an' go with a remote. Works like a charm."

He had to make a move, had to make it clear to her. "The brochure we got showed...uh...modern facilities. You know, a main office, and a central rec. hall. And lots of tall pine trees".

"Mr. McComb, we run a good clean camp here. No trouble, no crime, no frills. The flyer you saw is for all the Red Pine Resorts. There's five a'them, across the country. Some may be a little fancier than here, but then, they're pricier. All run by the same head office, all a little diff'runt. D y'all understand?"

This was news. Gord wondered if perhaps they had some legal grounds to back them up when they demanded their refund. False advertising, maybe?

45

"Y'all have lot # 9, down by the lake. Like y'asked. D'y'all wanta see it?" Gone now any delusions about a sweet southern belle.

"Okay, we'll take a look. Can I bring my car in now?"

"Lemme get y'all a remote." She rummaged in an old half-bushel basket under the phone shelf and chose a remote wrapped in electrical tape. She pointed it at the black box on the oil drum and the slender pole slid back to allow the passing of a vehicle.

"Uh, just before y'all go t' get yer car. We had to make a coupla changes. In yer booking."

"Such as?"

"Well, we couldn't get y'all the Citation. Problem with the dealer. But we got y'all a stand-by....little smaller. An' we had t' close the laundry room for a spell. Trouble with th' plumbin; the rec. center won't be open before Christmas.....we're renovatin' it, along with th'snack bar an' restaurant.... soon as Clayton Hodgins an his boys are done huntin'."

Gord brightened. This could be their out of the mess: all the services advertised, and none available. "I'll get the car," he said. "Do I follow you?"

He went back to the car. Judy's foul humor was like nothing he'd seen before. "What in heaven's name is going on?" she demanded. "Why were you so long?And who was that old hag?"

"That was Carla Blatchley....the manager. Our hostess."

"That's the woman on the phone?!! You said she was a real lady!! We're not staying here. This is a gawd awful dump. I'm not staying here!"

He looked at his wife, at the glossy brochure on the dashboard, and his impulse was to simply turn the car around and drive away. They'd find a place in Aberdeen, or Pinehurst. Call Richard and Wendy, tell them it was a dump and not to come. But he had to get the money back.

"Just a minute...hold on, Jude. Let's think how we're gonna do this. Right now, we'll follow her to the rig. We'll have a look at it....and then we'll find some way to get out of it. It's like a contract....we've gotta find a way to get our money back."

"My God...that's the manager!! You thought she was such a lady. She looks like she's been dragged through a hedge! I don't like this, Gord. Geez, what if we get stuck....this is awful. I'm scared. Just get our money, and get me outta here!"

He eased the car along a rutted path, following the bouncing golf cart. As they crawled along the rough track, they looked left and right to see nothing but vacant lots and the occasional dumpy trailer. Where were the gleaming motor homes, the smiling campers, the frolicking children–all so charmingly portrayed in the brochure.

46

They continued down a light grade, over rocky ground, hoping not to bottom out, and caught sight of water through the scraggly trees. They saw a grouping of four or five shacks beside a larger building at the water's edge. The closer they got to this grouping, the worse it looked. The 'lake' was a murky pond. From side to side, end to end, no greater distance than a mid-wedge. Weeds and reeds marked its edges, and a semblance of a dock – rotting planks on oil drums – jutted sadly twenty feet into the brackish water. The golf cart slewed around the larger building and Gord slowed even more to avoid a broken laundry hamper and a tricycle in the middle of the rock-strewn track. "Ah", he thought, "signs of human habitation". But it wasn't funny. The shacks turned out to be trailers converted in haphazard fashion to more or less permanent homes. They were set among anemic alders, boulders, and cast-off items of domesticity – old pots, broken chairs, a barbecue with rusted propane tank still attached, and a Pepsi cooler minus its top.

The 'lake' no more than a puddle, the buildings and trailers in a state of complete disrepair, or abandonment – the whole place was a shambles.

"Oh my God! Look at that, Gord. There, by the end shack," Judy whispered as they crept by the hovels on wheels. A stringy specter of a man clad only in filthy bib overalls and a grease-stained camouflage cap worked on an engine block suspended from a cedar pole tripod. A huge pasty-faced woman in a floral dress and unlaced work boots sat near the tripod on an overturned milk crate. There was a cat sidling around her legs, and a bundle of soiled clothes in a cracked yellow hamper on the ground beside her. She had a bottle of beer in one hand, and a cigarette in the other. The couple watched, expressionless, as Gord drove past.

"The washers and dryers aren't working," he said.

"That's not all that's not working," Judy replied, still in shock and whispering. "Oh, God, I wish we were outta here. This is like some hillbilly horror movie!"

"I agree. Let's just look at the R.V. Maybe we could stay one night. No, wait listen. We could stay one night, an' then, in the morning, I'll go up t' the office an' say we changed our minds...or something. Say we got called home for an emergency. Something. We'll think of something....."

It only got worse. Their 'motor home' turned out to be a well-traveled nineteen foot Winnebago, a fading brown trailer on cinder blocks moldering in a weedy lot beside an equally worn Dodge pick-up without doors and jacked up on cement blocks at the front and a couple of pine logs where the rear wheels should have been. A dirty canvas canopy over the front door served no purpose, with its tears and holes, other than to darken an already-dark interior.

They parked and sat in numbed silence. Carla Blatchley slid out of the golf cart and waited for them to emerge. "C'mon, Jude, we'll look at it an' find some way outta this mess." He was unsure how this would be effected, but knew it had to be done.

"Well, here she is. Y' all may have t' watch yer head, stoop a bit, with yer height." She mounted the steps, two concrete blocks, and tugged the door open. The odor of confined airless space wafted out. Judy shrank back, and Gord forced himself forward to look inside. The main area was kitchen and living room, walled off from the back of the trailer by a hanging beach towel from Vero Beach. "Look here, Jude," Gord called in a tone which he hoped conveyed some sense of outrage, "not quite as advertised, wouldn't you agree?"

Reluctantly, Judy stuck her head inside. She saw cracked, peeling, filthy linoleum, a small counter-top fridge propped open with an empty milk bottle, a dual element stove with one coil missing. The sink was hard-water stained and filthy. She gathered her courage and stepped inside, and went to stand beside her husband, whether to draw strength from him or to bolster his own deflated spirits, as they surveyed the squalor around them. Neither seemed willing to look behind the beach towel partition.

"It's worse than anything I've ever seen, " Judy whispered weakly, trying to hold back tears. Gord put an arm around her shoulders. He was bent to avoid the low ceiling, and for the moment he was speechless. He swept the room with a last look of despair and disgust, and said, "That's enough. We're not staying here. I'll settle this right now."

Carla Blatchley was waiting, smoking a cigarette and surveying her domain from the vantage point of her golf cart. She smiled thinly as the shaken couple emerged. Judy went back to the car and Gord approached the golf cart in what he hoped was the appearance of shock and indignation.

"Mrs. Blatchley, this is unacceptable. It's nothing like what you promised. It's not what's advertised. We can't stay here."

"Suit yerself," she said, starting the golf cart forward.

"Wait a minute!" He moved to block the cart, and she braked. "I want a refund. We want our deposit back. This is totally unacceptable."

"A refund!? You expect money back? I don't run my business that way, mister! Y' all booked a spot, an' I kept that spot fer y' all." She threw the cigarette aside and made to swing the cart around him. He moved again to stand in her way, grabbing at the roof pillar and hoping she wouldn't squash him against the old pick-up.

"Hold it!" he shouted, his anger over-coming his fear. "You can't do this. You have to give us our money!!"

48

"Look, you. I dunno how y' all do business where y' all come from. Y' all reserved a spot an' a trailer. I could'a rented it any number a' times. You don't like it...too bad. That's yer problem, not mine. We don't give refunds. Period. Read yer brochure! Now move!"

By now the couple from the end trailer had ambled over to see what the noise was about. The man had a heavy wrench in his hand. The woman went to lean on the front of the car. And as if they'd been summoned by the voices raised in anger, other denizens of the camp now appeared. A bearded man and what might have been his two slouching slope-shouldered sons rounded the corner of the rec hall and approached the two arguing at the golf cart. In the wake of these sinister newcomers, slinking along with a melon-headed baby on her hip, a haggard woman materialized. She, too, slouched over to the car and, with a baleful look at the now-terrified Judy cowering inside locked doors, she plunked the moon-faced baby down on the hood of the car. Her faded dress was streaked at the waist, soiled by the infant's dirty diaper.

The bearded man carried an axe, and the younger men, or boys, smaller copies of the bearded lout, fanned out and, along with the skinny man holding the wrench, effectively surrounded the two squared-off combatants. Heedless of consequences, Gord reached over and grabbed the steering wheel.

"You can't do this!" he shouted. "You have to give us our money. This is criminal. You know it is. This is nothing like what we paid for. You misled us from the start!"

The woman, assessing the situation and knowing that, with the back-up on scene, she had the upper hand, laughed at Gord. "Lookit....y' all called. Y' all asked fer a spot an' a trailer. An' by God, that's what yuh got. There's no refund. Yuh shoulda knowed that if yuh read the brochure. Besides, that money's spent. Now move!!" And this time she did drive ahead, forcing Gord to jump aside.

"This is fraud!" he yelled as she swung the cart around. "I'm going to the police!"

Judy rolled the window down a few inches, and called, "Gord, get in the car! Get in the car. Let's leave. Get in the car!"

He made his way to the car, hoping his rage would hold the knot of assembled campers in check. He realized that the golf cart had stopped partway up the slope. Mrs. Blatchley shouted down at him, "I wouldn't suggest y' all go t' any po-lice. Yuh got nothin' t' tell 'em, except y' all booked, an' sent a deposit, as required, y'all got what yuh booked. End of story, mister. No refunds. Company policy!"

He would have answered, but he saw the small group beginning to move toward the car. Heeding Judy's plea, he opened the door, hearing the last words from Mrs. Blatchley as he slid into the car.

"Besides," she hollered, "I'll tell the po-lice y' all threatened me.....tried t' grab me. An' I got witnesses!" Triumphantly she pointed to the grizzled mini-mob. And with that she chugged and bounced back up the rocky slope. Her minions, still silent, glowered at Gord and Judy until the golf cart was gone, and then they drifted away, back to wherever they'd come from.

"Let's get as far away from here as possible, Gord. We can get a lawyer, or something. But right now, all I want is to be away from here, never, ever, come anywhere near this hell hole again!!"

Gingerly, Gord backed the car into the weeds and rocks by the decrepit Winnebago. The last thing he wanted now was to get stuck. He swung the car slowly back into the track and they made their way up the slope and past the office. Mrs. Blatchley was waiting on her golf cart by the gate, and she worked the remote to allow their departure.

.32 SPECIAL

"Well.... mainly it's guns. Rifles an' shotguns. An' huntin'. I'd say we got more guns per person than any other county in th' State. Hell, prob'ly th' whole country!"

Sheriff Vern Townsend set his cup on the counter and pointed to the enlarged Beecham County map behind his desk. Max looked at the map. "Sure don't look like a real big area, Sheriff."

"It ain't. Fact, it's th' smallest county in th' State. Thirty-three hundred, last count."

Reporter Maxwell Duffy was in Cattonsville on assignment, gathering material for a feature on rural counties in southern Georgia. Beecham County was the last of his stops. He'd expected to be told about their Azalea Festival, or maybe their peach and soybean production. The sheriff left little doubt concerning Beecham's distinct character among her neighbors.

"Thirty-three hundred,"he repeated,"give or take. Now, y' consider th' number of women an' kids, an' we estimate they's more'n four thousand guns. Prob'ly ever' man 'n boy over fourteen got four or five guns, minimum."

"But ... how would you know that? I mean, how could you come up with that number?"

"Hell, I know ever' fam'ly in th' county. Been here all m'life, an' sheriff fer twenty-six years. Not much I couldn't say about what goes on around here."

"That's an awful lot of firepower, Sheriff. I mean, does it worry you at all?" Max wondered how this topic could be the focus of his Beecham segment. He doubted his editor would accept what might be an indictment of red-neck America.

"Son, in those twenty-six years, they's been what ... mebbe half a dozen what y'd call gun stories. Worry me? Not a little bit." He pulled out his plug of Red Man and moved over to his desk. "One incident sticks in m' mind." He nodded to the chair beside his desk and held out the plug. "Take a seat there ... Max, is it? I'll tell you a Beecham gun story."

Max waved off the proffered plug, settled into the seat, and opened his notebook. The sheriff called out to the adjoining room, "Doreen, bring us some coffee, would y' please."

He sat back and steepled his fingers and began, "You may or may not recall th' name Hector Coutts. Hec an' Celia Coutts lived two or three miles out th' Mill Road. This woulda bin eight or nine years ago..."

Max shook his head. Eight years ago he was fourteen and living in Greenville, South Carolina.

"Well, anyway, they had two kids, boy 'n a girl. Knowin' Hec an' Celia as I did, I'd a said th' Couttses shouldn't a had any kids at all. Y'see, Celia's kinda slow ... ain't got all her wits at th' best a times. An' Hec ... well, Hec Coutts was a hard case. Not yer 'ideal citizen'. Bad temper an mean. An' he weren't gonna change jus' b'cause he had kids."

The coffee came , and the sheriff paused while they took their cream and sugar. Max decided he wouldn't be taking notes. He took the cup and sat back to hear the story of Hec Coutts and guns.

"Leland was th' boy. He woulda bin sixteen when this happened. Leland was kinda ... uh ... what would y'say, kinda sissy-like. Not yer typical Beecham kid. Not inta th' usual stuff fer a boy. Y'know, sports , football, scrappin' with th' other boys. No friends at all. An' his momma was part t' blame, I'd say. She was always babyin' him, spoilin' him, not lettin' him grow up."

He took a sip, and blew on his coffee. "Y'gotta realize, Hec Coutts was a big, rough ol' boy ... a man's man, y'might say. Least, he saw hisself in that light. An' he had no time fer a kid, a boy, who wanted t'read books insteada playin' sports, or usin' tools, or goin' out t'hunt. An' th'more he saw ol' Celia pamperin' th' kid, th' more he bullied an' tormented him. Or ignored him altogether."

Max cringed inwardly: it sounded too familiar. His own father had never been accepting of his bookish interests and pursuits. "It can be pretty tough, tryin' to please a father," he said.

"You bet. An' there jus' weren't no pleasin' Hec Coutts. He wuz way over th' line with all that macho bullshit. Guys aroun' town, an' I'm talkin' reg'lar guys, beer-drinkin' an' huntin' guys, didn't want nuthin' t' do with Hec. He wuz always ridin' ever' one...pushin' 'em, always lookin' fer a scrap. An'that's jus' when he wuz sober. Get some booze in 'im, an' y'didn't want no part a Hec Coutts.. That ol' boy was one bad mean drunk!"

"And him with a momma's boy for a son."

"Yep. Not a good mix.. That boy suffered, I kin tell you. Anyone who weren't tough,or handy with guns 'r tools, 'r didn't like th' outdoors... well, he weren't a real man. An' Leland wuz never gonna be a man, in his daddy's eyes."

The sheriff reached to replenish his chaw, and worked the bite for a min-

52

ute or two before continuing. "Dunno how that boy kep' hisself t'gether, tell y' th' truth. Becomin' such a momma's boy 'cause a Celia ... a sissy, an' under Hec's roof. Celia never seen it, I guess, or mebbe that wuz her way a protectin' th' boy from Hec's pushin' an' teasin'. Kid musta bin miserable."

"I'm sure."

"An' gawd knows how it went at school, with th' other kids. They musta picked on him ... kids is like that. He wouldn't a bin one t'fight back, neither, him bein' so puny an' all. Prob'ly got more'n his share a black eyes an' busted lips. Y'know how it is when kids see somebody diff'rent. Dunno who's worse, th' little ones 'r th' high school kids. Either way, Leland couldn't get away from th' torment, at home or at th' school."

"I just can't believe a father would let that happen to his own child."

"Yeah, well .... Most daddies woulda toughened their kid up, got 'im to th' point where he could defend hisself, fight back. But Hec give up on that boy early on. Saw he weren't tough an' he weren't gonna get tough. Kid had no chance."

"A lot of good the mother did," Max said. "Seems to me she's gotta take some of the blame. Maybe a lot of the blame."

"Yeah, mebbe. Celia wuz weak. She wuz always weak, but she weren't mean. Ol' Hec broke her spirit from th' git-go. I gotta think she meant well ... with th' boy."

"You said this was a gun story."

"Yep. Hec Coutts prob'ly had more guns than we got here at th' station. Had at least three or four shotguns .... y'know, 12 gauge ... a 16 gauge an' a 20 gauge that I know fer sure. An' at least th' same number a rifles. Y'know .... a .22, a .30-.30, an' a .30-06. Th' usual. An' a Winchester .32 Special that wuz his daddy's. He loved that .32 Special. Carried it all th' time in th' rack in his truck. Gotta admit, it wuz a beauty. He loved that gun."

"You must have been concerned, him with so many guns and a mean temper. Not to mention how the booze affected him."

"Like I said, Max, all th' good ol' boys got guns, an' most of them like their Jim Beam now an' then. Tell y' what .... with Hec, I wuz more concerned with how he treated his fam'ly. Th' boy especially. More coffee?"

Max shook his head, and the sheriff continued. "It's a small community. Things like this stand out. Mebbe it's diff'rent in th' city ... things go unnoticed. But here, well, ever'body seen how th' boy wuz gettin' pushed an' pulled, Celia spoilin' 'im an' ol' Hec tormentin' 'im."

Max could only shake his head.

"An' then, when he wuz about ten, two things. Th' little girl, Amanda, wuz born. A sister fer Leland. An' most surprisin', Hec gives th' boy a gun. I s'pose it wuz a last attempt, y'might say, t'make a man of th' boy. Beautiful little Mossberg Over `n Under."

Max showed his bewilderment.

"Over `n Under... shotgun an' rifle, all in one. A twenty-two an' a .410, combined, like. A real beautiful little gun. Always wanted one m'self. Well sir, I don' b'lieve the boy ever fired that gun. Fact, Hec tol' me Leland wouldn't even take aholt a th' thing. Scared, I s'pose. Y'kin imagine how that set with his daddy!"

Max nodded.

" So now, Celia's got two kids .... a baby, an' Leland, an' both a them seemed t' be needin' her most a th' time. Hec's no help as a father. If he ain't at work, he's huntin' or down at The Blue Tick. Some nights he'd be stayin' over at Weldon Foster's hunt camp, steada goin' home."

"Tough on Celia and the kids...."

"Yep. Ol' Hec made ever'one miserable, hisself included. An' he makes sure ever'one knows how miserable he is."

"Don't think I want to meet this miserable s.o.b."

" You won't. But now, after th' girl comes along, little Amanda, it only gets worse. Celia's never been bright, an' now she's got two babies ... a infant an' th' ten-year-old. An' fer the next four or five years, we're all wonderin' how she's gonna cope. An' we wuz right t' wonder ... th' little girl got no more care ner attention than what wuz needed t'keep her alive. All th' mother's attention went t' Leland. Amanda, what chance did she have .... a loonie fer a mother, an' a father who she don' even know. An' a course, Leland's jus' about useless in his own way..."

Max could only shake his head.

"By th' time she's three or four, y'd see this little bit of a thing wanderin' around, nobody, it seemed, keepin' much of an eye on her. Least no parent. Th' boy did watch out fer her, I'll say that. I seen 'im take `er by th' hand a number a times. Prob'ly th' only care she got. An, hell, jus' as often I'd find her out on th' Mill Road, all by herself. 'Course, it ain't a busy road, but jus' th' same.

"What about Child Protective Services?"

"Here? In Cattonsville? Y'd have t' go t' Atlanta, or Brunswick, mebbe. Not sure y'd have a case, anyway. Th' child wuz fed an' clothed, an' they's no sign she wuz abused ... y'know, physically, like. Jus' didn't look like she wuz gettin' much motherin', y'know what I mean..."

"That's one rotten state of affairs! What's gonna become of kids , in a home like that? If you ask me, it's criminal."

"Yep, pretty near. This went on fer five years or more. Th' two kids with
54

only themselves, really, t' rely on. Zonked-out mother, an' a totally neglectful father. 'Course, in one way, it mighta been easier on ever'one with Hec away so much .... By th' time Amanda's six, Leland's almost sixteen, an' they're survivin' in a pretty sorry-ass hell hole. An' that's when it happened."

"It?"

"Yep. A real tragedy, I guess y'd call it."

"Preventable?" asked Max. "Seems to me this might have been set straight, if only somebody would have stood up to that bullyin' son of a bitch!"

The sheriff gave Max the look his statement deserved. "Stand up t'him, y'say? Y'mean, stand up physically? Or jus' t'discuss th' situation, like civilized gents discussin' th' crops 'r th' weather?"

"Well, I..."

"Lookee here, son. Weren't no discussin' with Hec Coutts. Last man t'try that was Gulley Neal, about ten years ago. Gulley caught Hec tryin' t'fence off part a his land fer himself, an' ...."

"Y'mean stealin' his land?"

"Not as Hec seen it. He seen that Gulley's back forty hadn't bin planted in a coupla years, an' he thought he'd put in some taters an' corn. Thought them acres sittin' fallow was a waste, I guess, an' corn might bring in some deer, mebbe."

"And what happened?"

"Gulley went t'see Hec at his place, an' Hec kicked his arse an' threw 'im off th' front porch. Gulley come t'me then an' I hadta straighten it all out. Got Hec t'take out the fence..."

"Simple as that?"

"Simple fer me. But not fer Gulley. Next time Hec seen Gulley drivin' up th'Mill Road he took after him an'drove 'im off th' road inta the deep ditch by McCarty's place. Wrecked Gulley's old Dodge pick-up an' they hadta cut Gulley outta th'truck. Busted three ribs on th' steerin' wheel."

"My God! What'd you do?"

"Couldn't do nuthin'. Gulley said he couldn't be sure who run 'im off, ner if it were deliberate or a accident."

"That man is mad. He's a menace!"

"Yep".

"And you said tragedy. What was that, and was it after the Gulley incident?"

"Yep. Happened about a month later, I recall it like it were yesterday. By this time, Leland's pretty well raisin' his little sister .... at least, keepin' an eye on her. An' on this particular day, Hec comes home all bruised up, an' in one gawdawful state a mind. Seems some a Gulley's friends, three 'r four

55

a them, jumped Hec outside The Blue Tick .... gonna teach 'im a lesson, I guess, fer what he done t'Gulley.Well, Hec got a few cuts an' bumps, but he pretty well destroyed them ol' boys. Put two a them in th' hospital. One a them ain't been right in th' head since. Anyway, Hec's all pumped up an' he comes inta th' house an' Leland's readin' a book 'r somethin', mebbe listenin' t'music 'r somethin'. An' Hec starts in on th' boy, yellin' an' cussin', an' Celia's too scared t'speak up, as usual. An' little Amanda gets real scared, seein' her daddy all bruised an' bloody an' all, an' she takes off. Nobody seen her leave. 'Course, Celia's scared Hec'll turn on her, an' Leland's gettin' all this abuse, an'....well, long story short, Hec cuffs th' boy around a bit, an' smacks Celia fer good measure, an' he heads back down t'th' Blue Tick. An hour or so later they realize th' little girl's gone. That is, Leland realizes it--- Celia's too zonked t'notice anything, an' Leland heads out t' bring her back."

"You did say the little girl often wandered off ....."

"Yep. But this time, it's late in th' day. Leland goes up 'n down th' Mill Road a mile 'r so each way. Over t' Gulley Neal's, an' up t' McCarty's. No sign. So he calls me. I got ahold a my deputy, an' we go t'get Tommy Delahunt with his dogs, an' we set out. Found 'er about eleven that night. She'd got as far as Jeb Hume's place, out back a th'Tube Mill"

He paused.

"She'd fell inta Horton Creek, in th' dark.. Musta hit her head when she fell in. Big boulders in that spot, back a th' mill...."

"She drowned?"

"Yep. Broke me up. All of us. Findin' her like that. An' then we hadta go an' tell Celia an' th' boy. Leland took it pretty hard. Celia jus' kinda rocked back 'n forth. Almost like she wasn't sure what we were sayin ..... like she wasn't really there. Strange ... if y'kin imagine."

"What about the father?Hec?"

"Well, it was about midnight ... a bit before. An' no surprise, Hec weren't home. I found 'im at The Blue Tick. Drunk. Didn't even know th' girl had wandered off."

"That is one miserable s.o.b., Sheriff!"

"Yep.But that ain't th' end of th' story."

"No?"

"Nosiree. Coupla days, they have th'wake fer th' little girl. An' Celia an' th' boy is so busted up an' sufferin', th' both a them, I didn't see how they'd get through th' lyin' in. Fact is, Celia never did come around t' normal, t' acceptin' th' little girl's death. She's over at th' Greenway Center now ... bin there ever since. Sorta in her own little world, y'might say."

"And the father?"

"Oh, Hec come drunk t' th' wake, an' t' th' fun'ral too. Didn't talk t' nobody. An' nobody was inclined t' talk t' him, neither. But Leland ... well, that boy got t'play a major part, all on his own.

"Leland!?"

"Yep. Day after th' fun'ral, I got a call from Everett Krumm, over at th' Tube Mill. Young Leland was up th' tower, wavin' a gun an' hollerin' fer his daddy."

"With a gun! His gun?"

"Not his .... he got his daddy's Winchester.32 Special. Th' one I tol' you about. An' ol' Everett sez I better get out there quick, b'fore he shoots somebody or falls off th' dam' tower."

"Where was his daddy?"

"At th' Blue Tick, where else? Anyway, I stopped an ' picked 'im up an' told 'im what was goin' on out at th'mill. He was pretty upset when he seen his .32 Special was gone from his truck. Starts tellin' me what he's gonna do to th' kid. Well, we got out there, an' tell y' th' truth, I was quite prepared t' let Hec climb that ol' tower. Better him than me, seein' as how Leland's got a rifle up there."

"What a story!"

"Yeah. Well, Hec starts hollerin' up at th' kid, tellin' him t'git his ass down with that Winchester or he'd be one sorry sumbitch.Y'kin imagine.'. ·.all threats, what he's gonna do t' th' kid an' all. An' Leland jus' hollers down t'Hec t'come up an' get it----if he's man enough."

"Damn!!

"Yep.'Course, that's all Hec has t'hear, his wimp of a son challengin' him, and with Hec's own gun .... his favorite gun!"

"Damn!"

"So ol' Hec starts up th' ladder, cussin' th' kid ever' step a th'way. An' Leland's givin' it right back t'th'old man, callin' him a coward an'a piece a shit ... Y'wouldn't a thought th' kid had that kinda grit. Darin' his daddy t' come on up, if he's man enough! By now, Hec's halfway up, an' he's in a major rage, I kin tell you. An' now I'm scared mebbe he'll throw th' kid off th' tower. So I grab th' bull horn an' call t' Hec t' come on down an' leave th' boy alone. I figgered it'd be best t' let th' kid come down on his own."

"And did that work?"

"Not nearly. By now Leland's laughin' at Hec, an' callin' him ever name y'kin imagine. Calls him a lazy drunken bum, an' a chickenshit an' I dunno what all. An' then he takes that Winchester an' starts bangin' it against th' steel rail, bangin' th' stock an' all, and that jus' drives ol' Hec to more of a rage, seein' his kid wreckin' that beautiful rifle. He's goin' on up, fast as he kin climb. Mebbe ten 'r twelve rungs from th' top, he looks up an' Leland's pointin' th' rifle at his daddy's head. Well, Hec stops fer a minute, an' I kin hear him tellin' th' kid he's yella an' a sissy an' he ain't man enough t'pull th' trigger ... all that kinda stuff."

"Wish I could have been there !!"

"An' then th' kid lays down th' rifle on th' platform, an' he sez c'mon up here ya sorry-ass drunken coward. C'mon up an' get yer dam' gun, if yer man enough .... An' then he jus' sits down, waitin'."

"What a scene!!! I can just imagine it".

"Yep. An' by now, half th' town's down b'low, watchin' an' listenin' t' Leland callin' out his old man. Callin' him a coward. Well sir, Hec scrambles up th' last few feet, an' when he grabs th' top rung, it comes off in his hand, an' down he goes, spinnin' an' flailin' an' hollerin'. That's a eighty foot tower, n' he bangs inta it a coupla times b'fore he hits th' ground."

"Kill him?"

"Not right away. But he's busted up pretty bad. Died on th' way t'th' hospital."

"Damn! What about Leland?"

"Well, Leland throws th' gun clear a th' tower an' climbs down, takin' care t'miss that top rung, of course. An y'know, he's no more shook up over his daddy fallin' than I dunno what. He seemed pretty much at peace, I'd say."

"That's one hell of a story, Sheriff. What became of the boy?"

"Last I heard, he was over in western Georgia, workin' with Jimmie Carter's group ... y'know, th' Habitat fer Humanity folks. He comes over here now 'n then, t'th'Greenway Clinic, t'see Celia. But I don't think she even knows who he is."

The reporter thanked the sheriff for his time, and for the story. The sheriff walked him to the door and waved as he drove off.

"Nice young fella'," he thought. "Wonder if he'll make mention of Cattonsville or Beecham County in his paper."

Of course, the sheriff had kept back one part of the tragic story. In fact, he hadn't told anyone what he'd discovered the day after the death of Hec Coutts, when he'd climbed the tower and found the hacksaw on the platform.

WRITERS CLASS

Whatever it was, a shout, or a shot or a car door slamming, it was only once, just enough to rouse him from sleep. He turned to read the beside clock: four-forty. Damn! The first deep sleep he'd had in over a week, and now this. He'd seen 1 o'clock, and 1:30, and 2:00. He'd finally drifted off, seemed like only minutes ago, and now some damn fool had snapped him out of the rest he so desperately needed, and he knew he'd never get back to sleep.

The first hint of dawn, and herky-jerky shadows danced across the room, ghostly patterns created by the live oaks and light curtains being rustled by a gentle early-morning breeze. It was un-seasonal, he noted, promising cool rain. A little rain, he thought, might be a good thing, considering the heat of passions that had raged during the last few weeks. Yep, a good rain just might clear the air, bring some relief to the island, maybe to the whole of Glynn County, so much in need of a cleansing.

Sheriff Vern Arbuckle loved the South. He often said the sky here had its own distinctive blue, the sun shone most days, and the rains fell on uninsulated roofs like the drumming of God's fingers, sometimes in gentle whispers, sometimes violent and insistent. But these days, he thought again, a cold rain might be just what everyone needed.

He lay back and made a futile attempt to clear his mind of the dream that had plagued his troubled sleep before he'd been jolted awake. The exact dream was gone, but only just, and it didn't seem to matter – it had been much the same as all the others. All variations of a theme. Inevitably he'd be teetering on the edge of some great abyss, some terrifying height, about to topple, and always he'd be reaching for some helping hand, or a beam, or a branch, and then he'd be plummeting and flailing. He'd fallen from cliffs, been sucked out of an aircraft banking over the Jekyll runway, swept off a tower of the Sidney Lanier bridge...Always, salvation had been close, but not near enough. Always he'd awake just in time, shivering and drenched in sweat. Awake, he tried to connect the dreams to the wretched events of the past seven weeks. There was a link, he knew, but he couldn't make it.

Return to sleep being impossible, he reasoned that wakefulness at least offered some relief from the torment. And lying now with one arm thrown across his eyes, he thought again of the woman in the cell. He wondered how she slept and if her nights were as hellish as his. Certainly, during the trial, her demeanor had given no hint of inner turmoil. Rather, she'd presented a model of serenity throughout the tortuous proceedings. The thought of the stereotypical Asian, inscrutable and impassive in the face of challenge and adversity. How little we know of them, he thought; how little I know of her. The whole sordid affair was a study in contrasts. On one hand, the genteel and easy charm of the setting, the Golden Isles of southeast Georgia. On the other, the vulgar tableau that had become Sheriff Arbuckle's sole focus over the past seven and a half weeks.

"Same thing again, Hon?" Vern's wife had awakened, too, and recognized the signs that had become part of their sleep-deprived nights. "No better, huh? Poor you. Are you gonna try to get some more sleep?"

"No...I'll get up in a minute or two. You stay here, Rosie. I'll put the coffee on in a little while. You get some more sleep."

He didn't get up immediately, but lay there letting his restless mind wander. At times like these, when the dreams seemed to threaten his very sanity and he'd waken disoriented and trembling, he'd think back to his old life, recalling the simple tranquility of his Yankee roots. He'd lived thirty years in the North, in up-State New York, in the town of Ogdensburg, where hockey and snowmobiling ruled the long cold winters, and the rest of the year seemed to be in preparation for more of the same next winter. He'd taught high school English and History, and coached football and hockey. Hard to believe he'd be missing that. But now, with the killing, and the trial, and the Klan, and the woman in the cell, those years up north began to look like the better deal. Then, his biggest problems had been marks deadlines, and team rosters, and how to motivate sluggish students. Then, he had hoped simply to get through his days without losing his temper, saying something he'd later regret. In those simpler times, he'd dreamt gentle dreams of sunny warm days in the South and wondered if and how he'd ever truly leave the North country.

His escape had come in his thirty-second year, the summer he'd gone with his brother to the Maritimes for a fly-fishing holiday. There, on the banks of the Miramichi he'd met Rose Woodley whose father owned a fishing camp and a half-mile of shoreline on that famous river. Their relationship bloomed and sped them through the two weeks, and on his return to Ogdensburg he'd sought her out at her home in Savannah. First by phone, daily, and then in person, in Savannah, he'd continued the courtship. He'd quit his teaching job and married Rose that October. It had been easy to turn his back on the North. Rose's father owned a papermill on the mainland, in Brunswick,

60

Georgia. The newlyweds moved to Jekyll Island just before Christmas, and Vern went to work in the mill in Brunswick. He stayed there for three years before joining the Glynn County police force, working in the Narcotics and Youth Crimes Division.

At age forty he had run successfully for sheriff of Glynn County, the job he'd held for the past eight years. The recent trial and conviction of Lucy Rhee for the murder of Ursel Kemp had been the toughest two months of Vern's life.

The media had been bloodthirsty, of course, relentless in dredging up every puerile and tawdry aspect of the lives of the accused and her victim. What might have been only mean and base in fact was embellished and lurid overblown detail in television and front page coverage from Savannah to Jacksonville. Police presence had been doubled in Brunswick, the State Police supplying three troopers each day of the trial to bolster the thin local ranks. Brunswick had attained, at least for a few weeks, big city status.

And the ingredients were perfect for sensationalism: sex, murder, and racism. The victim was a white man of means and stature in the community; the accused (now convicted) an Asian immigrant, a bag-packer and floor-sweeper at the Winn-Dixie managed by the man she was convicted of poisoning. Add to this the noisome presence of the Klan. Every T.V. snippet, every news photo, managed to include one or more of the Klansmen front and center, wrapped in or waving the Confederate flag and calling for swift Southern justice.

For the sheriff, the whole wretched fandango was, literally, more than he could stomach, and his Maalox intake had reached a level where Rose worried for his health. This was the South where gentility and grace were supposed to be second nature, with soft cadences falling from smiling lips like petals in a breeze. In his eight years of police work, Vern had encountered a range of depravity. Bar fights, stabbings, domestic violence, child neglect. He'd dealt with deaths, too, traffic fatalities and homicides. But this case was different and even now, with the trial over and the convicted killer awaiting sentencing, he was troubled by it. Deeply troubled, by harrowing dreams and a skin rash.

He got up, noting the time, half-past five and now light outside, and made his way to the kitchen..

Early on, when she saw how the case was affecting him, Rose had suggested he keep a record, personal reflections on all that transpired and pertained to the case. "Maybe it would be good therapy....make the dreams go away....take away the itchin' an' scratchin. An' who knows, maybe you could write it all up, when you retire. Might be a best seller." But he had no heart

61

for it; the very thought of somehow capitalizing on Lucy Rhee's misfortune was abhorrent to him. As he observed her, talked to her over the weeks of her incarceration, he had come to his own conclusion regarding her guilt or innocence. He was convinced this gentle self-deprecating girl was simply not capable of the crime of which she'd been convicted.

"I've never seen anyone like her", he'd told Rose. "She has no guile, no deceit in her. She's gentle, an' composed. She accepts the jail routine...no complaints, no demands. She sits there in court every day an' it's like she's waitin' for a bus. It's like....I dunno...like she either doesn't understand what's goin' on or she just doesn't care."

He made the coffee and then stood, waiting, at the kitchen sink. He looked out on the back yard, not seeing anything. He checked his watch, then turned the coffee machine off. He walked down the hall to the bedroom.

"Rosie...no, don't get up. You stay there for a while. I'm gonna drive over to th' jail for a few minutes..."

"Now?" She looked at the clock. "It's not even six....Have you had breakfast? I can..."

"No. Stay in bed. I'll eat when I get back. I won't be long."

"Something wrong, Vern?"

"No....it's just something I've gotta tend to. Won't take long. I made coffee....just needs t' be turned on."

Jesse put the last sheet down, straightened the pages, secured them with a paper clip, and sat back from the table. The others continued to sit quietly, expectantly, in various poses of attention and lethargy. When it became apparent that he had finished, they came to life.

"Whoa....wait..y' mean that's it? That can't be it, Jess." Karen the manicurist spoke first, looking around the table for support. "I mean...like...what's next? What's gonna happen, y' know, at th' jail an' all?"

"Right on! Y'can't stop there, man. Y' can't leave readers up in th' air like that. Y' gotta give us more info, like what an' why an' who. Know what I mean?" This from Mitch, the expert, the insufferable know-it-all Mitch.

"Yeah, I agree," chirped Cynthia, suddenly alert after a quarter hour of what had seemed very much like sleep during Jesse's reading. She sat up straight now, as if to underline her critical contribution. "I mean, what's up with this sheriff...is he some kind of nut? Who thinks like that? An' then, like, there's crime. Murder....But how did it happen, how did she get it to the guy, the poison? You didn't give us any facts, Jess."

"Well, it's meant to make you wonder, an' think," Jesse began, "and there's....."

"Wait....wait....," Audrey held up a delicate hand. "I've got it. The sheriff an' Lucy what's-her-name have somethin' going on. Y'know. She's his captive, right? An' he's the sheriff, right?" She lounged in her chair in what, Jesse assumed, was her effort at seductive posing, and breathed, "I mean, he's probably good-lookin; y'know...George Clooney kinda guy...an' she's probably, uh, y'know these Oriental women. She's available, an' it's his jail. Right?"

Mitch jumped back in. "Could be, but let's look first at th' weak spots. Y' know, Jess, this was supposed to be a character study. But you don't give us enough. Like, I mean, how tall is the sheriff, what's he weigh, what color is his wife's hair. That's character study. Y' don't give us stuff like that. That's important."

Jesse sat quiet and let them unload their critical barrage. If he had the answers they sought, he was not prepared to offer them. He looked at the instructor. Dr. Butterill sat steepling his long fingers, apparently marshalling his thoughts. But before the judgement came, Mitch continued, "An' another thing. How'd he get a job as a cop in the first place? What's his qualifications for that kinda work? An' then sheriff? I don't think it works that way."

"That's not important," Audrey sighed. "Who cares about a technicality. What's important is what the sheriff has on his mind. Like what he's got planned. Y' know, with Lucy..."

"Yeah. Is he gonna bust her outta jail, or what? But what about his wife, an' d'you think Rose knows what's goin' on....I know I'd be suspicious, my husband worryin' so much about some babe in jail." Karen, pleased with her insightful analysis, smiled around the table.

Finally Dr. Clive Butterill cleared his throat. Magisterial, pencil-thin, and pompous as a peacock, he taught communications at the Coastal Community College. And twice-weekly, on Monday and Thursday evenings, he encouraged writers-to-be in the basement of the Calvary Baptist Church. "Well, Jesse," he intoned, "that was interesting. But I think the class is, ah, fundamentally correct. As a story, well, here I have trouble. You haven't given us much. You hint and imply, but....well, that's not enough. You haven't given us substantive material." He paused, pleased with the word, and himself.

The assignment had been to create a short story set in the South, dealing with conflict and revealing character through action and dialogue. Each student would have thirty minutes. Jesse had been the first name drawn.

There were seven students. Jesse and Mitch were the only men. For the last two months they had been privileged to listen to Dr. Butterill's lectures on creative writing and ways to get published. All of them were struggling to "put the right words in the proper order", the learned professor's favorite phrase and mantra of encouragement. They attempted pen portraits, word associations, verse and prose, guided by their instructor's frequent references to his own writing achievements, some of which, he assured them, had been published in literary journals and none of which they ever got to see.

The women, hairdressers, salesclerks, and housewives, wrote dreadful pieces of fluff. Mitch had some experience, he was quick to point out. He wrote a weekly column on car maintenance for the *Tappets and Rods*. On the basis of this experience, he felt qualified to offer sage counsel, and in the two months the group had been together, his opinions had dominated their sessions. He picked up now where the instructor had left off. "That's it. A lack of substantive...uh....stuff. Y'know, it coulda been developed more like Audrey sez, get ol' Vern an' Lucy together. Whaddya think?"

Lorena, co-owner of L'il Critters pet shop, spoke up. "I liked it, Jess. But y' lost me when y' started talkin' about Oddenburg, er Oggersville, er whatever. What was that all about. An' then, the fishin' trip...y' lost me there. But I like th' idea of Vern an' Lucy...you know, gettin' together. An' could be ol' Rosie's got somethin' goin' on, too. Y' know, like with maybe a deputy er somethin! These days, y' know, who knows how long any marriage is gonna last..."

"Y' know, Jesse, you got the basis of a real story here," Mabel, mother of seven and well along her eighth pregnancy, added. "I like the way you make Vern so...uh....sensitive. But that ending....it's no ending at all."

Jesse nodded his thanks, and stole a look at his watch.

Dr. Butterill decided it was time for his final pronouncements. "Publishing is a tough business, people." He tugged at the knot of his tie. "And if there's one important thing I've learned, it's this: editors, publishers...they want substance. Tell the story, get it on the page. Let your reader see it, feel it. Don't get cute with suggestions and hints. The reader wants substance, not nuance." He sat back, mightily pleased with that note.

Jesse looked around the room, at his fellow students. He looked at the concrete-block wall, the church activities calendar on the wall behind the instructor's chair. And he felt the combined weight of anger and resignation flood over him. Was it worth trying to explain his intentions, defending his story?

"Well," he began, "I gave it a lot of thought. What I was trying..."

"Trying to get around the assignment, eh Jess!" Mitch was obviously enjoying the moment, inviting further participation in belittling Jesse's efforts. "Cutting corners works sometimes. But as Dr. B. says, you cut too many here. And we got nothin' t'go on..."

"Yeah, no fair, Jess," Cynthia snapped her gum, "I'd a wanted some action, y'know?"

Dr. B. held up his hand. Jesse noted the tremor, and wondered again if he drank. "Jesse, perhaps another go at it. I like the premise, and I really think you could develop something here. Something....uh...substantive. And try some character development. Let us see your sheriff. Make him real. And then, maybe we could hear your revision, with..uh...the additional stuff I've suggested. We'll hear the others first, an' I'll put you on again at the end. That gives you three weeks to come up with...uh...more plot, more character."

As he was speaking, Jesse's sense of desperation crystalized into the realization of what the last two months had been, a colossal waste of time.

"......and so, number two next week. That's..let's see...that's you, Audrey. And, Jesse, please don't be discouraged. You have some good points....good starting points. The story has potential. But I have to tell you, I know what editors look for. And, yes, I've had rejections along the way..along with successes. You pick yourself up and go at it again. You just have to give us more to sink our teeth into. Do you see?" He seemed almost to be pleading now, seeking agreement and support. Jesse just wanted it all to end, to be away from this place, this atmosphere of mediocrity.

The doctor wasn't finished. "Or maybe you could make a fresh start, find another idea to develop, another theme. And - just a thought - if you want to leave this first attempt with me, I could go over it, make notations that might be helpful. Y'know, a few good suggestions might put you back on track....."

"No, thanks. I'll take it with me. Thanks just the same." He put his story on the desk, along with his notes and pens, took his jacket off the back of the chair, and rose to leave.

Mitch reached over and touched his arm. "Tell y' what, Jess. Choose somethin' simpler. Y' know, straight story line, A to B...somethin' we kin all recognize. Not so much of that, uh, subconscious stuff. Y' know, no tricks er anything. I could give you some ideas on all that."

"Thanks, Mitch. I'll keep it in mind. I probably won't be seeing you again, though." And with that he was out of the room without a backward glance at the surprised faces behind him. Up the stairs, two at a time, and out of the church. He paused at the entrance to draw in a lungful of delicious fresh air. At the side of the parking lot, near the handicap spots, he spied a green trash barrel, and he headed straight for it. He dumped the story and all his notes into the barrel. "Guess I'll see what's goin' on at Chunky's," he thought as he wheeled his Mustang out of the lot.

Clive Butterill, leaving twenty-five minutes later and passing the trash barrel on the way to his car, saw something white on top of the accumulated garbage. Gingerly he reached in and extracted Jesse's notebooks and story. He looked around the now-deserted lot before slipping the pages into his bookbag.

He hummed happily as he drove home, thinking of the whisky-sour awaiting him, and knowing he had the basis of a dynamite short story.

Bourbon and Grits

DROUGHT

Most of the boys were in The Salty Dog the night after Burl McEvoy got shot. Jackson Buell left his bar open past closing time, and some of the boys stayed another hour or so, to show respect for Burl and appreciation for Jackie's gesture. Upton stayed late, and Billy the seed man, and Eddie Emmons. Joe Bob Hannah left, but Sheriff Townsend and Dewey Wales hung in. And Mason and Tommy Dodge.

Jackie turned out the main lights and the outside neon Budweiser and Miller lights, and ushered the boys into the back room. "It's one gawd-awful thing, boys. But to me, it's no great surprise, knowin' what ol' Burl's bin goin' through with that no-account half-breed. She's crazy, that one, an' she's bin gettin' loonier ever' day, ever since this drought began...."

Dewey agreed. "They say drought's the worst thing fer injuns. Makes 'em act crazy..."

"Wilma Jane Dooley ain't pure injun," Eddie said, pouring pretzels into dishes. "Her daddy was white. Merle, you knowed Paddy Dooley, didn't yuh?"

The sheriff snorted. "I shoulda knowed 'im. Threw his skinny ass inta jail more 'n a dozen times. 'Course, he lived like a injun, out there back a' Yulee."

"Well, injun er half-breed...what's the difference?" Jackie opened a cupboard and produced an unopened Famous Grouse and a nearly-full Jim Beam. "Help yerself, boys. Y' kin take my meanin', I'm pretty sure. That Wilma Jane Dooley's as crazy as any full-blood."

The regulars, beaten down by half a year of failed crops on land that wouldn't produce, payments that couldn't be made, nodded their sage agreement. Upton Radmore, once attorney-at-law, now disbarred, and by far the best educated among them, offered his analysis. "Weren't no way for this relationship to work out good, boys. The white man has no business gettin' mixed up with th' injun. Don't matter that it's a half-breed in this case. Never works, never will."

68

"Yer right, Up. I knowed ol' Burl was gonna regret takin' Wilma Jane in," Billy the seed man agreed, setting aside his Budweiser and reaching for the Scotch bottle. "Mind you," he added, "that Wilma Jane's the best-lookin' injun I ever seen."

"Yep, but them eyes," Dewey said, "them shifty eyes. I'd a' put money on it, she'd be nuthin' but trouble." He took a handful of peanuts, and added, "Real good looker. As my daddy usta say, 'I would not deny her in her hour of need'."

"Yeah, well, how did it all come down t' this, ol' Burl gettin' shot? I'd a' said Burl McEvoy was too smart t' get hisself shot. By a injun!" Eddie looked around the room for confirmation.

The boys sat silent for a few moments, each trying to picture the situation, trying t' imagine what might have prompted the near-fatal wounding of their friend. Mason broke the silence.

"Well, we kin pretty well guess. She took 'im by surprise. Y' know, it kin happen, yuh let down yer guard. Ol' Burl just turned his back at the wrong time an' that crazy half-breed let 'im have it."

"Yeah. 'Cept, she shot him in the front, Mason. Right, Merle?"

Sheriff Merle Townsend wiped froth from his moustache and nodded.

"Well," Dewey offered, "way I heard it, ol' Burl was pretty good to her, considering. I heard him an' Wilma Jane got along pretty good."

"Yer right, Dewey," Tommy said. "I seen th' two of 'em over t' th' Walmart last month, lookin' at them big-screen T.V.'s. An' y' know, next day er so, they got that big 'ol T.V. settin' right there in th' trailer. Hell if I know how they got it in there!"

Jackie came back from the bar with twelve more Buds and put them in a tub of ice. "Here y' are, boys. On the house. Or take the whiskey, if yuh prefer." He turned to the sheriff. "Wasn't all bad with Burl an' Wilma Jane. Some good times, eh, Merle?"

The sheriff nodded. "Yep. Kind of a day-to-day thing, y' might say. Me an' Hobie got called out t' th' trailer a number a' times, I kin tell yuh that. Weren't pretty, at times. An' one thing's fer sure, it got worse when the drought come. They seemed t' bang on each other more, the dryer it got. One time it'd be ol' Burl bleedin', next time it'd be ol' Wilma Jane all bloodied up." He paused to drain his Bud, and reached into the tub for another. "Yuh never knowed what t' expect. Got so's Hobie didn't wanta take them calls no more. Got scared ol' Wilma Jane was gonna go after him, one of them times."

Ed Emmons nodded. "Never trust a injun. An' then yuh gotta figure on two things, these days....a injun who's more 'n likely drunk, an' a goddam drought, worst in thirty-some years. That is one deadly combination, my friends!"

"Drought an' booze. An' a injun!" Billy the seed man poured more peanuts into a bowl, and took a handful. "I mind th' time, few years back, before th' drought, ol' Wilma Jane done a number on ol' Hammie Nuth."

Tommy Dodge's head snapped up. "I know'd Hammie Nuth. Usta live out t' Sprivey's Corners. Had a ol' green Fargo half ton. Won it in a poker game at Harrison McGruder's...."

"Yep. Well, Wilma Jane was bunkin' with Hammie, an' one day she up an' stuck him with a pitchfork." Billy the seed man had their undivided attention. Not even Sheriff Townsend had heard this one. "Heard it from Denzil Toombs. You boys remember Denzil, had one ear tore off in a fight with Clarence Hindman? Clarence caught 'im with his wife, out backa Carson Malloy's barn. Anyways, ol' Denzil was workin' at Hammie's that summer, an' he seen Wilma Jane stick ol' Hammie–."

"– He seen it?"

"Yep. She come outta th' barn while Hammie an' Denzil was workin' on Hammie's tractor. Old Ford Farm All, never did run good. An' she drove that pitchfork right into Hammie's backside. He never seen her comin'."

"Damn! Drunk, was she?"

"Prob'ly. Denzil told me he seen 'em fightin' earlier that mornin'. She was yellin' an' cussin'. Denzil said she took after ol' Hammie with a big ol' cast iron fry pan an' he had t' step lively, her swingin' at his head an' all. Said he finally got around behind her and knocked her down. Him an' Denzil sat on her 'til she went quiet like. An' then Hammie drug her inta th' house an' come back out t' work."

"Damn!"

"Yep. Hammie come out, an' they went t' work on th' tractor. Denzil figgered she was sleepin' it off, an' next thing he knowed, she's stickin' Hammie. He still walks kinda funny."

Sheriff Merle yawned and looked at his watch. "Reckon I oughta drive over an' check on Hobie. He come in dead tired t' night. I'll prob'ly find 'im sleepin' in one a' th' cells."

"Hobie's tired," Tommy laughed. "Hell, what I see, Hobie sleeps most of the day, ever' day."

"Yep, well, he's worse than usual t' night. He come in draggin', wore out. Tol' me he's been doin' some plumbin' fer widow Boone. But I don't like him sleepin' at the jail...."

"Plumbin', hell!" Tommy snorted. "Hobie Reese couldn't plumb a pisspot! I seen th' job he done over at Hap Daniel's place last month. Hap said he had t' git Beckinstalls in t' tear it all out an' start all over. Hobie had

70

th' crapper pipes runnin' inta th' kitchen drain an' I dunno what all....."

"I know. I heard all about it from Hap. But y' know Hobie's whole corn crop failed, an' his wife's over at the Greenway Clinic ever' second day, an' he's just tryin' t' bring in a few extra dollars....Ain't easy with no cash crop at all...."

They nodded. No need to explain what the drought was doing to Hobie Reese, to all of them. There was nothing anyone could say or do to change the hard times that seemed to suck the life out of all of them. They sat morose and reflective. Dewey Wales broke the silence.

"So yuh've got Wilma Jane down there now, Merle...yuh think they'll move her t' th' County Seat?"

"Dunno....guess it'll depend on Burl. Does he live or die."

"Any trouble bringin' her in?"

"Judas Priest, Ed, what you take me for? Think I can't make an arrest on a woman? Even if it is Wilma Jane Dooley?"

Tommy Dodge stood and stretched. "Guess I'll call it a night, boys. By gawd, this dam' drought's gotta end soon. Nothing goin' on...no work... nobody comin' t' town fer nuthin'. Nobody's buyin'. Only thing in the last six months is ol' Burl gettin' shot."

"Yep."

"Guess Burl's kids'll be comin' in. You talked t' any of 'em, Merle?" Upton asked. "I don't recall...how many kids is there, anyway?"

Merle leaned back and regarded the ceiling. "Couple in Atlanta. Two more gone out West somewheres. Hell if I know where. I tried t' call his sister in Statesville, but I couldn't get ahold of her. Hobie thinks she moved somewheres, mebbe Arkansas...."

"I remember Burl's oldest boy." Billy the seed man said. "A hell raiser, as I recall...Ursel I think his name was...."

"Yep. Ursel. He's servin' time, at Wadsworth."

"Wadsworth! What' d he do?"

"Well, grand theft auto when he was seventeen. An' he gets parole an' th' next week he tries t' sell some dope to a undercover cop!"

"But Wadsworth?!"

"Yep. They search his place after the dope bust an' they find stuff from more than a dozen burglaries, plus a bunch a' handguns and a coupla assault rifles. An' then he tried t' bust outta the remand center....."

"Yuh tell 'im about his daddy?"

"Uh, yeah. He was all fer comin' home. 'Course, the warden canned that. Long as ol' Burl's alive, Ursel's not goin' nowheres."

"They was two boys, twins I think," Billy the seed man said, "Ursel an'

Quentin...."

"Yep. Quentin's dead. Stabbed t' death, up in Richmond. Bar fight...."

"Mason, you had one a' th' McEvoy girls workin' fer you," Dewey said. "At th' RiteAid, wasn't it?"

"Yep. Carley Ann McEvoy. Musta bin eight or nine years ago. I put her on the cash, but that didn't work. Nice girl, but dumb as a post. Put 'er in the stock room. Woulda let her go, but ol' Burl done my roof fer half price. She married Cortland Bulger, if I remember right."

Eddie snorted. "There's a match made in heaven! Cort Bulger never done a day's work in his sorry life!"

"Him an' Burl hunted a lot, if I remember correct," Billy the seed man said, pouring himself another inch or two of Famous Grouse.

"Ain't seen Cort Bulger since he fell down Acey Jeeters' well," Upton said. "Broke both his legs. 'Course he was so drunk he was still singin' when they hauled 'im out."

"Yeah, well, never was a Bulger showed any more sense than a jackass." Billy the seed man took a long satisfying swallow. "Did yuh talk t' Carly Ann, Merle?"

"Couldn't get no one at the number Hobie give me. I'll try again in th' mornin'. Mebbe have t' send Hobie over t' Nahunta...."

"Uh," Mason spoke hesitantly, "yuh might wanta think about that, Sheriff. Carly Ann Bulger's....uh....she's gone kinda....peculiar. If y' know what I mean."

"No, I don't know, Mason. Gawd sake, I'm required to notify family. Gotta do it...it's the law. What're yuh tryin' t' tell me?"

"Well, I ain't seen this m' self, but....we...I heard things, an...well, Carly Ann's gone all voodoo."

"Voodoo! What in gawd's name are yuh talkin' about, voodoo!?"

"Millie's brother told me. He knows Cort Bulger. He sez Carly Ann's gone all funny. First sign we got, me an' Millie, we got our Christmas card sent back, Millie sends them a card ever' year, an' the card we sent had some crazy signs, some kinda symbols all over the baby Jesus in his crib. An' there was some kinda looney poem on th' back. Somethin' Carly Ann had wrote."

"Voodoo!? Crissake, Mason!" Merle drained his glass and reached for a refill. "By gawd, I got enough on my plate right now, an' you introduce voodoo!? C' mon, Mason."

"I know how it sounds, Merle. An' I didn't know what t' make of it all. I tell yuh, Millie's all shook up about them signs, an' that poem...."

"What's that got t' do with voodoo, fer crissake? An' with ol' Burl an' Wilma Jane?"

72

"I dunno, Merle. But I went an' seen Burl after the card come. Asked 'im what's goin' on with Carly Ann...."

"And?"

"An' he told me Carly Ann's gone cuckoo, since she had that baby born with no arms. She took that t' be some kinda sign er sumthin'. I dunno. Ol' Burl wasn't too sure himself....but...."

"C' mon, Mason!"

"No...listen. Burl tol' me himself. Said she started readin' all that crap about signs an' spells. Y' know...hexes an' th' like. She got ol' Cort t' take her down t' New Orleans, or somewheres. They took th' baby with 'em....got in touch with some sorry-ass medicine man or somethin'. Burl said they spent a month or more down there....listening to this looney cult bullshit an' all."

"Bullshit sounds about right, Mason."

"I know, I know. But Burl was sure she was hexed or sumthin'. Cort, he couldn't make her see no sense in anythin', an' he's goin' crazy hisself, seems. Ever' since th' baby, an' them goin' t' New Orleans, she's completely screwy. Wears some kinda black robe....an' she made Cort paint their trailer all black, even th' windas. An' she went an' painted them voodoo signs an' symbols all over th' trailer. And, uh...."

"Yeah, what? Go ahead."

"Well, she's stealin' chickens from her neighbors, an'–."

"Mason, you are startin' to piss me off!"

"Honest t' gawd, Merle. Folks seen her sneakin' around barn yards an' coops, all dressed funny an' totin' that little armless kid wrapped in some kinda black cocoon-thing an'stealin' chickens."

"Gimme another shot there, Jackie. Thanks." The sheriff ran a hand through his thinning hair and slumped back in his chair. "God knows what's next in this gawd-awful story. Go ahead, Mason......"

"Burl said she done more than just stealin' chickens. Said she commenced t' hissin' at folks, an' utterin'...."

"Utterin'!! What th' hell's 'utterin'?"

"Hell if I know. Burl said it's like puttin' a hex on ever' one she seen. Stoppin' folks in th' road, an' pointin', and givin' 'em th' evil eye. An' mumblin' at 'em, nothin' anybody could unnerstan'. Burl said it weren't no word of a lie. He give up on 'er, an' Cort finally give up on 'er...."

Billy the seed man laughed. " An' we thought Wilma Jane was looney! What you gonna do, Merle, get th' two of 'em together? A gun tuthii halit-hiced an' a voodoo princess....mebbe yuh could charge admission. People might forget about drought fer awhile!"

"Ain't funny, Billy. Maybe I swear you in an' send you over t' Nahunta

73

t' bring 'er in."

"Boys", Jackson said, "it's nearly three o'clock. I gotta git t' bed."

"Yep, time t' go." Dewey started gathering the empty bottles. "Thanks, Jackie. Dunno what we solved here t' night, but it felt good."

"Hope yuh kin solve yer problem, Merle," Jackie said, "Y' know, next-of-kin an' all. But I think Mason's right.....you don't want no voodoo daughter showin' up."

"Yeah, we'll see. If ol' Burl pulls through, we kin ferget all th' other business."

"An' what'll happen t' Wilma Jane?"

"Tell yuh th' truth, I surely do hope ol' Burl makes it. This county don't need no murder trial, not on top a' this drought an' all...."

"Jury gets paid, don't it?" Asked Eddie as he stacked the pretzel and peanut dishes.

"Yep...eight dollars a day."

"Eight bucks more 'n I'm pullin' in these days," said Billy the seed man.

"Now hold on boys," Merle said, reaching for his Stetson. "We get a murder trial, we gotta pay fer extra security. We gotta tie up people who might be makin' more 'n a lousy eight bucks a day. An' we got outsiders comin' in, just to gawk an....we don't want no murder trial!"

They made their way to the front of the saloon, and Mason held the door as they filed out.

"Anybody hear the forecast?"

"Same old, same old. God knows we need rain," said Dewey. "Donna Lou says we gotta move outta this dust bowl. She wants t' go live with her folks, up t' Minnesota. No drought in Minnesota."

"Hope yuh like ice an' snow!"

"Yeah, well, she may be goin' alone."

"Minnesota! Drought sounds okay, yuh start thinkin' about Minnesota."

"Got that right! G' night boys."

"G' night."

HUNT CAMP

"Oh yeah, it was a dumb idea. No argument there." Clayton banged the ashes from his long-cold pipe into his palm and dumped the remnants into the empty coffee can. He nodded agreement as Silas pulled four more Buds from the cooler. "But y' know," he continued, "a father can be pushed only so far, and then, by damn, y' gotta push back, take charge. I suppose y' could say I snapped. But who wouldn't, given them circumstances. They pushed, an' pushed....testin' me. An' they just pushed once too often."

"Kids," said Homer.

"Yeah. Would I do it again? I dunno. Prob' ly."

"I mind th' time my youngest got into a bottle a' my Wild Turkey," Silas said, placing the full bottles on the old steamer trunk. "Kid got absolutely hammered. I thought Bunny was gonna kill me. She went nuts. Y' d think I give 'im th' booze. She's a holy terror 'bout drinkin', that woman." And he lifted a cheek off the padded cushion to let a muffled fart sneak out, enriching the confined cabin air.

"Yep, they're all the same when it comes t' booze, I reckon." Clay settled back in the permanently half-open Laz-y-boy and patted his multi-pocketed vest for his tobacco pouch. "But Gawd almighty, that time with th' boys an' the t'baccy–that was a time!"

"Don't recall hearing that one," Homer said, reaching for another Bud. "How'd that one go? I do recall somethin' about one a' your guys upsettin' Jake Ebert's privy. With Jake in it."

"Judas Priest, who dropped that one?" Dillon suddenly exclaimed. "Silas, that was you, wasn't it! I b'lieve somethin' crawled up an' died inside a' you!"

"Yeah? Didja ever think it could be th' cookin' in this sorry-ass camp? Yer cookin', Homer....I hate t' complain, but I kin imagine tastier turds than that myst'ry yuh concocted t' night!"

"Get back t' them boys a' yers, Clay," Dillon said. "Wanna hear about th' t'baccy..."

Clay finally found the pouch and fished it out of a hip pocket. He filled the bowl and searched anew, for matches. His cronies waited, knowing he

75

would not be hurried, and they had all evening. The hunt camp, where they'd spent their last twenty or twenty-two Novembers, (they couldn't agree on the number of years), was a secluded three-room shanty fifteen miles from the town of Altonsburg, on the south branch of the Garlock River in North-East Tennessee. It was short on amenities, but warmed sufficiently by an old Vermont Castings stove. Its rough ambiance was perfectly conducive to the recollections and lies of the hunt club that once numbered seven and was now down to four. On this night, as always, the two old dogs slept fitfully in their corner by the wood pile, the rifles cleaned and readied for the morning leaned in another corner, the dishes were done, cleaned after a fashion, and the four old cronies sat around contentedly, ready for the usual lies and exaggerations. It was the first Fall hunt without Eldon, and they were determined to avoid mawkish memories of friends departed.

Clay drew contentedly on his mixture of Old Chum and Capt. Black and squinted through the smoke at his gnarled and whiskery companions.

"I s' pose y' could lay most of th' blame on Ol' Hitchcock," he said. "They'd been pesterin' me ever since they seen Ol' Hitchcock. Y' mind him, ol' Harvey Hitchcock, usta work fer Woodley, over at th' Co-op. Anyways, he come inta th' yard that time, me an' th' boys was workin' on the log splitter, an' he had a load a' squared timbers an' he's lookin' fer some creosote I had out in th' shed." He drew again on the sputtering Meer-Shaum and tamped the bowl with a roughened brown forefinger.

Dillon drained his Budweiser in a long swallow, loosed a resounding moist belch, and settled more comfortably into the broken loveseat. "Yep, I recall Ol' Hitchcock....Usta run with th' Garvie boys, back b'fore Miles Garvie set that fire t' Shackleton's barn. Killed some sheep...Ever'body thought it was Ol' Hitchcock set th' fire...."

"Lotta folks say it weren't Hitchcock set that fire. Never had no proof. An' he had a alibi," Homer said. "Claimed he was courtin' th' widow Tapley over t' Boone Creek that evenin'. An' she backed 'im up. Course Charlene Tapley was prob'ly capable of lyin'. Among other things."

"Yep," agreed Dillon, "I seen her with Abe Tinsley last month at th' Bennet's auction, an' y' know Abe's so near blind he'd go out with a alligator if it smelled good."

"Mebbe....but y' know Abe's no fool, an' th' widow's got lots a' dough, they say.."

"Let Clay tell th' story, boys," Silas rasped. "Clay, you want me t' put some more wood in th' stove?"

"No, hells bells, it's hotter 'n blazes in here as it is. Leave 'er be. Judas Priest, Homer, what'd you put in that gumbo, anyway?" And he took a long
76

pull on the Bud before returning to his pipe. "Now, you boys who knew Hitchcock remember he always had his jaw full a' t'baccy...chewing an' spittin' all day long. An' the boys just had t' see that particular show, and then they was at me all that summer. All 'cause of that one time....he's out there in th' yard, chewing an' cussin' an' spittin'. An' young Mikey, he's takin' it all in, an' y' can imagine how it's affectin' young Dermott...." He paused for another swig, and his listeners drained their bottles, too. "Silas, get me another one, will yuh."

Silas roused himself far enough off the floral covered rocker to reach into the cooler. "Lots left, boys. 'Course that's on account a' Eldon ain't here...."

"Yep, Eldon could put 'em down, that ol' boy. D' yuh mind th' summer he was courtin' Charley Dobson's sister? My gawd that was one homely woman!"

"Yeah, built like a sack a' moose antlers. But she could dance. An' Eldon did like t' dance..."

"Wasn't much that ol' boy didn't like," said Silas, and they all leaned in to clink their bottles.

"Anyways....," Clay brought them back to his story of the boys and Hitchcock and the tobacco. "There's Ol' Hitchcock out in th' yard, an' he's got his mouth full a' t'baccy an' he's cussin' t' beat hell an' spittin' his gobs ever' where. Good thing Agnes was off someplace...prob'ly gone t' bible study er somethin'....she couldn't abide Ol' Hitchcock. Course they wasn't many ol' boys from over t' Lowesville that she could abide."

"Yer Agnes was a hard woman, Clay." agreed Dillon. "I mind th' time she set th' dogs on ol' Herb Cooty's boy. Scared that ol' boy half t' death..... Don't know what scared 'im more, th' dogs or yer Agnes."

"Yep. Well, anyways, there we was, an' th' boys 'r gettin' th' whole show. An' a' course, Ol' Hitchcock's playin' it up, seein' th' effect he's havin' on th' boys. Musta gone through a whole plug a' Red Man while we's puttin' th' creosote t' them squared pieces. An' cussin'! Judas Priest, that man could cuss fer ten minutes an' never repeat hisself!"

"Kids got an earful, I reckon," said Homer, rubbing a sore on one blue-veined wrist. "I seen Ol' Hitchcock down t' Grady Lamb's place last Spring. It was cold, I recall....colder 'n a tart's farewell, an' Hitchcock an' Grady was tryin' to git th' power take off workin' on Grady's ol' Ford tractor. Havin' no end a' bad luck, an' they asked me was they anybody workin' th' fields over t' Willet's place."

"An' like yuh said, Ol' Hitchcock's cussin' a blue streak. An' y' know Grady's not happy about that at all. Grady don't like cussin', him bein' a fill-in-preacher over t' th' Baptist church at Danville, an' all. Looked like

Grady was fit t' bust 'im, but yuh don' wanta mess with Hitchcock, drunk 'r sober. An' he was sober as a judge that day!"

"Didja hear Grady Lamb's ol' lady run off?" Homer asked. "I heard it was some salesman, from Purina, I think it was."

"Y'ask me, I'd say Grady's better off. That Cora Lamb's about as ornery as I ever seen. Real mean, that one, and surely not one t' set yer heart a-racin'. Stick a cigar in her mouth an' y' got Groucho Marx." Dillon pulled a pouch of Half 'n Half from his shirt pocket and shook a measure of burleigh and bright onto a paper. He continued, "Yessir, I don't reckon Grady drew a happy breath all them years. Kin y' imagine life with a old bible-thumpin' hyena like that 'un?"

"But why not tell us what yuh really think of 'er, Dill?" asked Clay. "Yuh sure y'er not goin' a little soft on us, thinkin' about Grady's old lady?"

Dillon completed his ready-made, and prepared to light up. "Yeah, an' I really enjoy a good toothache! C'mon, Clay, let's hear the rest of yer story...."

"Well, after Hitchcock left, with all them timbers treated an' all, th' boys started in on me, about th' t'baccy juice. 'What's it taste like', 'd'yuh swallow it', 'where kin yuh git it', an' all. Couldn't keep 'em quiet. An' of course, could they try some. Course yuh kin imagine, if Agnes heard any a' this. Bad enough she can't abide Ol' Hitchcock, she's a terror on t'baccy fer chewing. An' spittin'.."

"It figures. Women!" Silas pulled a plug from his fleece-lined vest and bit off a small corner. "Bunny's brother Hilton chews, an' she won't have 'im in th' house, less'n he leaves his plug in th' truck."

"Lu-Anne's the same," said Homer. "Y'd think t'baccy's some almighty sin. I don' know what gits into some women, once they git their menfolk settled away, if y' know what I mean. B' fore we was married, ever' thin's jus' peaches 'n cream, y' kin smoke, er take a drink with th' boys. Then, y' git married t'em, an' y' see their true nature, their mean side. LuAnne's like a mean ol' dog when I wanta take a coupla drinks. An' do yer smokin' outside....an'...Judas Priest, I live eleven months a' th' year lookin' t' git up here, t' th' camp.....Women!"

"Yeah, well, y' make yer bed, yuh gotta sleep in it. Anyways, back t' th' boys. Them little monkeys kept pesterin' the whole time. They was bound they was gonna try th' chewin' t'baccy. 'Kin we git some t'day', 'what about t'morra', I tell yuh, tryin' to keep them quiet so Agnes don't get on no rampage, an' y' know she'd blame me....I tried t'tell 'em y'kin try it when y'kin buy yer own...."

"Well, sir, about that time they seen a baseball game, on tely vision, over t' Sid Wilson's place. They got one a' them tely vision sets, with a geezly

78

big tower beside th' house. An' my boys got t'see a ball game an' all them ball players is hawkin' and spittin' great gobs all over th' place..."

"Yeah, I seen a game one time me n' Bunny went inta Dayton. She had t'see about her bunions er' somethin', an' I went on over t' th' ballpark. Seen th' Dayton boys playin' the Havelock boys. Y'mind the Belcher twins, Dillon? They lived not too far from you, next concession if I remember right–Anyway, they was playin' fer th' Havelock team. An' Judas Priest, them boys liked their 'baccy!'" Silas's eyes glazed over for a few seconds as he brought to mind the glory days of the Dayton Bobcats, and baseball played on a regulation diamond, and bleachers that could hold up to a couple hundred spectators.

"Yeah, well," Clay growled, "d' yuh want this story or not?" They signaled for him to continue.

"Wait a minute, Clay," Dillon said. "I give that ol' Coleman a coupla pumps." The smoke-filled room had been getting darker, and Dillon coaxed the light back.

Clay continued, "So y' kin imagine how it's goin', Hitchcock an' then th' ball players, spittin' t' beat ol' hell. No way I could shut th' little buggers up now. I tried t' tell 'em if yer mother gets wind a' this there'll be the ab-so-lute hell t' pay, an' she won't be fit t' live with."

"Kids," Homer said, and lowered a gob into the coffee can.

"They got a hunderd questions, and I'm tellin' yuh, they like t'drove me t' desperation!"

"Yeah, somthin' like Harry Pratt's young lad," said Silas. "Had t' have a shot gun...had t' have a shot gun. Wouldn't give Harry a minute's peace.... just kept pestering fer a shot gun. Finally Harry's had enough, gets the lad a 12 gauge fer Christmas. Boy musta been ten 'r so...I think it was th' winter Shatner's dog bit Mable Connolley on the arse. Anyway, he got the dam' ol' 12 gauge, and wouldn't y' know it, first time out with it he blows his dam' foot off. I seen 'im just th' other day, over t' Jimmy Wall's place, workin' on a retainin' wall fer the new feed lot. Stumpin' around on that peg they got 'im fer a foot."

The four old-timers sat silent with their beers and tobacco and memories. One of the dogs, roused by their silence, looked up, sniffed the air, and flopped back down again. Homer, seeing that his bottle was again empty, made a move for the cooler and stopped. He said, "Think I'll switch fer a bit. Anybody want some rum, er a Jack?"

"Gimme a shot a' Jack, Homer, an' go easy on th' ice. I want t' taste it." Clay's pipe had gone out again, and he patted pockets in search of pipe cleaners and tobacco and matches.

"Well," said Silas, "see if we kin git this story finished b' fore midnight,

79

boys." And turning to Clay, "So, what about yer boys....did they git t' try 'er?"

"That's what I was gettin' to," said Clay, fishing out the pouch again. "It were sometime 'round mid-summer, near as I kin recall. One a' them days, y' know, when nothin' goes th' way y' want it to. There's a coupla dead chickens....fox, mebbe...th' water pump quit, they's a cow got mastitis, an' th' new feed prices come out. You know them kinda days."

"Anyways, the boys chose that particular day t' start in agin on the' t'baccy. I sez t' them, 'git in th' truck'. I goes t' th' front door and sez t' Agnes, 'We're goin' in t' Tommy Doyle's fer some wire, an' salve fer th' cow. Need anythin'?' An' she sez, 'Oh, mebbe some curds. Th' white ones, an' a new dish towel!' Or some such, I can't recall exactly."

"Anyways, off we go an' th' boys 're wonderin' what's up, 'cause I'm not sayin' nothin'. But y'kin imagine what I'm planning....gonna settle this 'baccy thing, an' mebbe that'll be th' end of it."

"So we git t' Tommy Doyle's, an' billy-be-dam' if Ol' Hitchcock ain't there!"

"Git out!"

"Yup. Like it musta been a sign er somethin'. Anyways, in we go, an' I sez 'Howdy' t' Tommy an' Ol' Hitchcock, an I sez t' Tommy, 'Gimme some a' them white curds, some udder salve, an' three plugs a' Red Man! Well sir, Ol' Hitchcock, he looks at me an' the boys, an' then I hand a plug t' each a' th' boys, an' he don't know whether t' shit 'er go blind! We head out t' th' truck, an' I see Ol' Hitchcock lookin' at us outta th' winda....I sez, have a go, boys!"

"I be damned," Homer breathed. "How old was them boys then, Clay? Couldn't a' bin real old...."

"I'd say Mikey was, mebbe ten, an' Dermott woulda bin about eight."

"Damn!"

"Yep....I started 'er up....seen Tommy an' Hitchcock watchin' it all, an' we pulled outta the lot an' headed fer home. All three of us got a plug, an' took a bite. An' I kin tell yuh....I don't chew, but I bin smokin' since I was twelve, an' that first bit is a helluva kick....made my eyes water...I look over at the boys, an' at first they's tryin' real hard t' be brave an' all. But th' tears is runnin' and they ain't sayin' a word. Prob'ly afraid t' swallow...an' we got five miles t' go....Y'kin imagine, coupla youngsters, an' a whole mouth full a' that stuff!"

"I keep lookin' over at 'em, an' they's tryin' like hell not t' yelp 'r holler. But they was sufferin. 'Wanta stop 'n spit er out?' I ask em. They just shake their heads....can't talk. An' Mikey says, with that geezly big gob in 'is mouth, an' th' tears runnin' down his face, he sez, 'We wanna git er soft so's

80

we kin spit, like Mr. Hitchcock.' An' poor little bugger, he's near t'chokin'. An' th' little guy, Dermott, he's turnin' kinda green. An' I gotta tell yuh, I wasn't enjoyin' m' own gob any too much by that time."

"By th' time we pulled inta th' yard, I was afraid I'd killed th' little buggers. Had t' go 'round th' truck t'open their door, let 'em out. They kinda slid 'n flopped out onta th' ground. An' I'm sure as hell havin' second thoughts, an' scared as hell Agnes was gonna look out an' see her babies lyin' on th' ground...."

"Damn!"

"Yeah, well....Agnes was down in the cellar, an' she never seen what was happenin' out in th' yard. I got 'em inta th' house, thought I could get 'em up t' their bedroom. But they just kinda collapsed agin on th' kitchen floor... nuthin' I could do..."

"Damn!"

"Yep, an' then, ol' Agnes appears, come up th' cellar steps, an'...well, it weren't pleasant."

"Upset, was she?"

"Y' might say so. She's yellin' at me, I poisoned her babies, an' th' like. By now th' boys is throwin' up all over th' kitchen floor, an' she's tryin' t' decide what t' do first, tend t' th' boys, bash me with a stick a' stove wood, 'r clean up th' mess."

"So what come next?"

"I reckoned my best place was somewheres else, an' I said 'Here's yer curds', an' I lit out fer th' barn t' tend t' th' cow."

"Women!" snorted Dillon. "They kin be difficult. That's why I steered clear of 'em. Couldn't see m'self bein' drove by no woman!"

"Yuh never did marry, Dillon...."

"Nope...seen too many a' m' friends payin' th' price. Lookit Clay, here, an' his story. Jus' tryin' t' teach th' boys a lesson, an' his ol' lady gives 'im no end a' grief fer it. No thankee!"

"Y' may have made th' right choice, there, Dill," said Silas. "You boys recall ol' Bucky Legris? His ol' lady was a reg'lar ring-tail terror, I kin tell ya. Always at ol' Bucky...'do this, don't do that'.....he couldn't do nuthin' right. Well, one day she's splittin' wood out back, an' Bucky decides he's had enough. Grabs a block a' maple an' crowns her with it. Like t'stove in 'er head..."

"I heard that, too," confirmed Clay, "an' they's more to it..."

"Yep. Down she goes. Bucky thinks he's killed her, an' he turns t' go back inta th' house. An' she gets up, still got th' axe in 'er hand, and she buries it right between his shoulder blades."

81

"Kill him?"

"Nope. But he ain't goin' t' no more dances. He's over at Green River now, been there for six, seven years. They have t' feed 'im through a straw."

"Guess I was lucky," Clay said. "Agnes was pretty hot over th' 'baccy business, but she never did git 'round t' bashin' me with the stick a' stove wood. And once she got th' boys t' bed an' got th' mess cleaned up in th' kitchen, I reckon she cooled down. Prob'ly realized what I done wasn't so bad. Th' boys was sick fer a day 'er two, but they come 'round. Hell, she prob'ly seen it as a good lesson fer th' boys...they never did take t' th' chewin' type a' t'baccy."

"Lessons is good fer young 'uns," Dillon opined. "Course, I never had none, as y' know. But, how they gonna learn, without lessons?"

"Yup."

"Yup."

"Haven't seen Agnes fer quite a spell," Clay continued. "She lit out, some time after that 'baccy incident. Sometimes I miss her, an' then I think, hell, I'm prob'ly better off runnin' th' place meself..."

"She's gone, then?"

"Yep. Heard she was seein' Arthur Colpitts fer a while. Arthur's dumb as a bag a' doorknobs, so they'd make a good pair. Dunno, though," he said reflectively, "if she wanted t' come back..." And he let the thought trail off.

Dillon got up for a refill. He went to the window and looked out on the blackness. "Reckon we might git some good shots tomorra, gents. Them apples oughta bring 'em in."

"Yup."

And they all knew they wouldn't get the shots....didn't want the shots. Didn't want to have to butcher and dress and lug and carry. One by one the old hunters went through the bed-time ritual, going outside to check the stars, to estimate the morrow's weather, to empty full bladders, and to hope the four of them would be on hand for next November's hunt.

RED SCHWINN

The woman from Macon was gone, finally, leaving behind her cloying scent of body odour and cheap perfume. Augie knew a migraine was on the way.

August Pruett II, city editor of the *Atlanta Ledger and Times*, continued to sit lost in thought and made no move for the codeine pills which might have forestalled the headache.

"Why now?", he thought. "Why now when the end is so near. I don't need this. Five weeks and I'm outta here ... and now this."

The woman from Macon had jolted him out of his dreams of fishing and days without deadlines, dreams which had become more persistent and alluring as retirement beckoned.

"Y'all remember Emerson Strutt," the woman had said, daring the newsman to contradict her as she settled her ample backside into the padded chair and fumbled her cigarettes out of a fake Gucci bag. Her unannounced entry had caught Augie by surprise, and the name she'd dropped had flustered him to the point where he failed to point out the No Smoking policy to the aggressive harridan before him.

"Uh..oh..yes. Dr. Emerson Strutt. Yes. I do recall. He was...uh...he was a close friend of my father. Many years ago."

"Well, he's my Daddy, an' I knew y'all would want to know. He's here. Here in Georgia." She drew deeply on her king-size Tarryton, leaned back, and regarded Augie triumphantly through a cloud of smoke, seemingly amused at this confusion.

"Uh...Ms..."

"It's Mrs. Mrs. Angelina Chambliss. Y'all can call me Angie."

"Yes. Well. Ah...Mrs. Chambliss. I wonder....I think you've confused me with my father, August Pruett Senior. He ran the paper here for years. And I know he and Dr. Strutt were very good friends. But, ah, that's some time ago. My father died twenty-seven years ago, and...."

The woman scarcely missed a beat. "Yes. Well I knew you'd want to know. Daddy's still alive, and I've found him!"

Was she deaf, or stupid?

83

"Uh, look, Mrs...Angie. Your father and I were never friends. I saw him a few times at our house. But he was friends with my father, and–."

"Me n' Daddy have not been close," she continued, oblivious to Augie's words, "not for some time. Many years, actually." She flicked ash on the carpet and smoothed a wrinkle in her skirt. "Fact of the matter, Daddy's been gone so long I assumed he was dead. But now, praise the Lord, I've found him, an' he's not so very far from here." She paused to dab theatrically at her eyes, now welling, apparently, with emotion. She sniffed loudly, and made a determined effort to regain composure. "An' I knew I had to tell y'all."

Augie sat back and stared at the woman. She had to be well into her sixties, he thought, and quite possibly completely mad. But if she was the daughter of Emerson Strutt, he owed her something, if only to hear her out. Emerson Strutt was a near-legendary figure in the South, and his disappearance some thirty years ago had been big news. But he had to convince her that the friendship she alluded to was between his father and her's.

He looked more closely now at the woman and saw, beneath the pushy confidence, someone rather pathetic in her attempts to hide her age. Ridiculous floppy-brim hat atop bottle-blonde tresses, heavy mascara and fake lashes, rings and bracelets enough to start a bazaar. Tammy Faye's in my office, he thought. And while they regarded each other across the expanse of his desk, Augie recalled in more detail the man in question, Emerson Strutt, a man of great accomplishment and seemingly unlimited potential for greatness. Brilliant scholar, gifted surgeon, generous philanthropist whose funding of scholarships and health facilities in the South was unmatched. And he recalled too the cruel vagaries of fate that had brought him low. It had been the tragedies in Emerson Strutt's life that had caused so much anguish in Augie's father's life, had drained him of his interest in work and, ultimately, in life itself. For years following Em Strutt's disappearance, Augie's father had made attempts to locate him. Always without success, and each failed attempt brought him closer to the end. The fall from grace suffered by Em Strutt, and his subsequent disappearance, had taken a mortal toll on Augie's father, and a massive stroke ended his suffering and his life in 1970.

And now, some thirty-five years after he'd disappeared, here was his daughter exulting that she'd found him. But why has she come to me, Augie wondered. No way she really thinks I'm her father's friend....

His reverie was interrupted when he realized the woman had spoken again.

"What ... oh, excuse me, Mrs...Angie. I was just trying to remember some of what my daddy told me about your father. What were you saying?"

"I said, mebbe y'all could do a piece. In y'all's paper. Y'know, a feature or somethin', on Daddy. Might be a real, whaddya call it, human interest piece.

84

People love that kinda stuff, y'know. Story about a great man, football star, bigshot doctor, all kinds a money, big war hero. An' then, all his troubles.... Big man becomes a bum, an' a drunk. An' then he just drops outta sight." She fished for another cigarette, and Augie let her go. "Nobody knows nothin' about him, where he's at, or nothin! An' then what, nearly forty years later, his daughter finds him, out in th' sticks. What a story! Whaddya think?" She looked around for an ashtray and Augie pushed the waste basket around the desk towards her. He wondered what she'd done with the first butt.

"Hmmm ... yes. Well...."

"Absolutely! Just a great story. An' who knows, you 'n Daddy might just pick up where y'all left off."

"Angie...look. You have to realize that it wasn't me. It was my father who—."

"Yes, whatever. But you did know Daddy, an'—well, it's just such a wonderful story. Folks'll love it. Should sell lotsa papers." And she gave Augie her sweetest smile.

The light began to dawn for Augie. She was here on a mission. Time to bring this to an end.

"Well, Mrs. Chambliss, it was good of you to come in." He rose to escort her to the door. "It was good to meet you, and to hear about Dr. Strutt after all these years. A pity my father couldn't know what became of his old friend. And...uh...where did you say he is now?"

"I didn't say. "Course, I was wonderin', Mr. Pruett, how much do y'all pay for stories like that?" Again, the sweet smile.

"Uh, well, we don't operate that way, payin' for stories..."

"Hmmm...well. Mebbe I oughta go on over to th' *Tribune*, or mebbe th' *Journal and Constitution*. Mebbe they'd be interested." She hoisted herself out of the chair, a slow and ponderous manoeuver, and turned towards the door.

Augie resisted the urge to make a testy retort and looked again at this daughter of his father's old friend. What he beheld softened his anger—a slattern trying with little success to play the Southern Belle. If she had ever possessed grace or charm, they were long gone. She exuded failure. Her walk was unsteady, and he saw how the light from the window etched the shadows around her jowls and highlighted the bags under her eyes. He saw, too, the pilling on her cheap scarf, the wear marks on the collar and at the elbows of her faux suede jacket.

"Tell you what, Mrs. Chambliss, we'll cover some of your expenses in coming here all the way from Macon. Cover your gas an' accommodations and the like. How'd that be?"

"Well..."

"We could cut you a check for two hundred dollars. Would that do it? You just tell me where Dr. Strutt's at, an' I'll call Sue Ellen down in accounting an' tell her to get that check ready."

"Daddy's in Wadley," she said.

Now, sitting still and alone in his office, hoping the migraine would subside on its own, Augie pushed a button on his console and leaned back, lacing his fingers behind his head and surveying the sprawling city below. He'd broken a rule, paying for a news story. But hell, two hundred bucks, and who knew—there might be a story in it. And at the very least, he'd find and talk to his father's old crony. The only close friend his father ever had. August Pruett Senior had been a hard man to know, even to his own family, and aloof and demanding of all who served him. He'd ruled his family and his paper from on high. It was only with Em Strutt that his father had been comfortable and at ease. Close friends since Emory, and the friendship had continued after college, when August Sr. had gone to the *Journal & Constitution* and Em had gone to open his practice in Chattanooga.

Em had been successful from the start, and was in a very short time, a very wealthy man. But money was only a means to an end, and his aim in life was service to mankind. He funded scholarships at Emory and Vanderbilt, and he financed medical centers and walk-in clinics in a number of small towns in Georgia and Tennessee.

When the U.S. entered the war, both men served overseas: Augie's father as a war correspondent and Em as chief surgeon with a mobile hospital unit. It was while he was serving in this capacity that Em Strutt was involved in a firefight that ended in seven enemy soldiers dead and the rescue of the wounded soldiers in his unit. For this act of valor, Em had been nominated for the Medal of Honor.

He returned a hero to Chattanooga, resumed his medical practice and his philanthropic endeavors. Approached to run for politics, he declined, preferring to serve his community in his chosen field.

And then, the fateful events that brought the friendship to an end. Faced with successive overwhelming personal tragedies, Em Strutt had, in 1962, simply disappeared. Augie's father, devastated by his friend's misfortunes and subsequent disappearance, tried desperately to find him. But all attempts failed, and eventually the sad story came to an end with the death of August Pruett Sr..

A knock disturbed Augie's reverie, and a young man entered. "You called, Sir?"

"Yes. Come in and sit down, Martin. I want you to do something for me.

86

Out of town. I want you to look up an old friend of my father. Over in Wadley."

"This is Atlanta news, Sir?"

"Could be. Could be quite a story...or it could be a dead end. The man's name is Emerson Strutt. You go find him. Shouldn't be too difficult, Wadley's just a dot on the map, more a crossroads than anything else. You ask around, you'll find him."

"And then?"

"Oh, I expect you'll find he's quite a character–unless his mind is completely gone. He's an old man, around ninety, I'd say. Tell him who sent you, and tell him I'll be getting in touch with him, real soon. I'm hoping he'll talk to you. He was quite a man..."

"Can you give me some background before I go?"

"Oh, you can look most of it up. College athlete, played football for Ohio State. One year anyway. Honor grad in medicine here at Emory. Top of his class. Had a practice over in Chattanooga before the war. Did all kinds of good with his money. And then he was a genuine war hero. You can look it all up."

"You knew him?"

"Barely. He and my father were close friends for twenty years or so. The friendship ended when Dr. Strutt's life went to pieces."

"Sir?"

"Yes. Terrible, what happened. Em had more than his share of grief. After the war, he killed a kid on a bike, over in Tennessee. Never saw the kid. He just never got over it. And then, a few years later, his wife and infant son were killed in a house fire."

"My God!".

"Yup. Well. He just couldn't cope, after all that. Shortly after the fire, about 1960 or '61 I think, he just disappeared. Looked like he mighta killed himself..who knew? Not a sign of any kind. That's thirty-five , thirty-six years ago. And now, apparently, he's over in Wadley. Do your research, Martin, and then get on over there, next day or so."

Two days later, as the setting sun cast the small town in make-believe contours like the set of an old Western movie, the reporter pulled into the Super 8 half a mile inside the Wadley town-limit sign. He booked a room and then asked the acne-scarred clerk if he knew Dr. Emerson Strutt.

"Doctor? Don't know nothin' about no Dr. Strutt. But they's an old man Em Strutt usta live back'a Si Gomery's Car Wash and Quick Lube."

"Used to? He's not there now?"

"Nope..He's dead. Died a week ago. Didn't look like no doctor to me."

"How old a man was he?"

"Who knows. Old. Could'a been ninety. Sure looked old..."

"Did you know him?"

The clerk snorted. "Nobody knowed 'im. Ol' Em was, whaddya call it, peculiar. Kept to himself all the time. Mebbe Si could tell ya more, seein' how he lived out back'a Si's place an' all."

"Wadley's pretty small. What, a coupla hundred or so? I'd a thought everybody would know everybody..."

"Yup, well, we do. 'Cept for Ol' Em. Paper said Winslow & Bagby done the buryin'. Didn't mention no family ner relatives. You could check with them, or go see Si Gomery."

"Mr. Pruett, Martin here. I'm in Wadley. I'll be leavin' in the morning. Some bad news for you, Sir. I found your man. Least, I found out about him. He's dead. Died last week."

Silence on the line, and Martin continued, "Wasn't sure it was the right man, at first ... listenin' to folks talk about him. But it's him... right age, and when he showed up here. I didn't get much you could use."

"Okay. When's the funeral? Oh ... I suppose they've already had it?"

"No funeral at all, Sir. He was just buried." The reporter paused. "Uh, seems he was buried at county expense. Seems he was destitute, and–"

"Martin, you come on back. Thank you for getting the information."

"I could stick around for a day or two, Sir. Maybe get some more..."

"No, you come on back." Augie hung up and buzzed his secretary. "Becky, get Winston up here, will you, please. Tell him he'll be coverin' for me for a day or two. I'll be over in Wadley. I'll give you the number when I get there."

The Car Wash and Quick Lube, est. 1951, would inspire no one to stop. A two-bay flat-roofed concrete block garage with grease pit on one side and an assortment of barrels, tires, tripod, tire change station, and rusted wheel rims in no semblance of order on the other. Along the back wall, over a greasy work bench loaded with tools and parts and cans, a '73 calendar from Webber Carbs featured a leggy blonde in cut-off Wranglers holding a goose-neck oil can in one hand and an adjustable wrench in the other.

Augie approached a cadaverous man in an oversized shop suit with Silas stitched above the left breast pocket. He was sorting through nuts and bolts in a Hills Bros. coffee can.

"Mr. Gomery? I'm August Pruett. Wonder if I might ask you a few ques-

88

tions about Emerson Strutt.. He was a friend of my father's, quite some time ago."

Si Gomery wiped his bony hands with a faded shop towel and squinted in the afternoon sun. "Another reporter? Reckon ol' Em never got this kinda notice when he was alive." He dragged a blue-veined hand across his upper lip, wiping a runny nose and leaving a moist streak across one dusty stubbled cheek. He spat and said, "Well, what kin I tell yuh?"

"You prob'ly knew him best. I was hopin' you could tell me a bit about him. Seems he was a mystery to most folks. He was here, livin' at your place, what, twenty years or more."

"Thirty-five! Come here in '63. I recall that 'cause it was just a coupla days after Kennedy got shot. He come into town lookin' fcr work an' a place t'stay. Somebody sent 'im here....I got a place out back." He nodded vaguely in the direction of the back wall. "An' he stayed there all them years."

"You'd think..all that time...you'd think he woulda made some kinda contact." It was more question than statement.

Si spit a medium gob into the grease pit. "You might think so, but you'd be dead wrong." He sat on an overturned grease drum and dug a pipe and pouch of Union Leader from his overalls pocket. He filled the bowl and flicked open an old Zippo with a Merchant Marine seal. He took a long draw and nodded Augie to a stool beside the workbench. "Yup, he was here alright, all thcm years, an' then again, he weren't here at all, if yuh take my meanin'." And he tapped the side of his head. "Didn't never talk t'no one, no more than a coupla words. Course, he'd give me a word or two when he come to pay the rent. Wasn't much, I kin tell yuh. An' mebbe he spoke to Harm Weatherby, over t' th' lumber yard. He worked there some."

"But I don't get it. Emerson Strutt was a great man. A great man, with a great mind. He was a doctor, a surgeon ... had a very successful practice over in Tennessee. He was a great community leader, gave all kinds of money to help the poor, and all. And he had an outstanding military record. This was a truly great man."

"You know'd him at one time, did ya say?".

"Not well. He and my father were friends. I'd see him at my daddy's house at times. But I know about him, know about all the things he did, the people he helped...."

"Hmmm...Well we had 'im here in Wadley fer quite a spell, an' he never helped nobody, an' he weren't friends with nobody, in illier." The old man drew contentedly on his pipe and regarded his visitor. "Seems to be quite a bit of interest in Ol' Em, now that he's dead. First th' woman, coupla weeks back, an' then that reporter." He spat reflectively, and continued, "Knowin'

Em, an' then hearin' your story. Somethin' don't quite fit."

Augie agreed, "It's more than pitiful. You make him sound like some kinda nut..."

"Yup. Pitiful. An 'y 'know, people tried t' be friendly, an' all. But it weren't no use. Ol' Em just lived in his own little world, an' finally people give up on' im. Kinda sad, ain't it. Just him an' that ol' bike."

"Bike?"

"Yup, a beat up ol' red bike. He was always pushin' that ol' Schwinn around town. Don't recall a time he didn't have it with him. Pushed it t' work, when he was workin'. At th' yard. Or when he was doin' janitor chores over at th' Handi-Mart. Workin' or not, it didn't matter t'Em, long as he had that ol' bike t'push. Seemed like it was everyday...he'd be up an' down every street an' alley in town. Dunno what he was thinkin' or where he was goin'. Didn't matter. Strangest thing y'ever seen. After a while, y'didn't even notice. Just a crazy ol' man pushin' an ol' red bike through town. Never seen 'im ridin' it. Always just pushin' it."

The old man saw that his words had upset Augie, and he stopped to suck on his pipe. "This weren't the man you an' yer daddy knew. This was a shell of a man, just barely gettin' by. Listen. You go on down to th' Court House. Go an' talk t' some of the boys. Ask them. You'll get some idea from th' boys. They'll be there. They're there ever' day. You'll find' em on the steps. Earl an' Harm an' Joe Willy. They'll be there. They kin tell yuh."

Later the same day, Augie approached a small group of whiskery gnarled old men sitting on the Court House steps. Weather-beaten and creased, in dusty worn denim and flannel, they watched the newcomer mount the steps with cautious indifference.

"Afternoon, gents," Augie began. "Another fine day, though I suppose we could use some rain."

"Yep."

"Looks like y' all got the best seats t' watch th' world go by."

"Got that right, mister. Where y' all from?"

"Atlanta. Fact is, I heard about the death of Emerson Strutt. Heard it just th' other day, an' so I thought I'd come see th' place where he lived."

"Y'all a friend of ol' Em?"

"Well, he and Daddy was good friends. Long time ago. I suppose you gents knew him. Bit of a character, was he?"

An old timer pulled a plug of Red Man from a shirt pocket, tore a thoughtful bit, and passed the plug to his neighbor. From the end of the ragged line a wrinkled gnome in bib Carhartts and soiled Farmall cap too big for his bony skull rasped, "Hell, yes, we knew 'im...knew 'im by sight. Seen 'im evr'
90

day, going' by, him with that rickety ol bike. But he never give no one an aye, nay, nor kiss my arse. Dam fool ol' coot!" He spat and wiped his mouth with the back of a bruised hand. "An' who're you, mister, and what're yuh asking about ol' Em fer, anyways?"

"Ah, well, I'm with the *Ledger and Times*, in Atlanta, an'...well, it may be hard to believe this, but your Old Em was really a pretty important man. At one time. Quite a while ago." A chorus of doubting snorts.

"Actually famous, at one time. Years ago. He was a doctor. Outstanding heart surgeon. Quite rich, too. Over in Tennessee...Chattanooga." He had their attention. "Did all kinds of great things, helpin' people, settin' up medical centers, free walk-in clinics an' the like. And he was decorated for bravery in the war...Second World War."

"Yuh sure yuh got th' right man, mister? Ol' Em was kinda simple, if yuh know what I mean. Not bright...."

"Oh, it's the same man, gents. What I can tell you I got from the research people at my paper an' from my daddy, before he died. Yep, it's Dr. Strutt, alright. I found out...did my research th' other day before comin' over here t' Wadley. We got all sorts a' old records at the paper. Em Strutt was the real deal. Had ever'thing going for him, back forty, fifty years ago. No tellin' where he mighta gone if he hadn't run into some pretty major setbacks. Real string a' bad luck."

They looked up. One, with a plug halfway to his mouth, spoke up. "Yer tellin' us that ol' Em was some kinda big shot doctor an' all. I dunno. All we ever seen was a loony ol' buzzard pushin' a beat-up ol' red bike all over town, going God knows where, ner why, an' never a word ner a nod t' anyone in his way. Contrary ol' coot!"

"Yer right there, Joe Willy. Never had a how-do ner th' time of day fer none of us. Crazy, I'd say. Or thought he was better'n any of us."

Another raspy voice continued, "Ol' Em was like some kinda spook... some kinda ghost comin' an' leavin' an' showin' up agin...."

"Yup...put me in mind of a ol' log floating' in an out with th' tide. Might see 'im ever' day for a month, an' then not fer a spell...mebbe gone for a coupla days an' then back agin, him an' that ol' bike .... an' like Earl says, never a word t'nobody."

"He must have had some reason to stay," Augie said, "he stayed here in Wadley for over thirty years. Musta had some good feelin' for the place."

They were silent, and he pressed on. "Didn't anyone get to know him at all?"

The one named Earl spat a particularly juicy gob. "How could we! He made it plain. He didn't want no company. Hell, he'd walk half a mile t'git around yuh." The old cronies spat their agreement.

"I know'd 'im, had words with 'im when he first come t' Wadley," an old timer in camouflage vest growled around his wad. "He come in, I was workin' at th' co-op,...sez he's lookin' fer work an' a place t' stay. That musta been thirty, thirty-five years ago. I recall it was just after Roy Pooley's barn burned down and his missus run off with Delbert Upshaw ... Anyways, I thought at th' time there was somethin' funny about th' guy. Somethin' about them eyes. They was dead lookin'.."

"Yer right, Floyd. I seen 'em too. Them eyes. Kind put yuh in mind of a fish...dead, like. Somebody sent 'im up t' Si Gomery's....I was workin' at th' Quick Lube then. Yup, I do recall them dead eyes. Anyway, he come up t' Si, an' Si give 'im that shack out back a' th' garage. Give 'im some work, too, I recall."

More nods and spits from the chorus. Camouflage continued, "Dunno if I'd a bin so quick t' accept 'im, th' look of 'im...with the wife an' kids an' all. Course, Si's daughter was not one to quicken yer pulse, if yuh know what I mean."

"What ever happened to that girl?"

"Dunno. Best thing fer her mighta bin t' join the circus!"

Snorts of agreement.

"I don't think Em would have been any kind of threat," Augie offered.

"Well, yuh never know. Drifter shows up...who is he...why's he here?"

Jo Willy spoke up, "One time my Effie says she's gonna talk t' him. Gonna stop 'im an' talk to 'im. Says he's hurtin' an' she's gonna find out why. Well, she done up some a' them peach preserves, somethin' like that, I don't recall exactly what, an' she goes out inta th' street in front a' our place. An' she stands right there, right in ol' Em's way. An' he's pushin' that ol' red Schwinn. No way she's gonna let 'im by. He'd hafta run 'er down. Anyway, she gets 'im t' stop, an' she sez, 'Mr. Strutt, I'd like y'all t' have these preserves. I surely hope yuh'll enjoy 'em.' An' she puts two jars in his basket. Mason jars. An' that ol' buzzard, he don' say nothin', just pushes 'round 'er, no more thankee than kiss my arse. An' next day, Missus Dillard down th' street, she brung Effie's peaches back. Em'd stuck 'em in her mailbox."

Augie felt compelled to defend the man for whom they so little sympathy, or understanding. "Y' know, gents, Dr. Strutt was a Northener"—they snorted their disdain—"but he chose to live here in the South. Went to medical school here, in Atlanta. And he chose to stay here and serve people here, in the South."

"Well, he didn't give us any sign a' that when he come here, t' Wadley."

"No—but his life changed. He enlisted, y' know, in '41. He headed a mo-

92

bile hospital unit. And in '43 he held off an enemy attack and took out seven enemy soldiers. Saved a couple of wounded G.I.'s. Got himself nominated for the Medal of Honor."

"Never guess it, seein' 'im shufflin' around town like some kinda derelict..."

"How would you? But after the war, he went back to Chattanooga, and he was driving himself...workin' overtime and all, tryin' to get the war out of his mind. And then, one night on his way home, he hit a nine-year-old kid on a bike. Killed the kid...never saw him. And I guess it just about killed the doctor. Never got over it, at least not to the point where he could go back to work. Nerves were shot to hell, with the war and all, and then killin' the kid. He left Tennessee an' went to work as an orderly in some small-town hospital in northern Georgia."

The group was silent, and Augie continued, "And then, more bad luck. He'd married a girl from somewhere up that way...South Carolina, I think. Small town girl. They had two kids...Em's not making much, and his wife's workin' part time at the Five 'n Dime. Two kids, a boy and a girl. Em's left the hospital by then, not sure why, and he's workin' in a lumber yard. Guess he was still goin' through some kinda hell...you know, the war, and then the kid on the bike. Anyway, one real cold mornin' in November, I think it was about '59 or '60, he's at work, the girl's in school, an' the wife and boy are at home. Boy woulda been about three, or four. Wasn't much of a house, tarpaper shack more like, an' they had space heaters, you know. Anyway, somethin' went wrong, the whole place went up in a matter of minutes, an' the two a'them never had a chance. Em heard the sirens when he was sortin' lumber, out in the yard."

The men shifted nervously now, unwilling or unable to comment, and Augie continued. "Well, you can imagine...more than Em, or anyone, could deal with. Went completely to pieces. Prob'ly woulda killed himself, but there was the girl. Angie's her name. He took to the bottle. Couldn't care for the girl...she woulda been about seven...authorities finally took her away. Sent her to St. Mary's, in Atlanta."

"So, how'd he end up here?"

"Well, that's what I've been tryin' to find out, last coupla days. Near as I can make out, he hung around town for a while, up north, near the South Carolina line. Livin' outta th' bottle, workin' odd jobs to pay for Jack Daniels. Did sweepin' an' lawn cuttin', that sorta thing. Folks tried to carry him, tide him over 'til he could get himself back together. But after a while it was plain he wasn't comin' around. Danville, that's where it was, I remember now. Anyway, folks got tired of tryin' to rescue Em from the misery he chose for himself."

The telling was draining Augie, and he paused, wishing mightily for a drink. But they wanted more.

"After a year or so of this, he left Danville...or was it Danburg...don't really matter...an' he began driftin'. Always broke, most of the time drunk, lookin' for enough work t' get t' th' next day. Went t' Homerville, then Ambrose, an' Chauncey, an' finally here, to Wadley."

"He musta had a service pension."

"Seems so. Government does its best to keep those records straight, I believe. He wouldn't be much help, considerin' how he drifted around. But he didn't want money, no more than just enough to live. Apparently he had it fixed so most of it went to the family of the youngster back in Chattanooga. And some went regular to the home in Atlanta...St. Mary's."

"What became of the daughter?"

"I met her, just a few days ago. She told me she'd been tryin' to find her daddy. Not sure how hard she tried. No great affection there—she sees him as a drunk who abandoned her when she was about six or seven. But give her credit, she did locate him, finally. Guess it was no great reunion. She found the man you all knew. She wasn't even sure he knew who she was. She came to me because she found out our daddies were friends."

"How'd she know that?"

"God knows."

A long silence while the group digested Augie's story. Then the one called Earl spoke. "Harm, I recollect th' time ol' Em come t' work fer you...."

"Yep. Woulda been '64, mebbe '65. Come into th' yard an' I give 'im work sortin lumber. Never said much. Liked t' be off by himself, out in th' yard. Pretty good worker. Don't recall him drinkin', least not on th' job."

"Did he keep the job long?" Augie asked.

Harm Weatherby let memory drift over him, specifically the memory of a drifter looking older than his years, needing a few bucks and a change of clothes. And as the memory firmed up, he recalled the day, early on, when Em had come to the office to ask a favor. Working on a pile at the far end of the yard, near the cypress trees and out of sight of the yard office, Em had found an old red bicycle half-buried in the boggy ground. He'd pulled it out and taken a cloth to it, revealing faded paint and rusty spokes. And he'd come in to ask Harm if he could have the bike. Assuming he'd use it to get to and from work, Harm had told him to take it.

Thinking back now, Harm realized that in those few minutes in his office, so long ago, he and Em Strutt had been as close to normal communication as Em had been since the awful tragedies Augie had described. And probably, as

94

close as anyone would ever get to Em Strutt for the rest of his lonely tortured life. There'd been more than just a bike on the man's mind. But Harm had missed the moment. And now he realized a sadness, a sense that he had let slip a chance to fulfil some vague need in his old employee. There had been one or two other similar moments, he recalled now, when Em seemed about to reveal something of himself, some pain perhaps that might have been alleviated through human contact. But Harm had been a busy man, and had not taken the time, made the effort. And the realization made him uncomfortable.

"No, not long," he said. "Mebbe a year or two. But I do recall he come back a few times, an' if I could, I give him whatever work I had. Short term, a few days now an' then. Like I said, Em was a good worker."

So, there you have it, Augie thought. Em brought his bike to work, pushing it the half-mile from the shack behind Si Gomery's garage to the lumber yard and back to the shack each day after work. And when there was no work, or Em decided he'd had enough of work, he'd push the bike through town. Day after day, in all weather, up and back through every street and back alley, pushing the old red balloon-tire Schwinn. An old man on a journey to nowhere.

Augie got up from the step. He brushed the seat of his pants and nodded to the group. He made his slow and thoughtful way to his car. He had his story, but he wasn't sure he'd print it.

POT LUCK

Except for hunting season, every Saturday the boys gathered at Lennie Carkner's barbershop for their catch-up on the local news. From Lennie's shop, at different times during the day, they'd wander off to the Co-op or the T.S.C. or McCaffrey's, but the barbershop was the acknowledged social hub of Altonsburg. For the boys, at least. They'd stop at Dunkin Donuts, maybe, to pick up a coffee and dozen assorted donuts–Lennie had a pot going all day but no one would touch his coffee–and then they'd settle in to solve the problems of the community, the country, or the world. Some, on occasion, even got their hair cut.

"Guess y'all heard about Wallace Dunleavy?" Lennie asked, searching through his scissors drawer, looking for a spoon for his coffee. "Sheriff finally had t' take his licence away."

"Ain't heard that," remarked Archie Sewall, the undertaker and taxidermist. "What'd 'ol Wallace do this time? Last I heard, he was gettin' ready t' go live with his daughter, over t' Speersburg."

"Yup, well, he was plannin' t' go there after th' Fall hunt." Lennie found a spoon and dipped it into his coffee. "But seems he lost his glasses, or stepped on 'em, or somethin', an' he was drivin' down t' th' Walmart fer some new ones, an–."

"–Drivin' hisself?!" Tommy Nash asked. "Hell, Wallace Dunleavy's blind as a dam' ol' bat even when he's wearin' his specs!"

"I know, Tommy. But you know Wallace....blind and stubborn!"

"Yeah," offered Brandon Dowie, wiping icing sugar on to the front of his bibbed Carhartts. "I had ol' Wallace helpin' me measure Clancy Farrell's feed lot last summer. Had 'im holdin' th' rod, an' he couldn't see me directin' 'im from fifty yards away, an' me wavin' that ol' orange flag. An' he had them glasses on that day. Dam' lotta good they done 'im."

"Yuh gonna stay with Denton Surveyin', Bran?" asked Tommy. "Seems I heard you was thinkin' a' goin' t' work fer Calderson's, over t' Stratsburg.".

"Yeah, well, I dunno. Calderson's ain't hiring fer awhile, since that trouble with the fire station bein' on Billy Bob Grissom's land, an' the audit, an' all.
96

B'sides, they don't give no time off fer the huntin' season."

Carlton Earnsley tried to get the talk back to Wallace Dunleavy. "So, Lennie, what about Wallace, an' his licence?"

"Oh, yeah. Well, he was drivin' hisself down t' Walmart last week. Drove through ever' stop sign an' traffic light on Jefferson. He nearly run over Myrtle Jinkinson out front a' th' Five an Dime. Run right acrost Early Little's front yard an' straight on up t' th' Walmart parkin' lot. Never stopped there neither 'til he smashed through th' front doors!"

"Damn!"

"Yup. Lucky it were a Tuesday mornin', early. Kin y' imagine if he'd a' gone on a Friday night or a Sata'day mornin', with all them Mexicans at th' Walmart?!"

The boys sat quietly contemplating Wallace Dunleavy's poor eyesight and what might have been. Then Carlton Earnsley got up and motioned Lennie out of the barber chair. "Guess yuh could gimme a trim, Lennie. Suppos'd t' take Earline t' th' church supper t' night. Just a trim."

He had their attention.

"I thought reverend Milliken said no more church suppers," Danny Hicks said. "Heard he was pretty upset, about Wilma an' all...."

"Yeah, well, he weren't happy, an' he did say there'd be no more pot lucks. But y' know," Carlton said, lifting his arms out from under the bib that Lennie was fixing at his neck, "yuh can't cut out them pot luck suppers. Might as well say yer gonna cut out th' Sunday service."

Danny reached for another donut. "I heard ol' Brady made 'em promise they'd be no more dancin' b' fore he'd let 'em have more pot lucks. Maybelle heard it from Cal Merriam's wife. Y'all may think Brady Milliken's pretty lib'ral, fer a Presbyterian, but he weren't gonna allow that kinda carryin' on anymore. An' it weren't just th' dancin'. Mostly it came down t' th' booze."

"How'd they get booze into a church supper?"

"Well, " said Archie, finishing his coffee and looking at Lennie's pot. He thought better of getting a refill, and continued, "y' kin guess....if ol' Wilma Broughton was there, y' kin be sure she'd a' brung a jug a' somethin'. She can't go t' no more pot lucks at th' Baptist church, on account of th' booze."

"Well, yer right....she was at th' last one, with th' dancin'. I seen her."

"I never seen that woman sober," Archie added. "An ol' Wilma's only too glad t' share her booze. Was Happy McColm there?"

"Hell, whaddya think?!" Brandon snorted, and patted his vest for his cigarettes. "Happy McColm ain't missed a pot luck in twenty years! Presbyterian, Lutheran, Catholic..he don't care, he goes t' all of 'em. An' he'll take a drink, that ol' boy!"

"Y' know," said Danny, "Wilma was a dancer up t' Darien fer a number a' years. I never seen her there, but some a' the boys at the Co-op remember her. Danced there, and then she danced at *The Last Chance* fer a coupla years."

"They closed that place down. Guess that was th' end a' Wilma's dancin' career," Tommy said, accepting the cigarette offered by Brandon. "She still looks pretty good, y' ask me."

"Yep. She's still got th' moves. An ol' Happy McColm thinks he kin dance. Gawd knows why.....if y'ever seen 'im on a dance floor."

"Don't matter," Lennie said, giving his scissors some experimental snipping moves around Carlton's ears. "Happy prob'ly had a snootful a' Wilma's booze. He never could hold his booze, that ol' boy. I recall th' time he threw up at th' dessert table at th' Methodist pot luck."

"I was there," Danny said. "Happy said he had the flu, but ever' body know'd he'd been in th' *Mayflower* all afternoon b'fore th' pot luck. Hell, he showed up in his sock feet!"

"Yup. Well, Hap an' Wilma was dancin' an' hollerin', tryin' t' git ever' body up t' dance...." Brandon pulled out his pack of Red Man, bit off a corner, and passed the plug to Tommy Nash. "Ain't surprisin' Reverend Milliken was pissed–pardon my French–an' he said afterwards that was th' end a' pot lucks...."

"Me an' Maybelle missed that one, with th' dancin'," Danny said, "but we bin goin' t' th' pot lucks ever since Brady Milliken come t' Altonsburg."

"When was that anyways?" Lennie asked. "Musta bin ten years ago...."

"Nope, more like fifteen," Carlton said.

"You don't go reg'lar t' th' pot lucks, do yuh, Lennie?"

"Ain't high on my list. Not since Dixie got food poisonin' at th' Luth'ran supper a few years back."

"Stick t' th' Presbyterians, Lennie. They got more class. 'Cept fer a few folks I could mention...."

"Yeah? Who might that be, Carlton?" Lennie wiped his scissors on his apron.

"Well, y'all know Germaine Vandyne. Married Rudd Vandyne after she run off from Porky Dumont, few years back....."

"Or mebbe Porky give' er the boot."

"Yeah, I know who y' mean." Archie fished out his makings and prepared to roll a cigarette. "That Germaine ain't missed too many meals, y'ask me. I seen her at th' wake fer Timmy Driscoll an' she near cleaned off th' refreshment table all by herself. An' far as I know, she an' Rudd didn't even know Timmy Driscoll."

"That ol' girl does like t' eat."

"Yeah, well, Earline tol' me they was thinkin' a' havin' some a' th' ladies servin' th' dishes. Y' know, instead a havin' folks serve themselves. All account a' ol' Germaine. That ol' girl'd go up an' load two plates ever' time. Said she's fixin' one fer Rudd....but Rudd don't eat much a' anythin' these days, not since he got th' worms, working' down there at Dockerty's."

"Yuh seen ol' Rudd lately?" asked Tommy. "Skinny as a ol' porch rail...."

"Well, Germain's makin' up fer Rudd not eatin'. An' that's th' reason the ladies is servin' out th' food...."

Danny laughed. "Tommy, yuh could bring yer back-hoe 'round t' feed ol' Germaine. My gawd that's a big ol' girl!"

"Pretty good grub at them pot lucks," Brandon said. "But yuh gotta get there early, get yer seat near th' servin' tables."

"Yup," agreed Carlton. "An' they've started bringin' speakers in. That was Brady Milliken's idea. Las' time we had some ol' gal from Lanesville, talkin' about scrapbooks if yuh kin believe it. An' while this ol' gal's talkin', ol' Germaine plunks herself down at th' dessert table. Took her chair right over there, an' I kept my eye on 'er...watched 'er jam down four 'er five a' them little dessert plates full a' ever'thin' they had on that ol' dessert table!"

"Tell yuh what," Archie said, finishing the roll-your-own and digging for a match," yuh gotta feel a mite sorry fer ol' Rudd. His Charlotte was a fine woman."

Another round of profound silence as the boys weighed the tribulations of Rudd Vandyne. Tommy the back-hoe man broke the silence. "Always a full house, though. Even if they gotta sit through th' speeches an' all...."

"Yep," Carlton agreed, "free food'll git 'em ever' time, speech' r no speech."

"Yep, an' I kin tell yuh one thing. Y' might think my undertakin' business has them set rules n' regulations, "Archie said, "but them pot lucks! Them ladies shoulda bin put t' runnin' th' work camps! Talk about yer right way a' doin' things. Gotta have ever'thin' just so...plates 'n spoons 'n knives 'n forks all lined up just so. An' th' napkins gotta be folded in one particular way..."

"Yeah," Danny said, " I seen 'em. I was helpin' Maybelle set up las' time...y'know, the tables an' chairs. An' I watched Jackie Wishart's wife goin' 'round th' room foldin' them napkins an' placin'em just so. An' I be dam'd if ol' Molly Gaithers ain't comin' along b'hind her changin' th' folds in th' napkins an' rearrangin' ever' dam' one a' th' plates an' spoons an' all!"

"Yep, Pretty partic'lar, them ol' gals. Ol' Tommy Harrelson was helpin' set up one time an' he tried t' set the tables acrost th' room insteada long-ways an' ol' Molly Gaithers hollered at 'im an' sezs who's he think he is, changin' things, th' tables is always set long ways. 'Course, ol' Tommy's deaf as a dead hawg, an' he just goes on settin' 'em up cross-ways. They just about had t' pull ol' Molly off 'im b'fore they got it all sorted out."

"Yeah. Good grub though, mostly."

"Yep, 'Cept th' time Gert Stotsbury choked on a chicken bone. I heard ol' Dooley Greeves reached down her throat an' pulled th' bone out...."

"Earline found a horse-shoe nail in one a' Louise Detmer's casseroles one time. Near busted a tooth on it."

"Damn! Reminds me a' th' time I was fixin' th' remains a' Chad Hammacher," Archie said, "an' I found a kitchen sponge stuck in his throat. His wife said ol' Chad died in his sleep."

"Yeah, I recall that trial. Them Hammachers lived out th' River Road, didn't they? Out past th' tannery."

Lennie whipped the cloth away from Carlton with a flourish. "There yuh go, Carl. Just right fer th' pot luck." He put the comb and scissors down and filled his cup with lukewarm sludge. "Anyone else goin' t' th' supper?"

"I dunno," Brandon said. "Loretta didn't say nuthin' about it, an' I'm not sure she'd go anyways. Not after that set-to with Frank Brimmer's wife."

"I heard about a fight," Tommy said, "heard Frank tellin' Ernie Evers down at the Co-op somethin' about a ruckus at one a' th' suppers. I didn't know it was his own wife he was talkin' about. An' sure as hell I didn't know it was yer Loretta, Bran. How'd that go, anyways?"

"Oh, nuthin' much to it. Loretta got a split lip. Not much. Loretta kin give as good as she gets...."

"Yeah, I heard Sally Ann Brimmer got a busted nose. 'Course, that mighta improved her looks somewhat. That is one homely girl," Danny said. "Makes ol' Frank look han'som, an' he's no prize!"

"What was they fightin' about?"

"Oh, nuthin much. Loretta brung her scallop 'taters an' a pot a' spicy meatballs. Worked most a' th' mornin' on them dishes, an' Sally Ann's in line t' get served. There's another ol' gal with a big appetite! An' Sally takes one a' them meatballs an' pops it in her mouth right there at th' servin' table, an' next thing y' know, she pops it out onta her plate an' sez these meatballs is all salty, an' well sir, Loretta's halfway acrost th' room an' she sees what Sally done, an' what she said, an' she goes cuttin' through th' line an' tells Sally Ann she's a dumb red neck who don't know good food from a horse turd an' th' next thing they're swingin' an' cussin'...."

"Damn!"

"Yep. An' ol' Bennie Ostendorf's in th' middle of it all. He don't know where t' turn t' get outta the way, an' Loretta got aholt a' Sally Ann by th' hair, an' Sally Ann's kickin' an' swingin'. An' a' course, they knock ol' Bennie

100

over onta th' table an' it comes crashin' down, all th' pots an' dishes an' all. Bennie's eighty-seven, y' know..."

"Damn!"

"Yep. Weren't pretty. Jimmie Bob Metcalf's got his fiddle–him an' Mac MacGregor was suppos'd t' provide some music later on....Mac with his accordion–an' well sir, ol' Bennie's covered with scallop 'taters an' bean salad, an' tryin' t' git up, an' Loretta an' Sally Ann are on top of 'im, an' Jimmie Bob an' Mac commence t' playin', an' th' reverend's tryin' t' pry th' ladies apart an' Molly Gaither's hollerin' t' keep calm....'Course no one's listenin' t' her...."

"Damn!! I never got t' see that kinda carryin' on," Danny said, "not at no church pot luck. Ever' time me an' Maybelle go t' th' pot lucks at th' Baptist church they got hymns an' all. But no fightin'. An' most times th' food's cold!"

"Yeah. Them Presbyterians. It's pretty well known, they put on the best pot lucks."

"Yep. Well, Carl, you an' Earline go on down an' enjoy th' pot luck t'night." Lennie shook the cloth before folding it and setting it on the counter with the combs and scissors and tonic bottles. "Mebbe me an' Dixie might go on down too.....'less yuh gotta sign up ahead a' time."

MATHEMATICAL PROBABILITY

The strike at the paper mill was taking its toll throughout Altonsburg, and nowhere more dramatically than at Denzil Upshaw's tavern.

"Dunno where th' boys is spendin' their time, but it sure as hell ain't here," Denzil told Denise, as he watched her going through her bar-maid routine, trying to look busy. "May hafta lay y'off fer a spell, least until they git 'er up an' runnin' agin. Hate t' do it, Denise...." They both knew what the strike meant, for them and for the whole town. Denise nodded and continued polishing the spotless bar.

The room was empty except for the back corner table where the three regulars sat. Strike or no, Amos and Tommy Ellacott rarely missed an evening at the Cherokee Rose, and the third drinker, Bucky Dinsmore, was just about as faithful. Except lately, when his three friends began to note a change in Bucky. Denzil had a pretty good idea what was wrong with their old friend. "He's tryin' t' git over LuAnn runnin' off....he'll be okay. Ask me, he's better off without 'er..."

"He don't seem t' want t' talk about it," Tommy said. "Just keeps starin' inta his beer an' won't say nuthin: Hell, she's been lit out fer weeks..."

"Give 'im time...sometimes a fella got t' do some re-adjustin', an' that's what ol' Buck's doin', sortin' ever' thin' out."

But on this evening the understanding and patience of the boys came to an end. "Nuff's enuff! Cryin' out loud, that ol' boy's gotta git aholt a' hisself 'fore he gets us all blubbering in our beer!" Amos rubbed his whiskery chin and motioned for a refill. "Gimme one more, Denzil, an' draw one fer Tommy. We'll give 'im another go-round, but I dunno....I ain't real optee-mistic."

"Some boys take longer 'n others, Amos." Denzil looked across the room to where Tommy sat with Bucky. "Yuh recall th' time Boyd Dilworth's ol' lady run off with that banjo player from Waycross? Boyd kep' sayin' he didn't care a whit, sez he had no use fer Mary-Jo anyways, an' then he ups an' follows her over t' Waycross an' finds her at th' bluegrass festival with her new man.....Guess it got a mite ugly, 'cause ol' Boyd near killed th' banjo

102

player an' got hisself throw'd in jail fer a month."

"Women! Cause a' more dam' trouble. Boyd ain't a bad sort, that ol' boy."

"Nope. But she got 'im pretty wound up that time, that Mary-Jo."

Denzil drew two more drafts and watched Amos make his unsteady way over to the table in the corner. He called to Denise, out back, "Denise, c'mon out here an' tend th' bar fer a bit...not that they's anybody t' tend to. I'm gonna go an' help th' boys with ol' Bucky." He poured two more drafts and came around the bar to join the others at the table in the corner.

Bucky barely looked up as first Amos and then Denzil, took seats at his lonely table. Amos took a long swallow, wiped again at his creased and stubbled chin, and said to no one in particular, "I be dam' glad when the mill starts up agin. Shut-down's no good fer no one."

"Yup, yer right there, Amos." Tommy Ellacott looked around the near-empty room and reached for the peanuts. "Some a' th' boys is already talkin' 'bout headin' South. Heard they was work down th' Panhandle. Dunno that I'd wanta live in that part a' th' world, though. Awful lotta a' old people, y' know, from up North. Heard th' traffic's a real bitch, ever' body creepin' along, goin' out fer supper at four o'clock.....th' early-bird deals. Gerry Don Burwash was down there last year, saw half a dozen accidents in two 'r three days....all them old folks no idea where they wanta go, an' running red lights an' never givin' a thought t' signalin' their turns....."

"Yup...but if they got work there, yuh can't blame th' boys. I was twenty years younger, that's where I'd be headin', prob'ly."

"Yup. Heard ol' Doyle Burney hadta let three more a' th' boys go, over t' th' lumber yard. No buildin' goin' on. Nuthin's goin' on....."

Denzil pushed a full glass across the table, "Here, Buck...on th' house." He raised his glass, inviting the others to join him. "Better times," he said.

Bucky Dinsmore curled a despondent fist around the glass, but didn't raise it. "Thankee, Den. But I ain't in no mood fer no toasts. No 'better times' fer me, boys. Not now, not never." And he wiped his red-rimmed eyes with a theatrical flourish.

Tommy patted his friend on the shoulder. "C' mon, Buck. No ol' gal's worth this kinda sufferin'." He looked around the table for support. "Right, boys?"

The boys nodded and grunted assent. They knew enough about the ways of women. Tommy continued, "Women! Y'all gotta understand, Buck, they ain't like us. They ain't solid, nor reliable. Yuh can't predict 'em, no how. Lookit Wanda-Jane....coupla years ago she tol' Amos she was leavin', had enuff a' life on th' farm. Said she was gonna go live in th' city....said she needed 'culture' er some dam' fool thing. Right, Amos?"

"Yup.....said she needed some a' th' finer things. Couldn't get 'em out here. I sez, go ahead. I knew she wouldn't stay away. Hell, 'culture'? She wouldn't know culture if it bit 'er on th' arse! An' I was right. She went t' her sister's place, over t' Brunswick. Sister works in one a' them beauty parlor places. Got Wanda-Jane a job there, cuttin' toe nails 'er some dam' thing."

"Yep....that's culture yuh kin keep. How'd yuh like t' cut toe nails fer a livin'?"

"I let 'er go....an' I tol' her she'd be back. An' sure enuff, she come back less 'n a month. Culture!"

"Yuh see, Bucky....they ain't like us. They don' know what they want, half th' time."

Tommy reached for the peanuts. "Lu Ann'll be back. Soon as she sees what kinda mean ol' boy that Delbert Backus kin be."

"Tommy's right." Denzil leaned forward, the better to accentuate his point. "Lu Ann's just goin' through some kinda woman-stage, Buck. She'll be back. Dam' funny things happen t' women at times. Y'all ain't th' first t' go through one a' their funny times. Wanda-Jane come back. Lu Ann'll come back. Yuh just gotta give yerself a shake....don't let no woman get yuh down like this."

Bucky sat up. He looked at his three friends, saw their genuine concern. He reached for his half-empty glass, drained it, and gave a resounding satisfying belch. He sat back, and said, "Y'all got it wrong, boys. It ain't losing Lu Ann that's got me in this state."

Their shock was obvious.

"Hell, no. Ol' Del Backus kin have 'er. Good riddance!" He reached for Denzil's fresh offering and took a long swallow.

"Well what in th' merry ol' hell y'all bin mopin' an' whinin' about fer th' last month? Worryin' us, an–.......hell, we thought–"

"–Boys, hell if I care 'bout Lu Ann an' Delbert. She's gone, he kin have 'er. But when she lit out, made me ree-a-lize what a waste my life has bin... an' I come t'see what I coulda bin!"

"Th' hell yuh talkin' about, waste?"

"Yep, a waste. I tell yuh, boys. I bin figgerin' a lot. Bin givin' m'life a lotta thought. An' yuh know, I kin see th' big picture now."

"Th' 'big picture'? What th' hell yuh talkin' 'bout?" Denzil signalled Denise for refills.

"It's clear t' me now, boys. It's what I coulda bin. All them wasted years. I tell yuh, 'stead a' workin' at th' Co-op, I coulda owned th' dam' place. Steada growin' taters 'n peas, I coulda had m'own dairy farm. Or horses...I coulda bin raisin' horses."

104

Having no immediate response, the boys sat back in dumbfound silence. Denise brought the tray, set down the fresh glasses, and took away the empties.

"Yep, I missed the boat, boys. I coulda bin somebody....a figger in th' community. Somebody big. Bigger 'n ol' Del Backus fer sure!"

Denzil found his voice. "Th' hell yuh talkin' about, Buck? Yuh got a good job. Yuh got yer place out there, what, five acres er more...Seems t' me yuh done purty good, even if Lu Ann lit out on yuh...."

"Lu Ann be dam'd! I'm tellin' y'all, boys, I slep' through them years when I coulda bin makin' sumthin' a' m'self. An' I'll tell yuh why. I never got th' mathy matics."

"Th' mathy matics? Th' addin' an' subtractin'?"

"More n'that, boys. Th' gee-om-etree, an' th' al-gee-bra. Ol' Miz Pickens, yuh remember her, she said, 'Buck, y'all ain't goin' nowheres 'less yuh got th' mathy matics...yer gee-om-etree an' yer al-gee-bra'. But was I listenin'? No dam' way. An' lookit me now."

They looked, skeptical and bemused.

"I tell yuh, boys, that mathy matics is th' key. An' I didn't git 'er. Let er go. Coulda bin anythin', with th' mathy matics, an' I wouldn't listen...."

Amos snorted. "That ol' Miz Pickens were one crotchety ol' terror. An' homely! Don' think I ever seen a homelier woman. She kep' a bunch a' cats, as I recall."

"Yep. An' I seen her one time down at th' Five n' Dime, she had ol' Albert Vane by th' ear, tellin' him he's gotta do his homework or she was gonna whip his sorry ass. An' ever' body cleared outta th' way, 'case she turned on someone else. She was mean!" Denzil turned to Tommy. "She was partial t' you, Tommy, weren't she?"

Tommy laughed. "Oh yeah. We were real chummy." He paused to recollect and take a sip. "Homely...an' mean as a mule with th' skitters. She pulled my ears more n' once. An' you tell me, Bucky, what's th' use a' long dee-vision in a man's world anyways?"

"Yer wrong, Tommy," Bucky said, reaching for one of the full glasses. "I bin givin 'er a lotta thought, since Lu Ann left....since she run off. Yuh gotta know all th' angles....all th' twists 'n turns in life. If I coulda know'd that Lu Ann was gittin' ready t' take off....Well, things mighta bin diff'rent. An' if I'd a' paid th' right attention t' th' mathy matics, my po-ten-shul coulda come through. I coulda went on....t' th' trade school, or th' agriculture school. Coulda got m' own shop, or mebbe m' own business....."

The boys looked at each other.

"Or mebbe I'da got me a big spread, y' know, a hunnert acres 'r more... property...like ol' Del Backus out t' other side a' Yulee."

"Well," Denzil agreed, "ol' Del done okay. S'pose that's why yer Lu Ann run off with 'im. Sure as hell weren't fer his looks, nor hisself....his personality, y'know. 'Bout as friendly as a dam' hy-ee-na. But he does have the doh-ray-me, ol' Del."

"Yep, well, somebody like ol' Del, y'all kin be sure he got th' mathy matics. He woulda stayed awake through them lessons. Hell, he prob'ly stayed awake through ol' Gump Sparling's science classes."

"D' yuh recall th' time Billy Branson left th' gas on in ol' Gump's lab and tol' Danny Muller it was th' best place t' go fer a smoke...tol' 'im ol Gump was away, an' it was safe to go in there t' light up...."

"That Billy! He liked t' get th' dumb bunnies inta trouble....last I heard, ol' Danny Muller was livin' with a uncle or somethin', over t'Perry."

"Yep. Deaf as a post. But at least he kin see outta one eye."

Bucky steered their reminiscences back to his theme. "Yeh, well, Billy an' Danny an' th' rest of us...we shoulda bin payin' more attention t' th' things that get yuh ahead. The mathy matics, an' th' science. Yuh git th' learnin', yuh git th' key t' success in life."

"This is somethin' y'all just worked out, Buck?"

"Yup. I seen th' light when ol' Lu Ann lit out. I kin thank 'er fer that, at least."

"Y'all missin' her, I'm guessin'."

"Hell, no. But I know now what I shoulda bin, t'hold onta 'er. Tell yuh, boys, ain't no stoppin' a man who got th' learnin'. With th' mathy matics, I mighta run fer election. Sheriff, mebbe, or town clerk. I bin figgerin' a lot, since she lit out. An' y' know, I shed some tears in m'beer, knowin' I missed out on so many years a' success. Coulda bin anythin' I wanted. Coulda bin a business man, wearin' a suit..."

"Ah, c'mon, Buck."

"I mean it, boys. I coulda drove t' work in a new Oldsmobile ever' day, jus' like Del Backus. Coulda had my picture in th' *Times Leader*. Hell, no tellin' where I coulda gone, with th' mathy matics."

The boys said nothing, but regarded their friend with new respect. As Bucky's eyes welled up anew, Amos spoke, hoping to ward off a fresh bout of mawkish snuffling.

"Lookit, Buck. Them days is gone. Mebbe yer right. Mebbe with th' mathy matics yuh mighta bin somebody. Mebbe. Mebbe yuh mighta kep' ol' Lu Ann in her place. But yuh didn't git the gee-om-etree, yuh didn't make nuthin' a' yerself, an' Lu Ann's gone off t' Yulee. But yer here, yuh got us, yuh still got yer job down t' th' Co-op. An' that's that. Ferget th' past an' what coulda bin. Be thankful...they's plenty a' ol' boys got it a lot worse."

106

It was a long speech by Ellacott standards, and Amos needed a refill. Denzil called for four more, and leaned back in to the table. "Amos got it right, Buck. There's them that got it, an' them that don't. That's jus' th' way it is. Lookit ol' Billy-Mack Creighton. R'member how he chased his old lady off last year? Tol' her t' git off his property, he was done with 'er, and she had t'get out. An' it was at night, d'yuh recall? Put her out one night last Spring, an' it was rainin'....Ol' Jenny Creighton weren't such a bad gal, y'ask me...." The boys nodded at the recollection, and Denzil continued. "Anyways, ol' Jenny lost her way, crossin' th' fields in th' rain, sheriff figgered she was headin' fer Frank Deegan's place. An' didn't she fall inta that ol' well on Harley Norton's place.....found her a coupla days later, heard her hollerin' once th' rain stopped. She's still in the State home, far as I know. An' yuh kin imagine how Billy-Mack feels. Heard they went after him t'pay some a' the bills fer her care."

He paused long enough to drain his glass, and continued. "I'm guessin' ol' Billy-Mack would be glad t' change places with yuh, Buck....with any of us. An' we didn't git th' mathy matics neither. But yuh know, could be we're the lucky ones even without th' learnin'."

Tommy leaned back and stretched. "Another round, boys?" And at their grunts of agreement, he waved four fingers at Denise. "Amos n' Denzil 'r right, Buck. We got each other. How many times y'all seen Delbert Backus in here havin' a beer with friends. Come t'think of it, can you name any ol' boy in this county ever sat down an' had a beer with Del? Don't think so. Yer Lu Ann's gonna find out soon enuff what kinda man she got. Her an' Del prob'ly sit there ever' night jus' lookin' at each other, an' gittin' sick a' th' sight a' each other. I know I would....get sick a' Del, that is. He kin have all th' mathy matics an' learnin' an' still be one mean ol' sumbitch."

The beers came and the four good old boys leaned back to digest this sound reasoning.

"Git us some a' them pickled eggs, Denise, and mebbe some peanuts, if they's any left." Denzil looked around the room, empty now. "Yep. No amount a' learnin', mathy matics, ner history 'n geography, gonna git yuh good times like these, boys."

Bucky Dinsmore, half-believing the well-intentioned counsel of his friends, reached for his glass. Maybe they're right, he thought. He looked at Denise watching the T.V. at the end of the bar. He looked at the Budweiser clock above the rows of bottles behind the bar. Ten-thirty-three. His thoughts turned to the cat at home, no doubt prowling the kitchen and sitting room, wondering where supper was. He thought again of Lu Ann and Del Backus. Lu Ann probably doing her crossword puzzle and asking Del for a three-letter word for a flowery garland. He thought again about the life he might have had, and the shiny black Oldsmobile Del Backus drove through town each day. He raised his glass and said, "Thanks fer all th' encouragin' words, boys. It means a lot t' me. Even if y'all are full a' shit. Next round's on me."

FOR BETTER OR FOR WORSE

"This just ain't workin' out, Sue Ellen." Floyd spat a greasy gob back onto his plate and pushed the glutinous mass away as he rose from the table. "Yuh tol' me yuh could cook, girl, an' gawd knows I ain't partic'lar, but sure as hell I can't swalla this stuff, whatever yuh call it."

Sue Ellen sat stoney-faced, determined not to let the incipient tears start flowing. It was her third attempt at meal preparation, and even before this rejection, his third, she'd been pretty sure the meat loaf was a failure.

"Gawd sake," Floyd continued, "yuh musta learned sumthin' from yer maw. Ain't ever' maw suppos'd t'teach a girl how t'cook? How did yuh manage t' miss all them lessons?"

A number of retorts swirled through Sue Ellen's mind, but none was uttered. She sat staring at her plate as Floyd, heading for the door, continued to berate her. "Yuh gotta do better 'n this, or I'll be sendin' yuh back t' yer daddy." He shucked into his denim jacket, and paused at the door. "That kinda vittles may be good 'nuff fer Carty an' Billy Joe, but it ain't good 'nuff fer me....fer a workin' man. I tol' yuh what I need. Meat an' potatas. Real food. Gimme meat an' potatas." And he was gone.

Floyd was right, she knew. The dinners had been barely edible, and this latest attempt was the worst so far, and things most definitely were not working out. In less than a week of married life, the newlyweds were approaching the realization that the marriage may have been a colossal mistake.

Her daddy had tried to warn her. "Yer makin' a big mistake, Sue Ellen. That Floyd McLinton's no dam' good. Never was, never will be. An' yuh know how he treated Ruth Ann Willows.....treated 'er like a dam' ol' dog. She had t' light out fer Atlanta or he'd a' killed th'poor girl. He's nuthin' but trouble..."

This from a father whose concern for his daughter extended no further than the assurance that floors would be swept, clothon washed, und girls and bacon made. His words were nowhere near enough to discourage the smitten seventeen-year-old. With joy in her heart and knowing that only happiness lay that way, Sue Ellen Dupree had flown to the arms of Floyd McLinton, her shining knight and saviour.

Eight years ago, Sue Ellen's daddy, Carty Dupree had been left with two youngsters to raise when his wife had run off with Smoot Hawkins, a travelling seed salesman from Waycross. Never much of a husband or father, Carty was left as sole parent to fourteen-year-old Billy Joe and nine-year-old Sue Ellen. His reaction to wife Zelda's departure was simply, "Good riddance! That lazy good-fer-nuthin' kin go t' hell with Smoot Hawkins. He'll be sick a' th' sight of 'er b' fore long. I kin guarantee it. I shoulda dumped her sorry ass outta here years ago." And in the eight years since, young Sue Ellen had been homemaker and cook for the three of them living in their drab and dismal shack on a weed-strewn half-acre a mile out of Bentonville, on the Mill Road.

Carty and his son managed the tire recycling depot on the rocky field adjacent to the gravel pit across the road. Worn truck and car tires from every retailer and service station within a hundred miles were dumped at the depot. Carty and Billy Joe stacked the tires and every month or so the piles were loaded and trucked away to the plant at Corrins where, supposedly, something productive came from the whole operation. Carty had no idea what the process involved, what its end products might be, nor was he interested. "Hell if I know what they do with 'em. Me an' Billy Joe just gotta be here t' load 'em when th' trucks come. Mebbe they cut 'em up, mebbe they burn 'em. Hell if I care."

Billy Joe shared his father's opinion, as well as his apathetic approach to life in general. Father and son brought minimal qualifications to the job. The piling and loading was sporadic work, requiring nothing more than a strong back and no imagination. With lots of time on their hands, they were content to laze around outside the tar paper shack that served as the recycling depot office, where they and their cronies from Bentonville passed the days. Wade Pickens and the Crawley brothers usually showed up with a case of Budweiser, and Carty and Billy Joe supplied the 'shine in mason jars.

"Yuh hear about Mose Turley?" Wade asked, snapping open a can.

"Last I heard, ol' Mose was headin' out west."

"Yup. Well, he got as far as Mobile, an' he got hisself shot tryin' t' rob a liquor store."

"Killed?"

"Nope. Got 'im in th' neck, though. Clerk shot 'im. Coulda killed him."

Billy Joe poured another couple of inches into his daddy's glass and then upended the nearly-empty mason jar. He wiped his chin and said, "Mose tol' me he was gonna be workin' fer Steggles in th' Spring...drivin a back hoe or a dozer or sumthin."

110

"Yeah, ol' Mose was gonna do a lotta things..."

And so the days went by, with half-hearted desultory conversation interrupted only occasionally by work brought on by the arrival of the trucks.

Carty's drinking buddies were no doubt aware of Sue Ellen. They had their eyes on her as she grew into her teen years. But either out of respect for, or fear of, Carty and Billy Joe, they never had more than a nod or a 'howdy' for the tired, overworked, and unresponsive daughter of their host.

Sue Ellen had left school after grade eight, and her knowledge and experience of the world, and especially of men, was limited to father and brother and the few hangers-on at the depot across the road. Only rarely did she cross the road, and then only to respond to the call of her father or brother. "Sue Ellen, go on out t' th' root cellar an' bring us another jar a' 'shine," or "Sue Ellen, come an' git these hamhocks Wade brung us. Yuh kin git 'em ready fer supper." And then, at the Labor Day dance, she met Floyd McLinton.

The afternoon festivities were winding down at the Aikens Fairgrounds, and the dance was just getting started. Sue Ellen was working at the lemonade stand on the side of the hall opposite the bar when Floyd came sauntering in, headed to the bar. This was a man respected for the work he did and for the long hours he put into it. A farrier in an agricultural community is never without a demand for his services, and Floyd was on call any hour of the night or day. But that respect bordered on fear, as he was known also for a quick temper. A firm but gentle hand with horses became an unpredictable force, especially when he had a few drinks in him. "He's around them horses all th' time....never did learn how t' git along with people," Carty had explained after Floyd broke Billy Joe's jaw when the unfortunate young man had accidentally bumped into Floyd at the Co-op. Billy Joe had been in the process of apologizing and never saw the punch coming.

"That's just Floyd," was the usual response to outbursts like the one that floored Billy Joe, and no one seemed inclined to discuss this quicksilver temperament with the muscular blacksmith.

He was not usually at gatherings like the Labor Day celebrations and dance, but he'd shoed eight horses for Dinny Olmsted that morning, and he was ready to enjoy some unaccustomed leisure time. He'd gone to the Baptist Ladies pie and tart booth where he'd put away half a peach pie and three or four of Miss Brownrigg's raspberry tarts, and he was ready for a drink. When he saw the girl in the polka-dot dress he made an abrupt stop and headed for the lemonade stand.

"Hey there, little girl, gimme a shot of yer best stuff." And he pulled a fistful of bills from his hip pocket. "Them pies out there was givin' me a powerful thirst. I'm dry as a ol' boot." And he leaned comfortably on the

111

counter, giving Sue Ellen his best side to contemplate as he surveyed the still largely-empty hall.

Sue Ellen, neither beautiful, confident, no worldly-wise, was not stupid. She made a remarkably accurate on-the-spot assessment of the man before her, aided no doubt by the wad of bills in the callused hand. She saw a posing, half-way handsome laborer, sure of himself and anxious to be admired The request for lemonade was transparent: this was a beer and whiskey man. But he had altered course to come to her, and it might be her only chance. She tucked a few loose hairs into place and tried a pose of her own.

"My best stuff?" she said. "You might hafta take me outta this booth t' git that!"

Where that came from she couldn't have said. But she was seventeen, and up to now she'd imagined only the same drab life stretching years ahead of her. And something told her this was it–make your move, girl, or live the rest of your sorry life of regret out the Mill Road.

"Well, little girl, them's just th' words any man wants t' hear." He leaned in now and gave her a conspiratorial wink as he lowered his voice. "Yuh gonna be here in this booth all night, or can yuh come out t' dance....with me?"

"I'm not much fer dancin'," she said, "but I'd sure be pleased t' learn."

Floyd could scarcely believe his luck. The girl, while far from beautiful, had at least that 'down-home wholesome quality' as his momma used to say. And not only was she responding to his flirtatious dandling, but she was playing the game every bit as well as he was. Well, he thought, let's just see where this leads. "Little girl, I'm just th' man t' teach yuh. When kin yuh git off work?"

Sue Ellen reached around and untied her apron, then raised the hinged section of counter and came out of the booth. "I'm off now," she said.

"Whoa...yuh gonna just leave th' booth an' all? What about yer cash? What about yer customers?"

"You see any customers? My name's Sue Ellen," she said, "an' you said somethin' about a dance...."

Hard to believe that was only six days ago, but sitting alone now at the kitchen table, with the unpalatable meatloaf hardening in the pan, Sue Ellen knew it was over. Or soon would be. Not just the whirlwind romance, not just the honeymoon–they'd gone for three days to Branson, Missouri–but probably the marriage itself.

Three days in Branson. Shows and dinners out. For Sue Ellen, who'd never been further from home than Aikens Corners, eight miles down the Mill Road, it was beyond anything she could have imagined. But the novelty and excitement were short-lived: Floyd had to get back to work. He was the

112

only farrier within fifty miles of Bentonville and his services were constantly in demand. For three days back home Sue Ellen tried to perform all aspects of the domestic role as she perceived it. Keep Floyd's rundown three-room shanty respectable and put good wholesome food on the table. Floyd's needs were simple, his directions explicit.

"Meat an' potatas, Sue Ellen. Nuthin' fancy. Grits an' bacon fer breakfast. I'm out all day, and when I git home at th' end of th' day, just gimme meat an' potatas."

Well, that sounded too much like the grub preferences of Carty and Billy Joe. She hadn't left the Mill Road meat an' potatas environment for more of the same. Maybe it was Branson, when in those three magical days they'd eaten exotic fare served on fine china set on tables covered in white linen. Maybe she was seeing her new husband as a figure of prestige in the community. He was a farrier, after all. Whatever the motivation, she was determined to provide Floyd with dinners more grand than simple 'meat an' potatas."

"What's this?" he'd asked on their first night back home.

"It's a omelet, Floyd. Eggs an' cheese an' cubed ham an' mushrooms. A omelet."

"Mushrooms!! I ain't eatin mushrooms, Sue Ellen." He'd dumped the omelet in the garbage pail. "I'll git a burger down at Kelsey's. An' fer tomorrow night, make it meat an' potatas!" And he was gone.

Sue Ellen was determined, and the next night she'd tried pork chops with rice in tomato sauce. The pork chops had been done to the consistency of hockey pucks.

"Rice!! Who tol' yuh I wanted rice! Gawd sakes, Sue Ellen, d' yuh think I'm a chinaman er somethin'? Meat an' potatas, girl. What's so dam' hard about that!" And he'd gone out again.

The meatloaf was the latest and probably last attempt Sue Ellen would be making to provide varied and wholesome meals for her man.

She got up from the table and picked up the pan of meatloaf. It seemed to have gotten heavier. Unable even to imagine scraping the plate clean, she dumped the whole thing in the pail under the sink. She opened the cupboard above the stove and took out a box of Cheerios. She filled a bowl, poured milk over the cereal, and went to the front room. She looked out and saw that Floyd's truck was gone. She sat and turned on the T.V., settling in for a few hours of mindless viewing.

The rap on the front door was so slight she wasn't sure it was a knock at all. She hit the mute button and heard the distinct rapping. "Who's there?" she called.

The door opened a crack. "It's just me, Dearie. Can I come in?"

"Mrs. Whorley?" Just what I need, she thought. But she went to the door to admit the elderly neighbor from across the street. "I wasn't sure I heard you knocking, Mrs. Whorley. Come in. Is everything all right?"

"You tell me, Dearie. That's why I'm here..." The aged crone edged into the room and headed for the kitchen. She set her cane in the corner and perched on one of the straight-back chairs.

"Kin I git you somethin, Mrs. Whorley? Mebbe some tea?"

"That would be nice, Dear." She folded her blue-veined blotchy hands on the table top and watched Sue Ellen fill the kettle. "First time we've had a chance t' visit," she said. "I'd of come over sooner, but I wanted t' give you an' Floyd some time t' settle in....."

"Uh huh, that's nice, Mrs. Whorley."

"You can call me Dora, Dearie. It's Theadora, but I never could abide that name...."

"All right....Dora. Do you like sugar, an' milk?"

"Oh, I'm not fussy, Dear. 'Course, if you had a drop of somethin' stronger...?"

"Ma' am?"

"Dearie, I've lived eighty-eight years because I allow m'self a little pick-me-up in my tea..."

"Oh, yes...of course. Lemme see what Floyd has here...." Sue Ellen began opening cupboards.

"Look in th' broom closet, Dearie. You'll find somethin' there."

"Yup...you're right. Looks like you got a choice..Dora." Sue Ellen began reading the bottle labels.

"Old Grand Dad would be a nice treat, Dear. Just a few drops. And while you're gettin' th' tea, let me tell you why I'm here."

Sue Ellen gave the old lady a quizzical look. Dora slid her cup across the table and began.

"I've known Floyd McLinton since he was a baby. Knew his momma an' daddy....Watched him grow up in this very house. Your kettle's boilin', Dear."

Sue Ellen got up to pour the water.

"You should put the bags in first, Dear. But that'll be fine. An' just a bit more of that bourbon. That's lovely, Dear. Don't forget t' turn off your stove."

Sue Ellen took her seat across from Dora and said, "I'm sorry Floyd's not here....he had t' go out an–."

"Yes, I know. I saw him go. And I saw him go last night, 'bout the same time. An' th' night before that....."

Sue Ellen wrapped her hands around her steaming cup and looked at the darkness outside the kitchen window.

114

"Y' know, Dear, marriage is sorta like those penny arcade games, the ones where you pay your money an' try to pick up a prize inside the glass case. What do they call it..."Treasure Hunt'....or somethin' like that. You work this sorta arm, like a fishin' pole, an' you try to hook on to somethin' nice..."

Sue Ellen nodded, even though she'd never seen the game her neighbor was describing.

"Sometimes you're lucky, an' you get a nice prize, like a bracelet, or a string of pearls. Not real pearls, of course. But nice enough to wear. But sometimes you get somethin' real cheap, somethin' no good for anything at all. An' sometimes you come up with nothing..."

Sue Ellen reached for the bourbon bottle and added a dollop to her own cup.

"Floyd's a good, hard-workin' man. He was headstrong an' a hell raiser, growin' up. Never did seem t' be able t' keep friends fer too long. I'm talkin about girl friends, Dearie. An' I saw how he treated Wanda Beecher. Mighta raised a hand to that poor girl a number of times. That wasn't right, an' he's lucky she didn't report him for it. An' then, Ruth Ann Willows. Just a lovely girl. Not much older 'n you, Dearie. How old are you, anyway?"

"Nearly eighteen. In four months."

"Yes. Well, Ruth Ann lasted a mite longer. But she left him too."

"I just met Floyd last week," Sue Ellen said. "He was awful good t' me. Took me t' Branson, an–."

"I know, Dear. I know. He can be a fine young man. A good husband. But...well...he's gotta come up with some kinda good prize from that Treasure tank. If y' take my meanin'."

"Well,....we do alright...y' know..."

"I know, Dear. I'm sure that part is just fine. Like it was for fifty-eight years for me an' Delbert. But I wonder if I could give you a little advice...... about the other parts of bein' married?"

Sue Ellen nodded, not at all sure where the old lady was taking her.

"Y'see, Dearie, some men don't need anythin' more than what y' might call the bare necessities." She took a long sip and twirled a bony finger to signal more whiskey. Sue Ellen poured enough to bring the tea back up to the brim.

"An' some men gotta have everything in the world done for 'em. Y' know, clean shirt every day, fancy times, an' all that life can offer...."

"But your Floyd's like the first one. An' you're doin' your best to give him the bare necessities. Prob' ly doing a real good job with that, I'd say. But Floyd does have some other needs that have to be filled." She gave Sue Ellen a squinty once-over. "You're fillin' his first need....but he's like my Delbert was....a meat an' potatoes man....Delbert only wanted two things outta mariage, an' the second was meat an' potatoes."

"But my daddy–."

"Oh, I know. Carty Dupree's always been a meat an' potatoes man. Like my Delbert an' your Floyd."

"I just thought–."

"You just thought you'd like t' change that with Floyd, didn't you?"

Sue Ellen nodded miserably.

"Dearie, you got a good man. Wanda tried to change him, an' she couldn't. Same with Ruth Ann. I don't want t' see you goin' down that road too. Give 'im what he wants. An' you two'll be happy, like me an' Delbert."

Floyd was still out when Sue Ellen went to bed that night. Before turning out her bedside lamp, she made out a grocery list for the next day's trip to Winn Dixie.

It was a short list.

The Horace Brant Stories

QUID PRO QUO

Dr. Horace Brant considered himself blessed. His practice in Wilkes-Barre provided him and his family with a fine home and all the material comforts of success in the city. And away from the city, up the mountain, he enjoyed his greatest satisfaction.

Six winding miles up #115 was a parcel of one thousand Pocono acres on Bear Mountain. He'd bought the land right after the war. And he'd determined from the outset that its pristine nature would be protected and preserved for the wildlife that abounded there. The thousand acres were heavily wooded with oak, beech, ash, and hickory. Here and there small clearings appeared, ten or fifteen acres each in most cases, fields cleared by early settlers, the resulting lots defined by impressive stone fences. In the mornings, often, groups of deer, sometimes fifteen or twenty at a time, came to drink from ponds and streams that tumbled through his woods and meadows, eventually to join the Susquehanna River far below.

The doctor's life was simple and orderly, spartan really, considering his prominence in the Wilkes-Barre medical community. He and his wife had a city role to play, a minimal number of social contacts, and almost all their attention was directed to their three children, daughter Barbara Ann and sons Bradley and Byron. It was up at the summit of Bear Mountain that the Brants seemed most in tune with life and their surroundings. The summer house, a fortess-like structure, Horace and the boys had built from the field stones and timber readily at hand on their majestic property.

Dr. Brant allowed himself the luxury of only two close friends. Up the mountain, it was old Delbert Buscomb, an 'original' as Horace described him, their ageless, tireless, and mostly-speechless, handyman-factotum. It was Del and Horace who had built the Brant house, with whatever help could be got from the boys, still not yet in their teen years at the time of construction. Del lived a couple of miles down the 115, and he kept watch over the Brant property when the city demanded their presence. He and Horace could work side by side and their exchanges would rarely exceed a dozen words through a whole day's work.

118

The other close friend was a Lebanese scrap dealer who lived quietly in a war-time bungalow near the freight yards, and who owned a square city block in the Mechanicsville section of Wilkes-Barre.. Eli Mansour had arrived penniless in America after the war and within ten years had grown a nondescript scrap business into a multi-million dollar enterprise trading in everything from salvaged rails to iron castings to reconditioned turbines and generators. The friendship dated from 1948 when the year-old daughter of the scrap metal man was brought to Dr. Brant with a life-threatening case of meningitis. Horace had saved the child's life. The friendship initiated by the grateful father and reciprocated by the usually taciturn doctor became, over the years, a treasured, private bond. In the early fifties Horace had invested heavily in his friend's business, and the results were more than satisfactory, for both men. One might assume this friendship was a simple matter of exchange for favours received. It was much more than that. Horace knew he had a close tie to someone on whom he could rely in any moment of need. The exact words were spoken on the occasion of Hanna Mansour's sixth birthday party. Horace had brought a small gift for the healthy little girl, and as he was leaving, Eli had taken him by the arm.

"Just before you go, Doctor," Eli had said, looking directly into Horace's eyes, "I want you to know something. I say this now, just this one time..." Horace had raised his eyebrows quizzically. His friend's demeanor was suddenly intense. The scrap man looked up and down the street. His grip on Horace's arm remained firm. "If there's ever a time when you need something....something done..." He paused, seeming to seek the proper words. "Anything," he continued. "You understand. Anything at all..you call on me."

In that moment Horace had felt no need for elaboration of the offer.

Over the years Horace had hiked over and through most of his thousand acres, marveled in its grandeur and beauty. He dreamed of passing it on to his children, with the implicit understanding that the character and appearance remain grand and untouched. On the edges of the cleared areas he had found stone foundations, fallen in, barely recognizable, silent testament to the struggles of settlers long ago.

It was a hunter's paradise, this part of northeast Pennsylvania, but he vowed there'd be no hunting on his land. He had posted the land himself and declared himself ready to chase off anyone who dared come to shoot the beautiful shy creatures he loved so well.

At the base of the other side of Bear Mountain, the side away from the city, and extending part way up neighboring Elk Mountain, was a small hamlet with the lofty name of West Alden Junction. There didn't seem to be an East or Main Alden. For some time in the first half of the twentieth century a single-track railway had run past the settlement. By the late forties the community had dwindled to less than a hundred souls living in a dozen or so run-down clapboard shanties lacking most of the amenities of modern life. There was no industry, no business, no postal address: the P.O. serving Nanticoke, itself barely more than a hamlet, also served the residents of West Alden. The inhabitants lived off the land in much the same fashion as the earliest settlers, hunting, trapping, and fishing in and out of any officially-sanctioned season. They were a coarse lot, unimpressed by law and order, especially as it pertained to private ownership of any part of the surrounding mountains.

Among these rough mountaineers none were coarser than the Gullions: Miles and Evelina, and their sons Emmett and Tyrone. Their house was, like all the West Alden houses, an unpainted listing frame shanty, with threatening hounds, clothesline, and wrecked shell of a rusting vehicle in a weed-strewn front yard. The only distinguishing feature of the Gullion yard was that the rusting Dodge pick-up wasn't up on cinder blocks, so one might assume it was capable of running.

Dirt, rush, and disrepair prevailed. A canted mailbox stood at the road, with *GULLION* hand painted on the one side and a close variation, *GULION,* on the other. On the ground at the base of the mail-box post was a half-sheet of quarter-inch plywood whose faded lettering proclaimed *GULLION & SONS, GEN'L CONTRACTING* and *NO JOB TO SMALL.*

The Gullion men were hunters, from a long line of hunters. On an unseasonably warm November afternoon Miles and his boys sat on the sagging back porch cleaning their .303's and discussing the disappointments of the hunt so far.

"I dunno....ne'er seen nuthin' like it. Not even a dam' track for two days now," Miles groused. "Can't figger it out...."

"Mebbe we oughta try up t'other side," said Tyrone, wiping an ever-dripping nose with an oily rag. "We could mebbe try up where Gill's daddy had his camp....years ago..."

"Worth a try," Emmett agreed.

"Yeah, well, we'll hafta bring Gill with us, an' that useless blue tick. "Course, Gill's prob'ly still drunk from th' auction over t'Puddicomb's last week." Miles spat a reflective gob, and continued, "An' if he's sober 'nuff t' walk up Bear, he'll more 'n likely have that no account walleyed Randy Post taggin' along ..."

"Hell if I care. We ain't gettin' jack in these godfersakin hills. An' Randy Post always has lotsa 'shine. Let's give 'er a try up Bear...."

120

On one of his exploratory circuits of his property early in his ownership, Horace had discovered a dilapidated shack on the edge of a small clearing just inside the property line on the slope leading down to West Alden Junction. And while he couldn't know it, this hovel was the old abandoned hunt camp of Webster Gill, of West Alden Junction. Little more than a shed, and almost completely hidden by brush and a protruding rock face, the ten by ten shack sat on a stone foundation and had thus been spared much of the ravages of time. Despite its obvious age, it revealed solid construction. Could have housed some settler family, Horace thought, maybe a hundred or more years ago. It crossed his mind to clear the brush and preserve this heritage dwelling, this spare one-door, one-window shanty, for the history it represented. But he was disturbed to notice signs of more recent use–a rough table, a couple of steel folding chairs, a mattress, as well as beer cans and an empty gin bottle.

Hunters, or kids, he thought; neither would be tolerated. He'd returned the following day with some lumber and hardware. The window he boarded up, and after reinforcing the door and replacing the hinges, he affixed a padlock and a sign prohibiting trespass on threat of prosecution.

Other jobs had demanded his time, and the shack was forgotten until, three years later, it occurred to him to check on it one Fall day.

What he found angered him. The boards had been torn off, the lock pried off, and a small pot-bellied stove sat in the middle of the room, its rickety chimney poking through a rough hole cut through the roof. Two filthy mattresses filled the remaining floor space. In a fury, Horace went for tools. He dragged the mattresses out, doused them with gas and set them afire. He re-boarded the window and door with four inch ardox nails. He left only after the mattresses were destroyed and the fire was safety out.

On his way down the mountain he stopped at the Wyoming County Sheriff's office to report the trespass and request police action in preventing further use of his property.

"Well, Doctor, what damage do you wish to report?" The clerk seemed bored.

"Damage? Well, there's some. But I'm reporting trespassing . This is my private property and I don't want people on my land."

"Do you have your land posted, Sir?"

"Of course it's posted. I'll put out more signs if I have to. But what I'm seeking here is assistance "

The blank unsympathetic stare of the duty officer was infuriating.

"Do your troopers drive through West Alden?"

"We do...they do."

"Well....couldn't they ask some questions...you know, maybe find out if anyone has information? Somebody must know who's been up on my land. I'd bet they're from West Alden. I'm prepared to press charges."

"Sir, we can't go in and accuse people like that. The land you're talking about...it's pretty remote, isn't it?"

Horace got nowhere and gained nothing but the conviction that the officer was probably well aware of who was using his property.

In the week before Christmas he decided on a Wednesday afternoon to check the property once again. He took the dogs, and instead of walking down from the house, he drove to West Alden Junction, parked the car at the end of a roughed-out bush road above town, and hiked up to the shack. The first thing he discovered was a number of posted signs torn down and strewn on the ground inside his property line. And then Jiggs and Monty started barking, their alarm echoed by the baying of other dogs in the direction of the shack. He stopped in his tracks. He wished he'd brought the .22 or a shovel, or a hammer, anything. But then, armed with righteous anger, he strode on.

Two men, both in checked bush shirts and Carhartt coveralls, stood in front of the shack. Smoke drifted lazily from the chimney. Four hounds with ears laid flat walked stiff-legged to sniff and challenge Horace's dogs. A gutted deer hung from a tri-pod by the door.

Horace spoke first, "I'm Horace Brant. You men are on my land. You're trespassing." No sign nor acknowledgment of his words. He spoke again, "This is private property. It's posted. You can't hunt or camp here."

A third face appeared in the doorway, bearded and scowling.

"I've informed the police. You men are trespassing. This is posted land," he repeated. "You can't hunt here....no hunting allowed."

As he said it, he realized that the hunting season was long over, had ended nearly a month ago. The fact that they were trespassing was only a small part of the picture, and this was no safe place to be and certainly not issuing threats to these dark, dirty, and, for all he knew, murderous mountain men. But he persisted.

"I'm giving you a warning this time. You have to leave. And you're not to come on this property again." The urge to flee rooted him to the spot. His eyes swept the immediate area. Laid across an old wooden crate were two rifles. A long-handled axe was buried in a stump which had served as a chopping block, and freshly-splintered kindling lay around the block. He knew his legs were trembling, and he wondered if he could speak again without his tremulous voice betraying him. He prayed his clean-shaven and gentlemanly demeanor would not reveal his fears to these dark and menacing brutes. Still they had not spoken.

122

"I'm leaving now. I want you gone when I come back tomorrow. This land is posted." He called the dogs, "Let's go, Biggs; come on, Monty...let's go...c'mon now." The dogs, completely subdued, were eager to turn away from the threatening hounds.

And then one of the men spoke, the older one in the doorway. "Well sir, mister doctor, seems t'me yuh got lotsa room fer yerself up t'other side a' this here mountain." He spat loudly and took a step down to the ground.

"I'm simply telling you, it's my land. It's posted and it's private. The police have been informed." He did not refer to their unlawful kill, and ended with, "You men have to get off my land."

"Yuh've said yer piece, Mister Fancy-man big shot doctor. An' now, yuh git....you an' yer yella-belly dogs. Git yer ass on down that trail!"

"You men have been warned!"

He was still shaking twenty-some minutes later when he pulled into the State Police depot. Another officer was on duty. As soon as Horace began, the trooper interrupted, "Sir, we have your complaint on file. And Trooper Howatt's been up there, twice, and he reports no sign of trespass on your land."

"I'm telling you, they're up there right now. I just came from there. I saw them. And they've got a deer!"

"We don't have a man available right now, Sir. I can send someone up in the morning. Did you get their names?"

"Of course not. There's three of them, an older man and two younger... and they've got rifles...."

"Did they threaten you, Sir?"

"Not..exactly. But it was a threatening situation. They're on my land. I want them put off, and charged!"

"Well, Sir...they're probably just local lads. Probably neighbors of yours. You might not want to stir up bad feelings, y' know, charging them. Are you sure you want that?"

Still shaking with residual fear and anger, Horace left the station with assurance that "one of the men'll look into it tomorrow..." But he knew nothing was going to be done.

Christmas came and went without a solution. Horace promised himself that the matter would be resolved, maybe in the Spring. He wanted no more to do with the police and their patronizing inefficiency. And he definitely did not want another face-to-face with the cretinous brutes on the other side of the mountain.

The police did call in mid-January to inform him that Trooper Howatt had again investigated, had found nothing, and his questions in West Alden had produced no useful information. The situation worsened before the winter ended. In March the police called again to report that someone had hiked up to the cabin and set it ablaze. It had burned to its rock foundation. Trooper Howatt, again the investigating officer, had found nothing to assist him in identifying those responsible.

The final chapter in the saga occurred four weeks after the fire. Horace had gone on a Saturday in April up the mountain to do some repair work on one of his storage sheds. He'd taken the dogs and they were free to roam while he and Delbert mixed the mortar and set the stones. The dogs had a routine: they'd tear through fields and woods for a couple of hours, returning exhausted and fulfilled when Horace whistled them back for the drive down to the city. Sometime around mid-afternoon they heard the dogs howling from a distance and assumed they'd treed a 'coon or porcupine. By four, with the job completed, Horace whistled and began cleaning the barrow and trowels. No dogs. The men shouted and whistled until darkness fell.

"Damn those dogs! Del, we can't wait here any longer. We'll leave the shed open. There's blankets in there. Put some water in...they can spend the night there. Can you come up in the morning to get them?" I'll come up t' your place in the morning..."

They weren't unduly concerned. It had happened before, and simply meant inconvenience for Horace and the old man.

Horace led the way out of the yard, old Del's Fargo clattering behind. Fifty yards from the main road the headlights framed a dog lying on the lane. It was Biggs. The Collie lay bedraggled and exhausted, barely able to raise its head. He'd been sick, and was unable to move out of the path of the vehicles. Horace jumped out and ran to the dog. He saw no signs of injury, but the dog lay limp in his arms as he carried it to the back seat. They called and whistled for another ten minutes, but there was no sign of the other dog.

Del called at seven the next morning.

"Yuh better c'mon up...t' th' house."

Del met Horace at the main house and pointed him to the shed. The lifeless body of Monty hung by his collar looped over the top corner of the open door. On the ground in front of the shed and just beneath the dog's body was one of the orange and black signs proclaiming 'This Land is Posted'.

"I loved that dog," Horace said, clasping the tumbler of bourbon. "They didn't have to kill the dog...."

Eli Mansour leaned forward and laid a gentle hand on his friend's arm. "I agree. A grievance is one thing....a quarrel...man to man. To take the quarrel out on a man's dog...that is the coward's way..."

"They came on my land....they destroyed my property. They threatened

124

me. I went to the police –."

"Doctor....you should know that certain...uh...situations are best handled without police involvement. They are not always reliable..."

"But, to do that....to Monty. What's next, my family?"

"Yes, what's next. Doctor, you must leave this to me. The police are no help. This is a matter that requires attention. These people, they must not think they can do these cowardly things and not be held accountable."

The import of these words snapped Horace to full attention. He sat straight up in his chair, spilling some of the whiskey on his pant leg. "What do...I mean, what are –."

"Please, Doctor. Calm yourself. We have no further need to discuss this outrage. Please, put your mind at ease. You and I have been good friends for so long now. It is a simple matter. I will make some arrangements. You have no need to worry about these barbaric people."

Horace settled back and allowed Eli to replenish the bourbon. At that moment he considered himself truly blessed.

PENNY WISE....

Having grown up in the Depression years, Dr. Horace Brant could never quite let go of the fear of hard times. He'd seen his father broken and bowed after a short working life in the mines, cast off without pension or security of any kind. And Horace had vowed to move heaven and earth to avoid such drudgery and to protect his own family from such penury.

From the age of twelve he worked two jobs while attending school. Through high school and college he continued to work, succeeding in putting himself through medical school. His rise from humble beginnings was achieved through self-discipline and unflagging determination. The material rewards achieved, he never changed. Nor did the theme of the lessons he sought to pass on to his own children.

The range of the lessons was quite predictable: the grit and moral strength of his father's generation, his own stern apprenticeship and ascendancy, the deplorable slide of the current generation of creampuffs, deadbeats, and welfare recipients.

"Work is noble." His opening was always some variation on the theme of honest labour. "Look around an' all you see these days is lazy bums. Leeches. Wantin' something for nothing. Handouts, welfare. That's not for us, not for you."

Horace's children could not avoid his counsel. It was daily fare with his audience captive at the dinner table. "You remember, boys. And you, too, Barbara Ann. There's no free lunch. You get what you work for. Lookit your gran' dad..." It may not have been the ideal model, as old Joe Brant had worked like a coolie and had, at the end of his shortened working life, nothing material to show for his back-breaking labour. No matter. Horace's lecture moved easily on to his own hard-earned success as the role to emulate.

"I never had a day without work or study. An' that's the way it should be. This country was built by the sweat an' toil of laborin' men. Not by welfare bums."

From uprightness and moral rectitude, he'd turn to the virtue of thrift.

"Always look for bargains. An' sales. I don't mean junk. Get quality, but get it on sale." For Horace, the doctor, a penny saved was as significant as a
126

fortune earned. Ever parsimonious, he'd drive ten miles to save a dollar on a pair of twenty-dollar shoes. Driving a four-year old Cadillac, he scouted out the gas stations to save a cent on a gallon of gas. With the help of his friend Eli the scrap dealer he was able to indulge his need for salvage: storage sheds, most of his garage, a lean-to behind the garage–all containing random piles of scrap materials, testimony to his thrift, frugality, and avarice.

He bought his suits from a mail-order firm in Hong Kong. "Shoes...you've gotta have shoes, but you don't need Florsheims. Get Sismans." It was a favorite line, and the kids always rolled their eyes at this point in the lecture. When Bradley and Byron were twelve and ten, he put them to work. He'd purchased a thousand acres up Bear Mountain above Wilkes-Barre with the intention of building a retreat for summers and weekends away from the city. "It'll be just the ticket...fresh air, an' all the work y' could ever want!" He'd hired a handyman, old Delbert Buscomb, to help prepare the site and to oversee the excavation for the foundation. The country home was to be built by Horace and Del over the next two or three years. "No hurry, boys. We'll do it on weekends and in the summer. And you'll learn lessons no school can teach...."

After the foundation was poured, and prior to the framing stage, Horace and Del had erected two out buildings, storage space for building materials and tools, and for the salvage items from Eli Mansour's scrap yard. These included dozens of rims, re-bars, con rods, pistons, I-beams, bumpers, and bolts. There were sections of fire escape, three sets of elevator doors, half a dozen brass beds in varying stages of disrepair......Most of the items were from a time and place beyond practical use. The only thing missing in the disarray was any semblance of organization.

"Del, that's your job when we're not workin' on the house," Horace explained. "Days when I can't be here, you an' the boys can get a start on some kind of inventory."

The boys rolled their eyes. Del simply nodded, knowing there was little likelihood of any order ever being imposed on the daunting mass of barrels and cables and planks and wheels.

One Saturday when Horace had to be in Carlisle he'd driven the boys up to the site and left them for the day with Del. He'd come across another bargain, courtesy of Eli, a truck load of lumber salvaged from a warehouse demolition. At this stage, he wanted the boards sorted and piled, after the removal and saving of all the nails. The lumber was sound and fit for any number of future needs.

"Dad," Bradley protested, "you're joking, right? Save the nails? Taking 'em out will take us a week. You could buy new nails...all you need."

Horace didn't even reply. He handed each boy a hammer and pry bar, spoke briefly to Delbert, and drove out of the yard and down the mountain. The old man and two unhappy boys surveyed the pile of lumber.

"Nobody saves nails," Byron whined. "We shouldn't have to do this." He watched Del pull a few boards free of the pile. "We'll never get this done." Del began to pull and straighten the extracted nails, dropping them into his red coffee can.

Bradley signed mightily and watched as the old man, head down and seemingly unaware of the two assistants, reached for another board. Shamed by the man's silent progress, the boys picked up their tools and began.

Gradually the pile of cleaned boards grew, the coffee cans filled, and the patience of the boys drew closer to its end. "This is so dumb," whispered Byron. "Do we really hafta finish this, Brad?"

"All the nails out...that's what he said. An' then we've gotta pile them."

"But it'll take forever...."

"I know. We've gotta think of something."

"Yeah. Lookit ol' Del. Doesn't seem to bother him a bit."

"Yeah, well, it doesn't take a lotta brains, does it?" Brad snickered. "Prob'ly th' only thing th' ol' fart's good for, pullin' nails an' sortin' boards."

By eleven the boys were just about played out. Their pile was woefully short of the old man's neatly-stacked nail free boards. Finally, after much theatrical sighing, Brad laid down his hammer and said, "This is so dumb. Why don't we just cut the ends off the boards?"

Del said nothing, but kept on extracting and straightening, bent over his work. His silence was a stinging reproof. The boys now felt foolish, and their ears tingled in shame. Brad bent again to the task and Byron followed the lead. Ten minutes passed. Del put down his hammer and reached for his water bottle. He took a couple of long swallows and then, in what was possibly his lengthiest utterance in years, he said, "Be it ever so lowly, all labor is holy. Just keep that in mind, boys."

By the time Horace drove into the yard at 4:30 that afternoon, the lumber, free of nails and sorted by width and length, was piled on skids under a canvas beside the storage shed.

A field-stone fortress, the mountain house took over two years to build. Brad, then fifteen, was able to give Del and his father a man's work with the heavy beams and stones. Twelve-year-old Byron was the gofer and hander-up of tools, the cleaner-up and put-away man.

"It's good hard work, boys," Horace told them at the outset and regularly during the construction. 'But good hard work built this country. And you'll never regret it. The world's full of lazy bums. They go nowhere. You're

128

gonna be satisfied, an' happy with your labors." And to this admonition he never failed to add, "Be doctors, boys. No finer calling, and th' pay is right."

On a Friday evening in the late summer of '52, Horace announced he was taking the boys to town the next morning for back-to-school apparel. He was going to introduce them to the latest trend in clothing retailing: discount warehouse shopping.

"The only way to go, boys. An' it's gonna take a chunk outta those places in town. The way of the future. You'll get value...good quality. An' nothin' like those bandits at The Hub an' Goldbergs." He assured them this was the forerunner of modern merchandising.

Their destination was a huge ugly grey brick warehouse on the north side of town. A blue and white marquee proclaimed Robert Hall Clothing–'The Best for Less.' Horace had been there at the Grand Opening, and saw immediately the savings potential. "Prices you won't believe," he promised.

Inside the unadorned barracks-like building were rows upon soldierly rows of racks displaying suits, top coats, jackets, and pants designed to fit every size and shape of man and boy in the country. A bargain barn covering two or three acres where fairly-correct fit and utilitarian style went with rock-bottom prices.

Two salesmen approached. "Good morning, gentlemen. You can serve yourselves, or we'd be happy to assist you with your selections." Within an hour, the three gentlemen were outfitted off the rack and in satisfied comfort. Dress and casual shirts, sports jackets and suits with two pairs of pants each....Socks, ties, belts, and underwear...The bill came to slightly over three hundred dollars.

Horace was ecstatic. "How can you go wrong? Look at what we got, and what we paid! No more shopping any place else, boys. Just too bad your mother and Barbara Ann can't get their stuff here. But y' know, I'll bet there'll be something for them, along these lines, real soon. People want reasonable prices."

As they packed their parcels in the trunk, he suggested a short trip. "Let's go over to th' hospital....I'll show you th' new addition. It's almost finished." He wheeled the big Cadillac out of the lot and out onto the 115 heading for the County Hospital.

"So.....how about that place. Crimy, I couldn't believe their prices, first time I went there! Winter coats at twenty-eight dollars!" Smart shopping always animated Horace, like discussion of socialized medicine, or mortar mix, or lawyers. "Y' know," he continued, "some of the docs I know won't go to a place like that. They'd rather pay some shyster a hundred bucks for a suit and twelve bucks for a shirt. Crimy, y' can get three suits there for what you'd pay for one at Goldberg's! A suit's a suit!"

They continued on toward the hospital. A red light flashed on the dashboard. "Crimy! I need gas. Meant to fill up yesterday....Let's see what they're chargin' at Shell." He wheeled down a side street and pulled up at a single-pump garage. A hand-lettered sign advertised gas at sixteen cents a gallon.

"Crimy! It was fifteen and a half last week. That's robbery. I'm not payin' that!" He pulled away as the attendant approached. 'We'll try the Texaco."

They pulled into the Texaco lot where there was a car already ahead of them at the pump. Gas–fifteen and a half. "That's better. Shoulda known that crook at Shell would try t' gouge another dime for a fill-up. I dunno how he–."

His indignation was cut off by a shout from Byron in the back seat. "Dad, lookit! Over there, at th' Esso!"

Across the street an Esso station proclaimed 'Gas - fifteen cents a gallon'.

"Crimy!" Horace turned the key and gunned the engine. He couldn't go forward because the car ahead was still fueling. He jammed into reverse and started to back out of the line, at the same time turning to negotiate the manoeuver. Too late. An old three-quarter ton Ford loaded with sand, gravel, and bags of concrete mix had pulled in behind the Cadillac, and in the split second before hitting the brake, Horace had rammed back into the bumper of the old truck. Not a major collision; the distance had been only five or six feet. The truck hadn't moved, its bumper absorbing most of the impact, and there seemed to be no damage at all, there. The Cadillac hadn't fared so well. On one side the tail-light housing was smashed, and the fender on that side had wrinkled as far forward as the back door. The bumper was pushed up into the trunk, rendering it impossible to open.

A huge black man in a grey woolen knot cap and torn army jacket sat placidly behind the wheel of the truck. He had a bottle of Orange Crush in one large hand and he seemed not in the least perturbed by the turn of events. With slow deliberation he climbed down and shuffled forward to survey the destruction.

"Man oh man, looks like you all got th' worst of it. Yo' Caddy's busted."

He was right. There wasn't a mark on the truck.

For the moment, and it was the only time either boy was to witness the phenomenon, Horace was at a loss for words. His mind, though, was fully occupied, racing through the possible ramifications of his predicament. First and foremost, and most vexatious, he was at fault and the station attendant was independent witness. There was no way to spread the blame. True, he'd been distracted by Byron's sudden shout, but it had been he who'd turned the key and stepped on the gas. He couldn't attach any blame to the other driver.

130

And him a darkie! Damn! He did some rapid calculations. The truck was undamaged, not even a mark on the bumper. The Caddy could be driven. The trunk would have to be pried open. He'd need a new trunk lid, fender, and bumper. Crimy.....this was adding up. He could report the accident, but that meant police to investigate and report, and insurance claims, and that probably meant higher rates....

He made an on-the-spot decision. "Back in the car, boys." The front car had filled up and gone. He gunned the Caddy out of the Texaco lot and across to the Esso pump, under the watchful amused eyes of the black truck driver and the Texaco attendant. They could still get the gas cap off, and he got his fifteen-cent fill up.

The trip to the hospital was put on hold. Instead, Horace drove the crippled Cadillac across town to the scrap yard of his friend Eli Mansour. There Eli had one of his men pry open the trunk with a crowbar. The packages from Robert Hall Clothing were thrown into the backseat. Three of the packages were badly crushed, but Horace told the boys to leave them alone. They'd check on them later. The mangled bumper was removed and hammered as straight as could be done with the equipment at hand. The rest would be the work of a dealer or body shop. The man wired the trunk shut. He could do nothing about the crumpled fender and broken tail light.

"Thanks, Eli. Wasn't much you could do, but that'll get us home." He waved off the offer of a substitute vehicle. He had considerably less to say on the drive home. The two boys sat quietly, knowing it was best not to intrude upon their father's thoughts. Half-way home he spoke.

"You boys learned something today. I want you to remember this; there's never any good comes out of an altercation with coloreds. There's nothing to be gained. There was no point, no sense in me arguing with that truck driver. Not worth it. So, what do you do when you're in a situation like that?" He paused briefly, and when neither boy responded, he continued. "We just chalk the whole business up to bad luck. Back luck happens, boys. And you have to deal with it. Now, today, there was nothing to be gained by getting into an argument. We'd never win that one." He glanced over at Brad to see if he was following the logic. It was hard to tell; the boy kept his eyes on the road ahead. Horace cleared his throat, and continued, " Now, I don't want you upsetting your mother about this. She likes to worry, and it's not necessary. We'll say nothing at all. Understand?"

The boys nodded and grunted agreement. They'd never seen their father like this. He finished as they pulled into their driveway. "We're going to forget the whole thing. Not one word. I mean this now, boys."

He ran the car into the garage while the boys carried the parcels in. Byron said, "What about the wrecked packages?" And Brad told him to keep quiet and take everything upstairs. Nothing was ever said to Eunice or Barbara Ann. The incident passed. Horace took the boys back to Robert Hall a few days later, and within a week of their ill-fated shopping trip, Horace had a new white Caddy. He told Eunice that the old one had been showing its age, and the mileage was creeping up to the point where its trade-in value might suffer.

PRODIGAL

Horace Brant's middle child was always number one. Siblings Barbara Ann and Byron got close-to-equal billing as far as affection and material comforts were concerned, but it was always obvious that their father's fondest hopes resided in Bradley.

That Brad would be an athlete, a scholar, and a doctor, was never in doubt. Horace had begun overseeing Brad's football development from Pop Warner days, through middle school, and up to varsity high school. "Crimy, that boy can't miss, Eun. He's got an arm like Sammy Baugh! You shoulda seen 'im picking Pittston's defense apart!" His mother never liked football, refused to attend his games, and relaxed only when Bradley was home, unhurt, after each practice or game.

"I can't see any point in ten boys piling on top of one boy. Someone's going to get hurt. Or killed. And that's a sport?" Eunice prayed daily for deliverance of her boy from football.

But Brad Brant loved the game and, encouraged by his father, excelled to the point where he was recognized across the state as a can't-miss college prospect.

"What a boy, Eun! He's got grit an' drive. Never quits. I knew he'd show 'em all. What an arm! I knew football was the best way for him to show what he's made of!" Horace could barely contain his enthusiasm when it came to envisaging the future for his children. Barbara Ann would, according to Horace's grand plan, enter pre-meds at Cornell. After his four years of high school Byron would go to the Wilkes Academy for maths and sciences, preparing him for medical school. And Brad, All-State footballer, would now be directing that grit and drive to succeed in a new direction.

"It's Lehigh, Brad. Two years of preparation, and you'll be ready to move right into a first-year program at any college in the country. And you'll do well. I know you will!"

"But no football, Pop? I've gotta play football."

"Brad, this is the time for studies. Time to move on to other great things."

"C'mon, Pop. I could play Level A."

"No doubt about it. But now's the time to start thinking about your future. You want a high-paying career....in medicine."

"But–."

"–That's all, Brad. You'll see, once you get there. You'll need all your energy for your studies."

The argument ended, like all others, with Horace in command. Brad Brant would be, at Lehigh Prep, a student first, foremost, and exclusively. Two attempts at circumventing Horace's plan crashed, predictably. In the first, Brad sought the assistance of his high school coach who he hoped might succeed in convincing Horace to let his son continue playing at the next level.

"Nope, Mac, he's through with football. He'll be preparing now for his career."

"Career, Doctor?"

"Yep. He's got his heart set on being a doctor. And football and medicine just don't mix."

Coach Mackey and Brad weren't beaten–yet. In a last-ditch manoeuver, Mac arranged for Joe DeMarco, head football coach a Lehigh, to call personally at the Brant home. He was talking to Brad and his mother when the doctor arrived home from work. He began his pitch, but was interrupted by Horace.

"I won't be rude, Mr. DeMarco. But I must make it clear. I...we've... chosen Lehigh for its academic program. My son has played his football. He gained state-wide recognition. But he is through with football. He's going to study medicine, and he's going to be a doctor. Thank you for coming, and for your interest. But we've made our decision."

Joe DeMarco had dinner that night with his friend Mac Mackey before returning to Lehigh. Both agreed that a good arm was an awful thing to waste.

Brad's two years at Lehigh were marked by barely-acceptable scholastic standing. Without the stimulus of football, his dedication to studies produced only D-level performance. That he might not become a doctor was never a conceivable factor in Horace's grand plan, but he did admit to concern.

"Well, athletes have a tough time setting academic sights, Eun. But he'll come around. We'll get him into Penn, or Pitt...He'll be fine."

"Mercy." Eunice replied, "as long as he's out of football, I'm happy whatever he does."

Mediocrity in a Brant was troubling, and Horace could not accept the possibility that Brad might not succeed. "He'll come around. He has to. He's gonna make a fine doctor. You'll see."

Brad came around. But not in the manner Horace predicted. In his second

134

year he was approached by Arnold Metzenbaum, owner of the Allentown Arrows, a semi-pro team playing in the Allegheny League. Eight teams from Pennsylvania, New York, and New Jersey formed the league; the players a mixture of washed-up pros, former college players who couldn't make the big league, and some hard-nosed blue-collar mine and factory workers who simply like the legal mayhem in what was known as 'the broken bone circuit'.

"We keep watch on all the football played in the state," Metzenbaum told Brad, "and we knew about you at Myers." This from the owner of a pro team. Brad was hooked. "You can fit right into our program," he continued. "Not much chance of injury. Our offence is run and shoot...you know, pulling guards and a rushing full back. With your arm, you just throw darts and bombs."

Legal niceties were not of paramount concern to Mr. Metzenbaum: Brad's problems were easily solved. Horace Brant need never know of his son's disobedience–a contract for $300 a game had Brad, identified as Mike Bullard, signing on for a seven-game schedule and a provision for up to three post-season games.

Brad could scarcely believe his luck–back in football, and getting paid to play! Inevitably, with games and practices his study schedule suffered, and he passed only three of five courses at Christmas time.

"I know the marks are lousy, Pop. But it's a lot tougher than I expected. You were right. But it'll be different at the end of the second term, you'll see."

The marks were, not surprisingly, nowhere near college-acceptance level, and a third year seemed the only recourse. Brad was secretly happy with the decision.

And Metzenbaum was happy too, offering a new contract calling for another hundred dollars per game. He suggested a deferred payment schedule, with a lump sum payable on completion of the season. "Common procedure, Brad. And safer, too, with the assumed identity. You know..."

Brad knew nothing about contracts.

"Sure, Mr. Metzenbaum, whatever you say. Whatever works." He found himself living on the edge of a strange sensation, a combination of exuberance and panic, with the thrill of the game, the threat of injury, and the dread of his father's discovery of his deceit.

And then he met Len Froebel. More accurately, Froebel met him. The thirty-five year old photographer did contract work for a number of small businesses in eastern Pennsylvania. Mainly, he produced brochures advertising community colleges, housing developments, private schools, and the like. His real interest was sports and he spent most of his time in arenas and on playing fields, taking pictures from sidelines and end zones, getting to know the players. Now and then he'd sell a stop-action picture to one of the local papers. Part of his beat was the Allegheny semi-pro league, although here his interest was minimal: he preferred the younger athletes and was a fixture at most of the high school events. His increased interest in the Arrows coincided with the appearance of quarterback Mike Bullard.

At first, he was taken by the youth of the new player. This was a league of men in their late twenties or thirties, and though the program listed Mike Bullard as twenty-five, Froebel could see that he was still a boy, probably eighteen or nineteen. A closer look and Froebel knew he was looking at a recent all-state high school player.

"Hey Brad. Brad Brant!"

Mr. Metzenbaum had told him to keep his helmet on while on the field or on the sidelines. In the first year, when he'd played sparingly, his anonymity had been maintained. Now, he was a starter and under more scrutiny. And here was a goateed man in turtleneck and tweed jacket, cameras around his neck, calling his name. He turned away. The caller persisted.

"Brad Brant...Myers High School!"

Tommy Duggan, one of the assistant coaches moved toward the man and Brad turned again to the passing drill. At the end of practice, Duggan took him aside.

"That guy wants to talk to you. He knows who you are."

"Who is he?"

"Name's Froebel. Lennie Froebel. A photographer. Sports nut...kinda wacko, if y' know what I mean. But he knows who you are. I can get rid of him..."

Froebel was waiting outside the clubhouse. "Brad....Len Froebel. Glad to meet you. I saw you at Myers...saw all your games, couple of years ago. Great arm....So, where did you go after Myers?"

"I'm at Lehigh Prep."

"And playin' here in Allentown. What's with the name change?"

Initially reluctant to give out much personal information, Brad felt an inexplicable trust and rapport. Perhaps it was the casual ease of the man as he remarked, "I always thought you belonged out there. Great poise. Most high school players are still developing. You had it all from the start." Perhaps it was the silver Porsche with the soft jazz drifting lightly through the open window. Some of the other players were filing out of the clubhouse, heading for their cars. They cast curious glances at Brad and Froebel as they passed.

"Uh, Mr. Froebel, could we talk somewhere else. These guys don't know about...uh....the name change."

"Sure, hop in. Where do you want to go? My place isn't too far from
136

here." And then, sensing Brad's unease, he said, "or how about the Lucky Strike? That's just a couple of blocks."

The car was unlike anything Brad had ever been in, low and snug and dark inside, smelling of leather. And when Froebel hit the gas, Brad entered a new world as the sudden smooth acceleration pinned him to the seat.

In a booth at the Lucky Strike, Froebel managed, by means that Brad could not have analyzed, to win the young man's full confidence. He exuded concern, interest, and empathy. For an hour, Brad told him, in full detail, the story of his nineteen years of life, in Wilkes-Barre, up Bear Mountain, on the playing fields, and in his less-than-distinguished academic setting at Lehigh Prep. It did not occur to him that Froebel had not yet told him the reason for their meeting, why he had been sought out by this worldly bon vivant. When the diner began to fill, Froebel suggested they move on to his apartment. He had a place in Woodlawn, he said. He'd fix them something to eat there, and he'd drive Brad back to Lehigh. The clincher came when, as they left the diner, he threw Brad the keys to the Porsche.

The apartment was captivating, a warm world of dark oak and brass accents, black leather, glass, crystal, and soft beige pile carpeting. An enormous Hi-Fi system, flanked by shelves filled with Froebel's picture albums, dominated one wall. The opposite side of the room was taken up with a mirror-backed liqueur cabinet. Modern jazz purred from speakers the size of washing machines.

"Sit here, Champ." Froebel pointed to the black leather couch. "I'll throw a salad together, put on a couple of steaks, an' then I want to show you some pictures."

An hour later he and Brad sat together on the couch and Froebel opened one of the picture albums, this one marked Football-High School. Brad was surprised to come across a picture taken during his final game at Myers. It showed Brad straight arming a tackler.

"Good shot, isn't it. One of the best zoom lenses you can buy." And he leaned forward and almost imperceptibly in toward Brad, pointing to features of the snapshots, carelessly draping his other arm around Brad's shoulder. The sensation that flashed through Brad's consciousness was new, a mixture of surprise, embarrassment, and discomfort. Then his host was again leaning back on the sofa and the moment had passed.

Another new thing to Brad was bourbon. Len had several different labels among his amazing array of whiskies, and on this occasion he recommended Maker's Mark. "Just sip it...let it roll gently on your tongue. That's it. Some like it straight, for the taste. I think you should start with some ice."

Brad agreed. It was warm and smooth. At ten, or eleven, he couldn't remember which, Len suggested it might be time for a quarterback with a game upcoming to get to bed, and he took Brad's third, or fourth–again, he couldn't remember precisely–whiskey from him and said he'd drive him home.

"C' mon, Champ," he said, with a steadying arm around the tipsy young man's waist, "time to hit the road. Easy does it now." And he held him upright as they made their way out to the car.

As he let himself into his room and prepared clumsily for bed, Brad's senses were tumbling and confused. But one fairly coherent thought did succeed in forming: he'd never known anyone like Len Froebel and he wanted to spend more time in the company of this worldly person.

Three weeks later, with five games remaining and the Arrows in position for a playoff spot, Len took Brad to the Mannheim Auto Auction. He told Brad to bring his check book. "You never know, Champ. Y' might see something worthwhile. You've got what, four or five grand now?"

The football money was good, Brad thought, and with the allowance from his father and few expenses, he was accumulating what to him was a small fortune. Halfway through his second season with the Arrows, he'd banked close to four thousand dollars.

The 'something worthwhile' turned out to be a four-year old Jaguar XK at $7,500. Len had pushed the only-partly reluctant Brad into the purchase. "It's a rock solid deal, Champ. Only 22,000 miles, it's as good as new. And not a mark on it....."

"Len....I've got four grand."

"Hell, Champ, I'll lend you $3,500. No problemo!"

And it really was as simple as that. One nagging thought, but like the football, Brad knew he could deal with it.

"If Pop finds out about the football before I get outta Lehigh, I'm a dead man anyway. A car shouldn't make that much difference. I hope."

His plan was to explain the football after his successful completion of studies. Horace would have to admit he'd been wrong, and that the old Brant grit and determination had, indeed, carried the day. And buying a car with his football money would be quite acceptable to a relieved and admiring father.

Len was now a major factor in Brad's life, a friend, guide, and mentor. Time which should have been devoted to study was spent more and more in Froebel's apartment. The age difference never crossed Brad's mind, other than to impress upon him his great fortune in having this worldly-wise man who could advise and encourage him while he was so far from home and fatherly influence.

On a Saturday in November in Binghampton, Brad called a reverse and before he could make the pivot he learned what Allegheny football really

138

meant. Blind sided, carried off the field with a blown knee, and as he lay on the sideline waiting for transportation, he knew his fate was sealed. Football was finished. His father would have to be told of the injury, and Brad could only guess the extent of Horace's fury. Then there was the abysmal scholastic record. Work and assignments neglected, and Christmas exams looming. And finally, a nearly new car, half paid for, with $3,500 owing.

Len picked him up at the hospital and brought him back to Woodlawn. Just getting into the Porsche had been a painful adventure. Tommy Duggan was waiting outside Lennie's apartment.

"Hey, Kid," he said, handing Brad an envelope. "Some bad news, on top of the knee, I'm afraid."

"What's this, Tommy?"

"Listen, Kid. This isn't really part of my job, but I like you, an' I said I'd do it. This here's your pay, but you're gonna be disappointed."

"How come? What's up, Tommy?"

"Look, Metzenbaum's a lawyer, Kid, an' he knows all the tricks. You're gettin' pay for the games you played. That's all. Your season's over, an'....."

"What does that mean?"

"It's in the contract, Kid. Some contract! Y' ask me, it stinks. But that's Metzenbaum. An' you signed for deferred pay. But that's for a whole season. Six games in, an' you're done. He screwed you, Kid." He gave Brad a fatherly pat on the shoulder and headed down the walkway to his car.

"What are we gonna do, Lennie? It's a lousy twelve hundred bucks. Is there something we can do?"

"I dunno. It doesn't look good, Champ. Unethical...immoral, but probably legal." Len poured two stiff drinks. "Metzenbaum knows the law. And he got you under-age. The league's for guys over twenty."

"Geez, Lennie. There's gotta be something."

"Yeah, but what. And how? Are you gonna sue him? He's a lawyer. And who's Mike Bullard? See what I mean?"

"I've gotta have that money, Lennie, or I'm screwed. What am I gonna do?" His voice cracked with fear and desperation.

"C' mon, Brad, it could be worse. Put your head back. Relax for a while." He shifted over to the couch where Brad sat, leg extended on a hassock, head back and one arm thrown over his eyes. "It's gonna be okay, Champ." And he patted Brad's good knee.

Brad's eyes popped open. The room was suddenly too hot, the music too low, his friend and counselor too close.

"Uh, I dunno, Len." He tried to shift away, but he was at the end of the sofa. "How could it be any worse? My dad, the whole football mess, and

139

the car. And the money...."

Len put his hand again on Brad's knee and rubbed gently. "Listen to me, Brad. There's nothing here we can't set straight. Believe me, we can work it out."

Brad wanted desperately to get up and walk around. But he was trapped, pinned like a bug. "Uh, Len....." He tried to manoeuver his leg away from Len's touch. "The money...What about the money? I don't have the money, and I don't know how I can ask my father...."

"That's okay, Champ. That's no problem. I can wait." And he placed his hand on Brad's thigh.

"C' mon, Lennie. C' mon! Don't!" He grabbed Len's hand to remove it from his leg. Lennie leaned in closer, and spoke reassuringly into Brad's ear.

"That's a lot of money, Champ. Thirty-five hundred bucks. Y' know, we can work out a real good way to make that payback. Just–."

"Get off me, Len! Get off this couch! Get away from me!" He shrugged away from the contact and struggled to get to his feet.

"Don't do something you'll regret, Champ."

"Gimme my crutches!"

"Think about this, Champ. Don't do something stupid. Stop and think."

"Gimme my goddam crutches!"

"What are you gonna do? Where are you gonna go?"

"I'm outta here. I'm not stayin' here. I'm goin' back to the school."

"That's a big mistake, Brad."

"Yeah? You made the mistake, Pal!"

"You owe me money, Champ. And I mean real money. Thirty-five hundred bucks. And I want my money!"

Brad called a cab from the lobby.

The call to home came just after breakfast on a Friday morning catching Horace on his way out the door.

"Emergency? What kind of emergency?"

Brad rushed his answer. "I'm in a jam, Pop, an' I need your help. I have to see you."

"Brad, what's this all about? Are you hurt? No? Sounds like you're hurt."

Brad drew a long breath. "Pop, I'm in trouble. I got myself in a real mess. I've gotta see you."

"All right. I can be there tonight,. I've got two operations today. I'll be there by eight or nine." He hung up abruptly, and to Eunice's look of puzzlement and concern, he said, "What's next? He's not hurt....but he has to see me. Crimy! As if I didn't have enough to worry about!"

"Should I come with you?"

140

"No. I'll go alone. I won't be staying."

Horace sat stony and silent as his son began. The cast had been the first shock. Brad had decided the best route was the direct one, complete with specifics. But he saw the progressive nature of his father's alarm and anger, and his resolve faded as the tale unfolded.

"You are here for one purpose. To study. To prepare for college. To prepare for the rest of your life."

"Yes, Pop."

"And you knew what I said about football. No football. Period. And you defied me. After what I went through to get you in here. You went against my direct stated order!"

Each utterance compounded Brad's misery. "Now you've wrecked your knee. And it wasn't even college football."

"Uh,...there's more, Pop."

Horace snorted. "There's always is, with lying. Well, what is it?"

"Oh, God–."

"–And never mind the blasphemy....God's not going to help you here!"

If only it could be over now, with that mixture of disappointment, scorn, and anger in his father's face and voice. But he'd summoned Horace for full absolution, and they were just getting started. If there was any measure of parental love in his father's tone, he could not detect it, and he despaired of finding it again.

"Uh...I've missed some of my classes this term, and –." Horace rose and went to the window, shutting his son out of his sight and looking, unseeing, out on the darkened campus. Brad continued, "And I've met this guy, he's a photographer, and –." He saw his father's hands, clasped behind his back, clinch visibly and viciously. "He said I –."

Horace turned and fixed his son with a glance of pure cold venom. "For the love of Christ! I don't care if you met God himself! You have defied me! You have lied and deceived me and your mother. You've wasted two years of your life, at my expense. Considerable expense. You've done what we had agreed you would not do. You risked permanent injury. And you've failed. Miserably! I can barely look on you as a son of mine!"

"But, Pop, I'm –."

"I'm not through! So listen. Your classes, and tests-."

"–Pop, I need money." There, it was out.

Horace suddenly sat down on the bed as though he'd been kicked in the back of the knees. "Money? What do you mean, money?"

"I bought a car, and –."

"A car?! What do you mean, you bought a car?! You don't need a car!"

"I bought a car when I was playing an' I had money, an' I thought I could do both things, you know, school an' football, an' –."

"How much?"

"What?"

"How much did you pay for a car which I knew nothing about, playing football which I had expressly forbidden, when you were sent here, by me, to learn how to become a worthwhile person?!" He drove the words like nails.

"It's a used car, an –."

"How much?"

"Seven thousand dollars."

"Seven thousand!" Horace exploded. "You had seven thousand for a car!? What kind of used car costs seven thousand dollars?! You had seven thousand?!"

"Uh...not exactly. I ....put some down an' I owe the rest. I coulda paid, but I lost the football job, an' I've gotta pay the rest, an' –."

"Hold it! Hold! You bought a car. God knows why. And God knows what used car is worth seven thousand dollars. And you still owe money. Give me this again. Clearly."

"A friend lent me the money."

"What friend?"

"An' I was gonna pay him back. An' now I've got no money, an' –."

"Brad, what in heaven's name have you done?!"

The tears came then. Horace was not moved. "Never mind the sniveling. Give me the whole story. Everything."

"Pop...please. I wasn't trying to hurt you. Or mom. I thought I could do it an' that you'd be proud–."

"Proud?! Proud of a son who lies to me. How could you think I'd be proud of that?"

"It was wrong. I'm sorry."

"Yeah. Well, get on with it. The money. You had money from football. But not enough for this seven thousand dollar car. Where'd the money come from, the rest of the money?"

Horace took a brown leather-bound notebook from his jacket pocket. "Give me this again. Name, address, exact amount owing. And where is this wonderful....what is it...a Rolls Royce?"

The notebook was a frightening touch.

"It's a Jag. It's at Lennie's place. What are you gonna do, Pop?"

"I'm going to bring some sanity and control into your life, since you've shown yourself quite incapable of it. Okay, let's have the details....."

Horace left shortly thereafter, leaving Brad chastened and relieved. He was to expect a call from his father next morning.

The phone rang at 10:07. Brad had been awake for hours. Horace wasted no time. "Get your car. Today. Bring it up to Wilkes-Barre this afternoon. The debt has been taken care of. I'll be expecting you here later today." He hung up.

With a mixture of trepidation and elation Brad drove that late afternoon to Wilkes-Barre. Byron and Eunice were at the mountain house when he got to the city. Horace did nothing to make his son comfortable, ushering him into the office where he received and counseled patients.

"Sit or stand....suit yourself," he said without ceremony as he lowered himself into the swivel chair behind the cluttered desk. There was a human skeleton on a rod in one corner beside a huge flip chart of anatomical diagrams. A grandfather clock stood against a paneled wall, beside a glass-fronted bookcase. Brad chose to stand: he hoped to minimize eye contact.

Horace waited while the clock chimed off the hour. Brad thought briefly that he'd never seen his father look so old. And then Horace began. "This house is owned and paid for. With furnishings, it's probably worth four hundred thousand." He'd caught his son off guard. "My car, while it's not a Jaguar, is worth about six thousand. It's paid for. I have personal savings, cash on hand, of three hundred and forty-three thousand. There's no money in any bank, but Eli Mansour is aware of another four hundred thousand that I have invested."

Brad had no idea where his was going; vaguely he imagined it must be preamble to a lecture on money management. His father continued, "The property up the mountain is worth....oh.....at least two or three million."

He paused, and toyed briefly with the pointer he used to illustrate anatomical features. "Did you have any idea of these values? And do you have any idea why I'm telling you these things?"

"No, Pop." And it was the truth.

"I'll tell you. And I want you to understand very clearly. Let there be no misunderstanding. If it's not clear to you, tell me, and I'll explain it again. I am fully prepared to write you out of any inheritance that you might have thought was coming to you."

Brad found breathing suddenly difficult; he sat down on one of the two patient chairs in front of his father's desk. Horace continued in a voice devoid of emotion; he might have been counseling the skeleton. "If you persist in any football schemes, now or in the future, you will be written out of my will. If you attempt to see Mr. Len Froebel again, at his home, in your dorm, or God forbid anywhere on property of mine, you will be written out. These are two simple and very clear conditions. Do you understand them?

"Yes, Pop. But what about the loan?"

"It's been repaid. And he has been informed that you are a medical student too busy for any further social contact with him."

"Okay, Pop."

"I've made inquiries about your photographer friend. I won't go into specifics, but I will tell you that you made a most unfortunate choice of friend. Most unfortunate. This man has a past that does not bear too close scrutiny. You'll not be seeing him again. He has his money. Is this understood?"

"Yes."

"You may or may not succeed in your medical pursuits. But at least you'll be making the effort now unimpeded by unsavory social associations or attempts to play a game where risk of serious injury is a constant factor. You'll return to the school. You'll leave your car up the mountain. You'll make an honest attempt at this one thing, your schooling, and in so doing you'll maintain your status in this family. If you fail to follow my order in this, you're out. Am I understood in this? I mean every word."

Brad made the return trip to Lehigh by bus on Sunday afternoon. His sleep that night was the first unbroken rest he'd had in two years.

DAVID

Monica Ebbs was a single mother. Her husband, a type-setter working for the Philadelphia Inquirer, had long since tired of her wearisome whining and their cretinous son's malevolence. Years ago, having already suffered through ten years that felt like twenty in her mean and strident presence and that of their monstrous child, he'd walked out of a life that threatened his sanity on a daily basis. He left her with a nine-year-old, who gave every promise of becoming even more insufferable than his neurotic mother. He'd tried, God knew, tried valiantly to love both wife and child, but neither proved worth the effort.

Monica's character had been molded from an early age by her older cousin, Carlene McGonigle. For twelve years the two girls had lived on the same street in Wilkes-Barre, Pennsylvania, before Carlene married a Texas roustabout and moved to Abilene in 1947. In those growing-up years, when both girls found themselves largely free of any kind of parental love and guidance, the older Carlene was able to pass on a mean-spirited disposition to the impressionable younger Monica. The result was a young woman who seemed to know only gloom and disappointment and expected nothing good or positive from life.

"Men are monsters," her cousin had taught her. "Don't get fooled by them. They're all the same. If you ever do get married, you've gotta be the boss from the get go."

That Monica married at all was more testament to her skill at dissembling than to anything attractive or pleasant in her make-up.

Early on, Ralph and Monica had liked each other. Very early on. Despite her cousin's tutelage and influence, Monica had entered marriage with a hopeful mind. He was a decent man, industrious and unfailingly honest. Monica was his first girlfriend; he never felt that he'd been deceived, and he settled easily into married life. His greatest hope, then, had been built around the idea of family happy times with a nice good wife and two children, a girl to adore, who would adore him in return, and a boy whom he could teach to fish and play ball and built campfires. The Norman Rockwell dream. It never materialized.

145

Monica lost interest and grew distant during the honeymoon. On their third night in Niagara Falls, she told him she needed cigarettes.

"It's almost midnight, Hon. Where do I get them at this hour?" And then he made the mistake of suggesting she quit anyway.

"Oh, fer Chrissake!" She snarled at him, "you're gettin' what you want. An' when I ask fer somethin', what do I get–nothin'. Well, it'll be nuthin' fer you, y' cheapskate!"

Inauspicious, but not insurmountable. They weathered the first tumultuous months, and the marriage settled into a routine of give-and-take: Ralph gave and Monica took. Ralph was hopeful that the arrival of their first child would soften the hard edges.

David was born squawking at half-past midnight. Monica sweated, twisted, and swore through twenty hours of labour, and when the eleven pound load finally emerged, she lapsed into grim resentful petulance that bordered on disavowal. At first she refused even to look on the child, let alone cuddle him to her breast.

The baby cried a lot, but Ralph assumed the ceaseless howling was part of a normal pattern. But as the months passed, the child's disposition worsened, and by the time he was old enough to manifest anything like a personality, his father was beginning to doubt good times would ever come.

He played in his own excrement, and his parents were unable to find any preventive measures, short of tying his arms to his side. The stink permeated their tiny apartment. His father might have been able to overcome this tribulation if he'd had any help or support from Monica. Her reaction was, from the first instance, a shriek of disgust, a slap to the child's head, and a direction to her husband to "clean up this little Christer...." And the cleaning up had been Ralph's responsibility from that day on as his son progressed from infant scatology to more sophisticated levels of despoilment and destruction.

It's unlikely David would have picked up on the strange sense of unease and foreboding that overcame those few visitors who looked down upon the creature with the outsized head and baleful stare. Such powers in a baby would go a long way in explaining the outlook he manifested growing up. His initial grotesqueness only increased through his first four or five years. In earlier times he'd have been regarded as a troll or cretin, rejected by society, maybe even abandoned by family.

His mother's miserable disposition became her chief trait from the day he was born. His father tried to see beyond the boy's physical blemishes, tried to forge a normal father-son bond. But his hours of play, of reading, of encouraging, trying to love the miserable wretch, produced nothing better than a whiney, loathsome slug who seemed incapable of happiness.

146

By the time he was talking, David's inclinations were clear. When his father brought home a Lincoln Log set, he promptly took a hammer and smashed it to splinters, proclaiming it "a geezly piece a' junk." His father got him a four-month-old spaniel. It went back after two days in the house with David; his treatment of the unfortunate pup went beyond torment. He pulled its ears, hit it with a steel ruler, jabbed it with scissors, and tried to set it on fire with his mother's lighter. Removal of the pup bothered him not at all: he "never wanted the geezly thing in the first place."

Playmates fared no better: he used his size to terrorize the younger kids in the neighborhood, appropriating their toys and taking delight in their tears. Play-visits to the Ebbs house were once-only experiences and on the few occasions that Monica ventured forth with her bad seed to visit neighbors, she found curtains drawn and her knock unanswered.

By age six David Ebbs was a legend in the Roundhouse Flats area of Philadelphia, feared and avoided. He seemed happy only when he could cause someone else's distress and misery. Ralph continued to try to find normalcy for the boy. Nothing worked. Baseball meant bat-throwing tantrums and nose-picking in the outfield. He was too big to play football in his age group. By his ninth year he had just about convinced his father that all attempts were futile. But Ralph continued to hope that one day the surly child would respond to the love his father piled on him, so out of proportion to his deserving.

It was the fishing rod that did it, that and the album. All his life, Ralph Ebbs had loved fishing. His grandfather, an avid angler, had introduced him to it, and Ralph and his father had spent countless pleasant hours together in this wonderful pastime. His prized possession was a very expensive Orvis rod which he kept in his den in a fine leather case lined with green felt. He dreamed fondly of one day passing the rod on to his deserving and appreciative son. In addition, he had a leather-bound album of pictures commemorating happy times, fishing experiences involving himself, his father, and his grandfather. The rod and album represented the truly happy times in his life, times that predated his marriage and fatherhood.

He would take David fishing. That would be the key to unlocking David's positive disposition. However, the boy's interest was piqued only when he first saw the hooks and began speculating on hurtful ways to use them. He threw his new Daiwa rod into the lake, and spent the next twenty minutes throwing rocks into the water near his father's line. This ended when the exasperated father dragged him kicking and cursing back to the car for the howling trip home. They went once more, at the end of the summer, with virtually the same outcome. Ralph was just about at the end of his rope.

"Ah, leave 'im be, the little bugger," Monica advised. "You should know by now...nuthin's gonna work with th' little Christer. I'd be damned before I'd do anythin' for 'im."

David overheard, and her words inspired him to further malevolence. The next day, with Ralph at work and Monica dozing through a gin-soaked afternoon, he took the album and the Orvis rod from the den closet. The book he set alight in the sand-box. The rod he smashed into splintery pieces, flailing it against the maple in the back corner of the yard. He didn't try to hide his destruction. The remains of the album smouldered through the rest of the afternoon–leather does not burn easily–and when his father went to investigate the lazy curl of smoke he found pieces of the Orvis rod scattered around the yard.

Ralph was heartbroken, of course, distraught and furious, all in one. It may have been the lack of remorse more than the act itself that motivated the shattered man. The wonton destruction, the blank indifference to his anger and hurt, and the lack of concern shown by Monica all pointed to the only solution guaranteed to save his sanity–he had to get out. Monica eased the pain of parting.

"Oh, go, for Chrissake. A lotta good y' do around here anyways. Good riddance!"

If she'd been thinking on her feet, she might have added that he take the boy with him. Not that David's father would have entertained the thought; he'd spent nearly ten years trying, entirely on his own, to understand, love, and encourage a child incapable of anything like love. He left them both, taking only the clothes on his back and a picture of him and Monica in happier times, before David's birth.

Monica got a job in a bowling alley. It enabled her to absent herself from David for hours at a time. He did pretty well what he wanted to do, attending school or not, as the mood struck him. The truant officer and Monica saw each other more frequently than either wished. David and his mother co-existed in a state of mutual disinterest, sharing a hatred for a world that owed them something and people who seemed happier than they. This included everyone they knew, saw, or heard about.

His bullying continued, with David looming over hapless schoolmates, always smaller, who tried their best to steer clear of the cretinous brute. The most serious instance occurred when, at age eleven, he assaulted two younger girls playing hopscotch in the school yard. It was late on a Friday afternoon in a darkening and deserted play area.

"Git over here, you two. Right now! Git over here!" He grabbed one of the girls by the hair and shoved the other one before him further into the

148

back corner of the yard where a huge maple hung over the school equipment shed. "Now, you bitches, you take yer clothes off. Do it! Do it, or I'll smash yer faces! Take yer clothes off. Lemme see......"

Petrified, the girls could neither move, nor speak. He yanked on a fistful of hair, and his captive shrieked. It was enough to jolt her companion into action. She bolted by her friend, pushing David as she wheeled around the tree and dashed through the adjacent back yard. Her flight, and the frantic screams of the girl still in his grasp, unnerved David. He gave his captive a vicious shove, kicked at her as she fell, and ran across the school yard and through back yards to his home.

He was in his room when Monica answered the door that evening to a policeman and two men from the neighborhood.

"I want to speak to your son, Mrs. Ebbs," the officer said.

"Why? What's he done" I told them I'd pay for those windows...."

"It's a lot more serious than broken windows, Mrs. Ebbs."

"A hell of a lot more serious," one of the men said, stepping forward. "This time that boy of yours is in real trouble."

The officer waved the man back. "Two girls were assaulted by your son this afternoon. In the school yard. Where is your son, Mrs. Ebbs?"

Monica trembled, ashed-faced, struggling to find voice. Her belligerence drained, she turned and hollered, "David, git down here! Now!"

David Ebbs was, at age twelve, placed on two years probation, under the supervision of his mother. He was prohibited from frequenting any of the play areas where neighborhood children would congregate. He was transferred to another public school for the remaining year of his elementary education. And until his fourteenth birthday he was to be in his home every evening under his mother's eye and control.

He entered Jefferson High at age fourteen, and for his first two years there he was himself a victim of the bullying he'd meted out through his public school years. He hated all classmates, all teachers, equally. He learned to toady up to the teachers who wanted that; he faded to complete obscurity in the classes of instructors who had no time for his repulsive servility. He neither had nor wanted friends.

In his last two years at Jefferson, his size afforded sufficient protection from the seniors who might have picked on him for his maladroitness and peculiar ways. They ignored him. And he, not surprisingly, took his delight in tormenting the hapless junior students who crossed his path.

The orientation week in September, when incoming students were forced into absurd initiation rituals, gave him his greatest pleasure. Then he could inflict misery and sometimes real physical hurt under the aegis of the school

149

administration which permitted these shameful rites of introduction. More than one youngster has had his welcome to high school turned into a hellish event by the loathsome creatures who crawl out to inflict pain upon defenseless victims, all under the guise of good clean fun. And in this indefensible practice, none was more loathsome than the odious David Ebbs. His favorite was to force some helpless wretch to push a penny down the hall with his nose. If the child failed to show proper respect as he was performing this act, David would, after checking to see that no staff or other seniors were present, encourage better performance with a kick in the rear end. Mercifully, there were enough calls to the school from outraged parents that this particular practice was eliminated from allowable initiation rituals. David didn't mind: he had had his fun with it, and besides, the ceremonies lasted only a week anyway. He preferred maneuvers that left him in safety and obscurity, far from the scene of the action. He really enjoyed squirting ink through the ventilation slits in lockers, when he was sure the halls were empty. He had succeeded in destroying dozens of library books by tearing out pages or defacing them with juvenile graffiti.

In his last year, he seemed to find some direction other than the perverse. In accounting class, especially, he sought to make a name for himself as someone able to debate with the teacher, someone with a quick tongue and keen insights. Of course, he'd been the object of scorn and ridicule over three years, but now he imagined the other students saw him as an admirable fellow. His exchanges with the teacher now became frequent, and, he imagined, a signal of his boredom with both subject and instructor.

"Ah yes, Mr. Billows, that's all quite obvious," he offered, lounging half in, half out of his seat and stroking the ridiculous tuft of vandyke he'd been nurturing for half the term. "But really, Sir, I fail to see its relevance in today's market economy."

Or, "Surely, Mr. Billows, such basic entries should be left to a clerk.... some minor functionary. You know, a bean-counter." He'd thought that one especially witty.

He took a daytime job in a warehouse after obtaining his high school diploma. At night, three times a week, he took courses towards a bachelor's degree. He had discovered direction in life: his sole ambition now was to become a lawyer. He reasoned that a profession that attracted such pejorative attention must surely be the calling for him. Also, he thought, a lawyer could become very wealthy, very fast. And finally, he believed it to be the surest way to get back at a world that had slighted him for far too long.

The two years following his departure from Jefferson did not see any appreciable betterment of David's temperament. He and his mother continued to inhabit a small universe of petty grievance and cynical detachment from the world of common decent folks. His progress toward his law degree would be the sole positive accomplishment he could identify. His mother waited patiently for the day when he would start his practice. Maybe then, she thought, she'd get some degree of compensation for putting up with his miserable self through all these years.

He read a lot, soaking in case histories, statements, rulings. He intended to learn about the workings, applications, and manipulations of the law. The drudgery of his present situation was temporary: he would learn the lingo, the stances, the posturing; he would soar above the dreary stages of apprenticeship. He would know the law and how to use it. In his mind he already had the label on his cape–'master of circumvention'.

A first major step along his chosen career path was his theft of a leather Law faculty jacket, size XXL, from the Rutgers Campus Book Store. He was on his way.

TURNABOUT

In Horace Brant's grand design, wherein physicians and clergymen occupied life's top rung of importance to society, his three children would follow him into careers in medicine. From infancy they were admonished, counselled, and guided towards this goal with its prestige, satisfaction, and remuneration.

As eldest, Barbara Ann was first to embark on the path Horace had chosen for her. Rather than entering her final year at Myers High School, where she had most enjoyed art, music, and literature, she was to change school and courses. He sent her across town to the Wilkes Academy, where Horace sat as a member of the Board, for her two year program, designed to qualify her for pre-meds at Cornell, offering mainly math and science courses, all of which she detested.

"It's the necessary foundation, Barbara Ann. I know you did well at Myers. But those artsy courses....well...Now you'll be getting into the real stuff. And you'll be glad you did, when you're at Cornell."

"But why can't I take some music? And Art? And surely literature is important, Daddy! I can't stand math. I can't do science."

"You can. You will. And you'll see...once you get into it."

"But–."

"–No buts. Time will tell you I'm right. And you'll thank me. When you're a doctor, an..."

"Mom...can't you see I have to take courses I like....courses I can do well in?"

Eunice never did participate in her husband's planning, having realized early on the futility of any such attempts. She could try to ease the tension, but as far as the great plan was concerned, she had no part. "Your father knows best, Barbara Ann. And he loves you. He wants the best for you. Barbara....Barbara....?" And she could not convince her daughter, because her own heart ached at the one-sidedness of Horace's organization of his daughter's life.

All concern and resentment notwithstanding, Barbara Ann entered the

152

private prep school in the Fall of '51. She settled into a fixed routine–off to school, and home to her room. The dinner table conversations, once lively with the three Brant children filling the air with laughter and banter, were now forced and abbreviated. Horace and oldest son Bradley talked football. Eunice, sensing and sharing her daughter's melancholy, went silently through wifely and motherly motions and hoped for better days. Only ten-year old Byron seemed unaffected, oblivious to the pall that had descended over the family. He had a standard line, one which he knew pleased his father, "When I'm a doctor, I'm gonna be rich an' live in a big house, an'..."

By the time mid-term exams rolled around, it was obvious that Barbara Ann was in hopelessly over her head.

"What's going on, Barbara Ann?" Horace demanded. "I know what you're capable of. You're a good worker, a good student. How do you explain this...this mess?!" He held her first report by the tips of his fingers, as if he were handling a turd.

Barbara Ann had nothing to offer. Her marks reflected her spirits, low and dismal.

"I'm telling you. And you know it...this has to stop. I want results. I want you succeeding."

"Daddy....I try, I'm trying. But..."

"Well?"

"It's just not the kind of work I like..."

"What you like!! You may not 'like' chemistry an' trigonometry and physics, but by God, that's what it takes to get into medicine. 'Like'!! Like it or not, that's the path to success. And I want you on that path. This has to change. Do you understand me!?"

Eunice, washing dishes, hung her head and muttered a silent prayer for her daughter's deliverance.

The course Barbara Ann most despised was physics, taught by Carlene McGonigle, a single mother who'd left an abusive husband in Texas and returned in 1950 to her home and a teaching job in Wilkes-Barre. Two nights a week she lectured at Wilkes College' she taught secondary level physics at the Academy each morning. A calamitous marriage had hardened Mrs. McGonigle and soured her in all matters pertaining to men. She was keenly attuned to perceived slights and wounds inflicted by men upon girls and women. If she suspected any form of aggression, control, or abuse, she waded into the affairs and made it her own. She had her antennae up where Barbara Ann Brant was concerned: she suspected an unhealthy reason for the girl's taciturn and gloomy behaviour. Determined to sort out and set straight, she took action. With any luck, she knew, she'd identify some male as cause of the girl's problems.

"Barbara Ann, this is unacceptable. Please see me in my office," she had written across the top of the failing test paper. There had been enough sign in class and during lab sessions, when Barbara Ann had shown intelligence, to convince her that the test effort was an aberration. There had to be some sinister reason for her poor performance. Mrs. McGonigle would get to the bottom of it. At the admin. Office she'd read through Barbara Ann's student record, noting with satisfaction that her assessment had been accurate–the marks from Myers High School were outstanding. Here at the Academy the girl was headed for failure. What was puzzling was her program, with its disproportionate emphasis on math and science courses. Her only good marks were in English literature.

The quiet knock came promptly at one o'clock. Barbara Ann entered and waited for the invitation to sit down.

"Barbara Ann, I've asked you to see me because there's something wrong and I think it can be fixed." She prided herself in what she took to be straight-forward no-nonsense candour. Some, less inclined to generosity, called her a pushy bitch.

"Miss?"

"I've had problems of my own, and I've always found solutions. I can tell when someone else has a problem, and I can help you find a solution to your problem. Or problems."

"I know my work has been pretty bad, Miss....I guess I just don't understand physics..."

"Look, Barbara Ann, I checked on all your work....and on your two years at Myers. You're a bright girl. It's not really a question of understanding. Am I right?"

"Well..."

"You can be honest with me. Is there a problem with a boyfriend? That's often the way it is. A boyfriend can cause all kinds of problems...trouble..."

"No, Miss....."

"Well, then, is it something at home? I don't intend to pry into personal affairs, but I'm convinced there's a reason for your failing grades. You're capable of so much more. I can help if you'll let me."

"Well...I miss my friends..."

Carlene McGonigle had read the student record carefully, and had been struck by the note of a guidance counsellor at Myers who had written, 'Barbara Ann, apparently by choice, lacks social contact with her peers'. She was not going to be put off by this false assertion.

"Friends may or may not be a factor, Barbara Ann. I feel it's something

154

other than friends in your case." She pushed further. "Your father is a very intelligent man. A very successful man....a doctor, I understand. I'm wondering if maybe you're getting pressure at home. From your father, I mean."

She knew she had scored; Barbara Ann's body stiffened, and she was now struggling for composure and unsure how to respond.

"This happens a lot. You're not the only one who's been pushed into a program you don't want. There are–."

"It's not that bad, Miss. I can try harder."

"Yes, you can. But is that what you want? You're the one who should be deciding these things. Believe me, these problems occur all the time, and they can be sorted out. You've simply been put in the wrong program, and it's just a matter of putting you in the right one."

Barbara Ann allowed herself a momentary ray of hope. Maybe Mrs. McGonigle was right. Maybe her father could be persuaded to allow her to choose her own courses...

"Well, I'm not sure..."

"It's not has hard as you think. I just wish I'd been there when you and your father registered. We would have made the proper course selections then." She knew very well that the registration had been done entirely by Dr. Brant, that Barbara Ann had not even been present, but she wanted the girl to acknowledge that as the first step in the process of renouncing her father's domination of her life.

Barbara Ann was distressed, her mind in turmoil. Here was this calm professional educator telling her she could successfully defy her father, while fifteen year's experience of total guidance told her that no such thing was possible.

"What courses would you like to take?" She knew pretty well what the answer would be. This talented girl had no place in a science program. At Myers she had excelled in literature and music studies. It could be/should be, the same at Wilkes. Enough ground work laid; it was time for the girl to make some decisions. And the potential for a confrontation with another bullying male–this time a man of prestige in the community–was an exciting prospect, full compensation, Mrs. McGonigle felt, for her loss of a student.

"Oh, gosh...I'm not sure. My father wants us all to be doctors. Me, and my brothers. I really should be in these courses...math...and science...."

"Barbara An, let me be honest with you. You're letting your father ruin your life. No, wait   wait a minute. Hear me out. You're not going to pass. You're failing physics, algebra, and trigonometry. There's no way you can do what he wants. You've got to change your courses and succeed in what *you* want to study."

"But Daddy will–."

"Do you want me to speak to him? You should be the one...but I can do it if you want."

"Oh...I....I really don't know..."

"You could be taking art, or music, or drama...."

"Well, I do like music, and poetry. And I–."

"There you are! You know, you should see yourself, Barbara Ann. Your whole face lights up when you talk about things you like."

It was all over. Only the details were left to be worked out, and they were frightening, pointing to a showdown. But Carlene McGonigle knew she'd won. And for Barbara Ann, the doctor's daughter, it was a heady moment, unlike any she'd known. Was it really happening? Was it possible to be free, after all? How could she face her father when she knew the only thing he wanted was a medical career for each of his children? But the happiness that flooded over her..she felt strong enough right now. Could she sustain the feeling and the determination until dinner time, five hours from now? And what would her break out, if she did pull it off, do to the brothers who were yet to embark on their paths to medicine? Would they point to her betrayal, and rebel as well?

Carlene saw the radiance fading, and sensed the train of thoughts that threatened to block the girl's defiant act. She struck again.

"It will be difficult, Barbara Ann, but only at first. Just until your father realizes how serious you are in this. You still love and respect him. And you still want to make him proud of you. But he has to let you live your own life. Believe me, when he sees you doing well in your new program, he'll still love you. He'll see that you've done the right thing. It won't take that long."

"But how do I actually tell him? Do I just go in and tell him?"

As much as she might have enjoyed the actual show-down, Carlene knew that she could not be the one to deliver this devastating thunderbolt. It would have to be done through the admin office. The thought of the delicate soft-spoken daughter standing up in defiance, declaring her independence, striking yet another blow for women's emancipation...it was a delicious thought. But, regretfully, the teacher could not be the flagbearer in this particular battle scene, so she gave Barbara Ann the steps to follow.

"The registrar will give you the course-change forms. You fill them out and get your father to sign them. Bring them back to the office. And you can be in your new classes, taking courses you like, by the end of the week. How does that sound?"

"Good...I think...But...oh, I just can't see Daddy going along..."

"He will, Barbara Ann. Just let him get over his anger. Men are like that.

He'll come around. He'll see that it's the right way. The forms will have Dr. Anglin's signature.....she's the registrar. Your father will remember her."

"I just wish–."

"Wishing won't work. This will. Get the forms today. Give them to your father right away. How about dinner time?"

"Oh, I hope so...."

"What about your mother? Will she back you up on this?"

"Well....I think she'd like me to take courses I like..."

"There you go. Good. You'll be glad you did this. And you know, your father will, too, when he sees your getting good high marks. I know I'll lose you from my class, but I'll be keeping an eye on you. I'm glad we had this discussion today, Barbara Ann, and I hope you'll come in again, let me know how things are going...here, and at home." She stood and extended a strong hand to her latest convert. She smiled inwardly, thinking of the futile ranting that would precede Dr. Horace Brant's capitulation.

Horace's response was swift, unequivocal, and irrevocable.

Barbara Ann had barely eaten, fearful and tremulous under the dreadful burden placed upon her.

"Goodness, Barbara Ann, you haven't touched your food. Are you coming down with something? I certainly hope not, with Christmas just two weeks away." Eunice felt her daughter's brow and said to Horace, "This child is not well. I think she's worrying herself sick over all that school work. It never bothered her before she went to Wilkes." It was the closest she ever came to questioning Horace's decision regarding Barbara Ann's schooling.

It was now or never. Her mother had given her the opening, and if she let it pass, she knew she'd never be up to the moment again.

"Uh...it is about school. Daddy, I spoke to a counsellor today, and she said I could pass if I change some of my courses. She sent these forms for you to sign." There, she'd done it.

"What's this all about..." He began to read. It didn't take long to grasp the significance of the material before him. Barbara Ann held her breath and clenched her fists in her lap, bracing herself for the onslaught. She remembered the words of her counsellor, that he'd 'be mad at first, but'–.

"And who is this C. McMonigle?"

"It's McGonigle, Daddy. She's my advisor. And she's my physics teacher. And she–."

Horace's open hand came down on the table with force enough to rattle the cups and saucers. He rose abruptly, knocking his chair over backwards, and strode to the front hall where the phone sat in an alcove under the stairs.

A call to his brother Bert in Philadelphia elicited the name of Hazeldean, a private school in Berwyn, a suburb just west of the city. From his brother also he got the name and number of the principal of Hazeldean. A second call followed immediately thereafter, to this gentleman who assured him that his daughter would be accepted for the second term, and that all that was required was a transcript of her marks from Myers and Wilkes. She could start the winter term on January fifth.

Horace's third call was to Irene Anglin, Registrar of Wilkes Academy.

Carlene McGonigle's three-year-old daughter played on the floor as her mother sat at their kitchen table, staring blankly at the wall in front of her. In her hand she clasped a torn envelope and a sheet of 8 by 11 pink paper, notice of immediate termination of her services at Wilkes Academy. The child had never seen her mother in this state, and nervously approached.

"Mummy...want to play with me?" She was unsure how to deal with a mother so distant and distracted. Normally, Carlene lavished affection and attention on her daughter.

"Not now, Sweetie. I'm busy. You go ahead...you play."

"But we could–."

"Did you hear me?! Not now! Leave me alone!"

Tears welled in the child's eyes, and Carlene was immediately ashamed of her sharpness.

"Come here, Sweetie. It's okay...Mummy's not feeling well. I can't play right now. You go play. I just need a few quiet minutes. Okay?"

For another ten minutes or so, she sat, watching her daughter, re-reading the notice from the registrar, and trying to gain control of her emotions. And then she reached for the phone on the counter at her elbow. She dialed, and heard three rings before a woman answered.

"Monica....it's me, cousin Carlene."

"How are you, Carlene?" Monica Ebbs replied in a tired voice, empty of feeling.

"Good...could be better...oh, you know, getting ready for Christmas an' all."

Monica hadn't heard from her cousin in months. They rarely spoke, having almost nothing in common, other than a shared sour disposition.

"Last I heard, you had two jobs on the go...teaching..."

"Yes. Well, I did. But, uh, I've left the Academy." Carlene was in no mood for full disclosure. "And you, and David: how is that son of yours? He must be....what, seventeen, eighteen by now?"

"He'll be eighteen next March. He's trying to get his high school diploma at night school An' I've got a new job, at a bowling alley near here."

"I've been thinking of both of you," Carlene said. "You live fairly close

158

to Hazeldean, don't you?"

Monica snorted. "That's the fancy-ass private school? Yeah. 'Course, we're on th' wrong side of the tracks, y' know what I mean? Hazeldean.... yeah, it's a mile or so, up Broadview Avenue....why the interest?"

"Oh, I just wondered. The daughter of a friend of mine is going there after Christmas, and I thought maybe David would like to meet her....."

"Carlene! You're not trying to set something up, are you?! I never pictured you as a match-maker!"

"Oh, no. But...you never know. I just thought....well, she'll be living there, away from home, an' I thought she might be lonely, an' maybe it would be nice for her to meet someone like David."

"Well, I dunno. I can tell him....."

"Okay...good to talk to you again, Monica. Say hello to David for me. Oh, by the way, this girl....she's loaded. Her daddy's loaded."

BEST LAID SCHEMES

"A lawyer!! An' part of my family!! God help us....a lawyer." Horace Brant's life was, basically, black and white. He loved his wife and children, his mountain paradise, and stone masonry. Among the objects of his scorn and loathing were welfare, trespassers, communists, bankers, and lawyers.

He was a self-made man who had held down two or three jobs at a time since he was fourteen to put himself through university and then medical school. He'd set up his practice in Wilkes-Barre, and in short order had been made head of thoracic surgery at Wyoming County General, and had purchased, in addition to his large city residence, a thousand acre parcel atop Bear Mountain in the Poconos above Wilkes-Barre. Having pulled himself up and through the Depression years, he had no sympathy for those who owed their existence solely to government handouts. Bankers were not to be trusted under any circumstance. And lawyers, conniving cheats and liars all, were an abomination. And his daughter Barbara Ann was going to marry one!

Her fiancee, David Ebbs, was, to all outward appearance, fairly normal, with two arms and two legs, etc. He had an aversion to exercise, and he seemed unwilling to look anyone in the eye. But those were mere quibbles when Horace learned of his loathsome calling. "A lawyer. A sneaking no good blood-sucking lawyer! Barbara Ann, you might as well tell me you're marryin' an axe-murderer. Or a baby molester. A lawyer!!"

Barbara Ann, though, was in love and immune to her father's antipathy. David Ebbs was her knight, her prince.

The marriage took place on Horace's fifty-first birthday. The bride was radiant. An all- day rain kept the festivities indoors. David's mother was there and her latest boyfriend served, awkwardly, as best man. Barbara Ann's brothers, a few school friends, and the immediate neighbors on either side–a small gathering all of whom seemed unsure how to make merry in the face of Horace's obdurate gloom. He'd had his way in only one aspect of the gloomy affair. "They'll be married at the house here, in the city. I'll not have that insufferable shyster up the mountain."

160

The happy couple went to live in Scranton, where David worked in the firm of Harper, Weltman, and Kilrea. Barbara Ann got a job teaching art and music in an elementary school, and David picked up where he'd left off before marriage, handling bankruptcies and foreclosures and aggressively philandering at every opportunity. Within six months Barbara Ann knew what kind of prince she'd married, but pride and refusal to admit that daddy had been right kept her imprisoned in her own hellish domestic quagmire.

That Barbara Ann knew of his tomcatting concerned him not a whit. He knew he'd got his ticket punched with a simple 'I do' and he was sure of his ultimate reward whether married to or divorced from the daughter of Doctor Horace Brant.

"The old man's an asshole, but he's a rich asshole, and sooner or later I'll be cashin' in." he'd told his mother, Monica. Monica Ebbs had her own particular sour disposition and jaundiced view of life, and she applauded her son's opportunistic plan.

"Well," she said, "make sure it's worth it. Take th' old fool fer all y' kin get."

"Tell y' the truth," David said, "what I'm really hopin' t' get is a chunk a' that mountain property. That's prime land."

"Yeah? Well, you deserve some kinda pay back, married to that horse-faced daughter of his..."

"Yeah, isn't she somethin'? But she's in line for a third of everything the old bastard's got."

Five years after Barbara Ann's wedding, Horace's oldest son Bradley, having finished his internship, started his own practice in Wilkes-Barre, family medicine with hospital privileges at Wyoming General, his father's hospital. Horace's spirits soared. Barbara Ann had become almost a non-factor in their lives, living twenty miles away and married to a man whose very name caused bile and revulsion in the old man. Horace still had hopes for youngest son Byron whose academic path was still in the meandering stage. While impatient for the boy, now in his mid-twenties, to make some firm decision and get on with it, Horace believed in the boy. "He's not Brad," he'd told his wife a hundred times. "Doesn't have the grit nor the drive Brad has. But God willing, he'll get there. One day."

Time passed, and with the passing, Horace showed signs of slowing down. He met more frequently with his old friend Eli Mansour as both men aged and became more philosophical. The two old cronies, as Brad called them, Horace nearing sixty-six and Eli a couple of years older, would sip their Maker's Mark and reflect on life in general and families in particular. On balance, they agreed, they'd fared pretty well.

161

"Your boys," said Eli, as much statement as question, "they enjoy success at this stage." He poured another ounce in each glass.

"Oh, that youngest one of mine...he'll probably get there. At least he seems settled....I was beginning to wonder if he'd ever get himself on track. Says he's decided....radiology. Not my choice, but he thinks that's where the money is..."

"You've given your boys every chance, Doctor. Every opportunity. They will repay your efforts. You'll see. Character will tell. You'll see."

"Bradley's doing well," Horace said, permitting himself a half smile. "He's marrying Douglas Taplin's daughter. Next month. They've bought a house, in Saddlebrook. First girl he ever dated...."

"The Taplins," Eli nodded. "These are good people. Douglas Taplin is a good, honest business man. Your son has done well."

"You're telling me. He's given millions to th' hospital over the years."

Eli knew about Barbara Ann's less-than-ideal marriage. There wasn't much that the scrap man wasn't aware of. But the topic was painful, he knew, and they had discussed it only once, a few years back, when Horace had first learned of Ebb's treatment of his daughter.

"He's worse than I feared, Eli, and God knows I wasn't expecting much. He's the lowest form of life. He's a bully and a coward. Treats Barbara Ann like dirt. And she takes it! Tells me it's all okay, they're working it out..." Horace's voice broke with the pain of telling, and Eli let him unburden himself. "I'd like to kill the slipp'ry son-of-a-bitch. I can't bear to think he'll get any part of anything I own...."

And Eli had said, at the time, "Doctor, this is a problem that can be solved. You need only ask...." He'd left it at that. It was all he'd needed to say. And the years had continued to pass, with Barbara Ann's situation unchanging and Eli's implicit offer always on the table.

With energy and desire fading, Horace went more and more to the mountain where he could still perform simple chores, mixing mortar and setting stones with old Del Buscomb, the ageless handyman. And quite unknown to the doctor and his oldest son, a subtle insidious shift was at work in the marriage of Dr. Brad Brant and his wife Charlotte.

Charlotte Taplin had grown up surrounded by great wealth and privilege, in the home, at the private schools, on the European vacations. While Brad could offer much more than most young wives would know in a lifetime, she felt increasingly limited and confined in her marriage. After five stultifying years, she declared, "I have a degree in sociology. That will get me into law school."

"In heaven's name, why?"

162

"Brad, isn't it obvious? We need more money. You know we need new cars, both of us. And this property....think what some landscaping could do... and a new circular driveway..." It was news to Brad that they were in such straightened means, but once launched, her mission for more money became a passion. "You know," she said, "once I get some money coming in, we could move over to Paddock Heights. The lots are much bigger. Daddy's building over there. Maybe we could get a horse, maybe a few horses. They're five acre lots and...."

A few months later it was, "The Warrentons are going to Portugal for two months. I haven't been to Portugal for years...." And then it was the investments theme. "Abby Drysdale says we could double our money with Rio Norwalk. She said they put half a mil in last week and it's already up eighteen percent."

Brad had thought they were doing pretty well. He'd nearly paid off the cost of equipping his office and examining rooms. The mortgage payments on their Saddlebrook house were manageable, just, but he knew the next few years would see steady betterment of their financial situation. But Charlotte's needs were immediate.

"I'll get a good position. Then we'll be able to start living."

She did get a position, partly through her superior performance in her classes and partly through her father's influence. She signed on with Denny, Cooperman, and Hayes. The job was in the real estate division, and the case load and time commitment were, it seemed, just what she'd wanted. She said to Brad, in her third week on the job, "There's real money to be made here. Finally, I can see some light at the end of the tunnel. We'll soon be able to live like normal people."

Both Charlotte Taplin and David Ebbs had married into the Brant family, and initially, Charlotte had accepted the judgement of the rest of the family, that Ebbs was a low-life philandering opportunist. And from David's point of view, Charlotte was of interest because she was drop-dead gorgeous and came from an immensely wealthy family. That one bears watching, he'd thought the first time he'd seen her, at the wedding of Brad and Charlotte. She'll respond to anything that smells of money, he'd figured, and he'd filed the thought away for possible future use.

He'd discussed Charlotte with his mother, his confidant in most matters pertaining to women, money, and the attainment of each commodity. "Oh, she's got her nose up in the air all right, but the rest of her is put out there for us all to see," he told her, "an' I'm pretty sure that deadass Bradly'll never be able to get her blue blood flowing."

"Mebbe you'll be the one to do it."

"Gimme time, mother dear–gimme time." He enjoyed these times together with Monica. It seemed they were always on the same wave length.

"You'll never guess what the delicious Charlotte is doing now, " he threw out one afternoon as he and his mother shared a Southern Comfort before he headed out to The Hare and Hound. "She's gone back to school. Law school."

Monica guffawed with delight. "Law! Old Horace'll have a coronary yet!"

"We can only hope."

"But why? She's got more money than she can spend. You suppose–."

"–Damn right I suppose. I suppose she's bored witless with that candy ass she's married to. And then, of course, it's the money. Once you've had all the money in the world, you've just gotta keep it coming."

At this point, David was already embarked on his grand scheme, a plan to pay back all the slights he'd suffered in the Brant family, and to enrich himself in the process.

Two years into her new world of work, and making almost as much as her husband, Charlotte was ready for the big move.

"Brad, this house is simply too small. I was talking to Wendy Haime today, and she and Richard have moved to Pocono Heights. They've got over four acres, and a pond, and a coach house. Wendy has a full-time maid, and–."

"–Whoa, Char. I don't want to move. What's wrong with this house anyway? You liked it....before you went to work."

"Oh Brad....it's so confining. I just feel closed in.....cramped. I need space to breathe. Wendy's got a studio, and an exercise room...."

And this was a scene that played out with increasing frequency and urgency as Brad struggled to grow his practice and Charlotte struggled, successfully, to bring in more and more money.

Horace Brant was felled by a massive stroke three months short of his seventy-fifth birthday. He and Eli had spent the afternoon up the mountain drinking bourbon and enjoying the sun on the autumn glory around. Eli's son Frank had driven them up, as he did whenever his father wanted to go anywhere those days. By mid-afternoon Horace had given in to fatigue and asked to leave earlier than they'd intended. He'd said little on the drive down, and once inside the house he'd collapsed on his way to the recliner in the T.V. room. He died around eleven that night.

Three days later, Charlotte Brant took a call that surprised her.

"Charlotte, how are you?" David Ebbs here. I saw you at Horace's funeral. A terrible shock wasn't it...."

"Hello, David. Yes.....a shock."

"Ruling the world of property investments yet, Charlotte?"

164

"Business is good," she said, not yet comfortable with the call.

"Charlotte....I have something here that might be of interest to you. It has to do with a piece of property and, uh, potentially, a lot of money. It would be worth your while to...uh, could we meet, real soon?"

They met at Donneker's, in Ephrata, far enough out that the chances of being recognized were slim.

Charlotte had worn her moss green Geiger jacket with a peach silk blouse and a single strand of pearls. Her golden hair shone in the tinted lights of the bar as she entered the room. Two salesmen at the bar swivelled in unison to watch her pass, and David rose from the small corner table to greet her. She checked his gleaming Bruno Malis and gold Rolex as he pulled out a chair for her.

"Charlotte, you look ravishing!"

"Flattery always works with me, David. How are you?"

"Fine, just fine. I'm glad you could come, Charlotte. I have something that I think could make both of us even finer." He signaled for drinks. "I'm having a martini. What will you have?"

"That would be fine, thank you."

When they'd been served, he began. "Horace's mountain property, and that big city house...a pretty handsome estate, wouldn't you agree?"

Charlotte nodded, non-commitally. "It's not a fortune, David."

"Maybe....maybe not. You probably know city property values, but...," he paused to sip his cocktail, "I have some information that Barbara Ann and Byron and Bradley don't have. Information about the mountain property."

He had her attention. "There's a small group out of Pittsburgh, four guys, very well heeled, who've been buying up potential resort properties....here and in Virginia, mainly. They've met with Abe Harper. They're looking at the thousand acres up Bear Mountain. Abe spoke to me...y' know....because I was so close to Horace." He smiled.

"Where's this going, David? And are you supposed to be discussing this at all?"

"Look, Horace had no idea. I doubt Brad or Byron have, an' I know Barbara Ann doesn't have a clue. About anything. But I'm talking real money here. Last time Horace put a value on that land, he thought maybe a million, or a million four, maybe. He didn't have a clue."

"So?"

"So these Pittsburgh boys see maybe ten times that much. They have some connection with Palmer's group. You know, upscale golf and housing. And at this stage, it's all speculative, and all very secret."

"You're saying–."

165

"Yep. We could be talking twenty mil here, Char. And I'm thinking there could be some way you and I are the ones holding the cards when these big boys come calling."

Charlotte realized that all previous reports had sold David Ebbs short. She saw his appeal. She leaned across the small table and covered his hand with her own. "You know, David, Brad doesn't like you very much."

"Well, that's okay, Char. Brad and I don't have much in common. Except for a real appreciation of beauty." And he placed his other hand over their clasped hands. "I've taken the liberty of reserving one of the upstairs rooms. Maybe we could get into the details...you know...away from prying eyes and all."

It really was as simple as that. On that first tryst, David explained the convoluted process he'd worked out whereby the two of them could become co-owners of the thousand acre parcel.

"Well," she'd breathed, lying back on the rumpled sheets, "I don't know about all the legal fine points. But if you can pull this off, you're a genius. You do have talents, Mr. Ebbs, in many areas."

David smiled contentedly, taking in again the stunning beauty of the body lying beside him. Charlotte stroked his arm. "It seems so simple. I guess that's why it frightens me. And it does depend on two assumptions, doesn't it?"

"I know....the will has to go the way I think it should."

"Yes," she agreed, "that seems pretty solid...pretty easy to predict."

"What's the other assumption?" he asked.

"Well...that you and I can make our, ah, personal relationship work."

"And....," he prompted.

"I'd say, at this point, there's a pretty good chance." And she drew him down again on the rumpled sheets.

The reading of the will shot the grand scheme to pieces. Horace had not made the allotments as David and Charlotte had predicted, and it appeared that they were dead in the water. In the year after his wife had died, Horace had taken another look at the big picture, and had discarded the idea of equal treatment for all three children.

Barbara Ann was to receive most of the cash from her father's investments. Fifty thousand of that very considerable sum he bequeathed to the Wyoming County General Hospital. The city house, valued at just under a million, went to son Byron described in Horace's last words as 'somewhat adrift and uncommitted to life goals'. The real kicker as far as the scheme of David and the pliant Charlotte was concerned, was the decision regarding the coveted

Pocono mountain land. The property would be held under a joint ownership plan, its owners to be Bradley Brant, Byron Brant, and Eli Mansour. Its final disposition to be a matter of agreement among the three owners.

David called Charlotte at work the next day. "This is a total shock,"he said. "I...uh...we didn't...ah...who would have predicted this?"

"Let me call you back," she said. Charlotte had some serious thinking to do. She punched the console and said, 'Lisa, no calls, please. And what do I have, two appointments today? Cancel them, please. No...reschedule them. Some time next week. Thank you." She took a yellow lined pad from a drawer, and picked up a pen. For a long time she sat still, made no move to write, just tried to marshal her thoughts. He was right...it was a shock, and Horace's allotments meant, probably, abandonment of the plans crafted by David. She had to admit to a certain relief, now that it seemed to be a dead issue. She'd had doubts about the practicality of the scheme from the outset, never mind the issues of morality or legality. But now a much larger issue imposed itself in her thinking: if the money was not to be on the table, did she still have any feelings at all for David Ebbs? The answer was stark and simple. No.

So, all she had to do, really, was clear her mind (her conscience did not appear to be a major consideration), and settle back into the role of loving and faithful wife. She'd made no notes. She knew what she had to do, and what she wanted to say. She looked at her watch. Eleven fifteen. That hadn't taken long.

David picked up on the first ring. "Charlotte, thank God. I tried calling you. Listen. I think we–."

"David, wait. Let me talk...."

"Yeah, but listen, we can–."

"No,.....you listen, David. Please. I've given this serious thought, and I've made a decision."

"Whaddya mean, *you've* made a decision?! We're in this together; *we* make decisions."

"David, listen to me. It's over. It won't work. Not the land deal, and not us."

"What! Whaddya mean. What are you tryin' to say?!"

"The plan you had...it can't work. It could never work. And I'm.....I'm staying with Bradley....with my husband."

"But we had, you know.....you said...."

"I said nothing, David. Please, don't make this difficult. I've made up my mind."

"We've gotta meet."

"No. No more meetings. It's over."

"Charlotte. C' mon, you're not thinking this through. We can work on this. This is only a little hitch in the plan–."

"David, we discussed some possibilities. But things have changed. I've changed my mind....that's it. It's over."

"Changed!! The hell you mean?" He willed his voice down and spoke slowly and distinctly, "We had an agreement. A deal, for chrissake. I've got the paperwork started. And besides, there's you 'n me."

"David, listen to me. Think for a minute. We talked. Nothing was ever sure, or finalized. We talked, that's all."

"That's all?! Lemme tell you something, Charlotte. I brought you a deal, you saw it. You agreed to it. It was a hell of a lot more than 'just talk'."

"It's over, David." She had to end this. "I've made up my mind. It's over. It never was. I'm staying with Bradley."

"You cheap slut! You cheap bitch slut! You...who do you think you're jerking around?! You can't do this–."

"I'm going to hang up, David. I've tried to–."

"You back out on this, you bitch, you screw up my plan, Charlotte, you're gonna be sorry. Very sorry!"

"Are you threatening me, David? I suggest you give that careful thought." She considered summoning Lisa to listen in, but decided to let him run his anger down.

"Charlotte," his desperation was evident now, and she relaxed in her chair. "Charlotte...geez....it's a deal. You'n me. We agreed."

"No, David. You assumed. And you rushed into...oh God...who knows what you thought you could pull off. We met, we talked, and nothing was ever agreed. Nothing was ever signed, by me. I'm not interested. I'm happily married, and I'm staying that way, with my husband. Now, if–."

"You're dead, you bitch. I'll ruin you. You and your candy ass...I'll tell Brad everything. I'll tell him how easy it was to get his high class slut wife into the sack! And how you loved it! You dumb bitch, you easy lay. You asked for it. You're dead, Charlotte!"

She eased the phone down. She sat still, idly rearranged some papers on her desk, bringing order to memo pads as she considered the seriousness of his threats. Funny, she thought, it hadn't gone as badly as she'd anticipated. She'd made the break. To be honest, she thought, a future with David Ebbs, whatever the financial rewards, was unthinkable. He really was a classless slug. She had been giddy with the intrigue, with the illicit nature of their coupling. But she knew now that life with Bradley was infinitely preferable to what David Ebbs represented. A few minutes of abuse over the phone
168

seemed a simple price to pay for her decision.

One monumental problem remained. Would David make good on his threat. What to do? How much time did she have? Could she simply deny everything? Would Bradley ever trust her again? Not likely. All she knew for certain was that David must be stopped. And as quickly as that thought materialized–that David must be stopped–she had the answer.

"Lisa, can you get me a number, please? The name is Mansour, here in Wilkes-Barre. I want Eli Mansour. Thanks, Lisa."

Her call had elicited neither shock, surprise, nor cordiality. The old man told Charlotte only that she could come to his office at the square-block scrap yard if she wanted a meeting. He'd said nothing when she explained that she required a service that only he could provide.

She was mildly annoyed when, on entering the office, she found a second, younger, man in the room.

"My son Frank is in charge here now, Mrs. Brant. All my affairs are handled by him. You may feel free to talk to both of us. And be assured, all business discussed in this room is kept in strict confidence." The old man eased himself slowly into the arm chair behind the desk, shifting slowly, seeking the least painful position for his aching lower back and buttocks. The younger man produced a bottle of bourbon and three glasses. He poured three drinks straight.

Charlotte perched on the front edge of the straight-back chair and began. What she'd planned to say came out in halting spasmodic fragments.

"There's this man...he's a lawyer married to my husband's sister. He's not, ah...he's a liar and I think he's dishonest. His name is Ebbs, David Ebbs. He tried to get me to take part in some crooked land deal. He wants to cheat us, me and my husband. And when I wouldn't go along with his crazy plan, he threatened me....he's threatening to tell my husband a bunch of lies about me. You know who my husband is. He's Bradley Brant. You knew his father quite well, I believe...." She was almost out of breath. Eli nodded, and she continued, "And if Ebbs tells Bradley these lies about me, it'll ruin me. He'll ruin our marriage...."

The old man held up a hand to slow her careening discourse. He signaled to his son to pour more whiskey. Charlotte was trembling. She'd been stopped in full flight and she was desperate to resume. Her eyes never left the old man as she took a hurried swallow. The straight bourbon burned its way down and she gasped. When she was able to speak again, she rushed on.

"He says he'll tell Brad we had an agreement, him and me. But it's all lies. There was no agreement. About anything. I assure you. But this morning he said he'd tell my husband I was planning this deal, behind his back, and –."

"You say 'deal', Mrs. Brant. Can you be more specific?"

"It was supposed to be some trick, oh, I don't know. He asked me to meet him, and I went because he said it was a property matter, and that's my work. But then, he said it was some shady way he'd cooked up to get the mountain property that Horace owns....owned...and he was going to get that property somehow. He had some wild plan, and I said it was wrong, and I wasn't the least interested....." She paused to breathe, "It was some crazy plan, and he's going to say I was in on it, or something. Oh God...I don't know what he's going to say. And I'm afraid. Afraid Bradley will think I'd go along with this evil man....."

The two men showed neither surprise nor sympathy, but regarded her with sober disinterest. Surely her plight merited some sign of concern. She paused on the edge of full disclosure. Desperation pushed her over.

"And there's more. He said he'll tell Bradley I was....I mean...that it was more than just some sneaky business deal." She gulped more of the burning liquid. And now she was unable to meet the old man's eyes. She looked down, away. He sees right through me, she thought. "He said he'll tell Bradley we were....intimate. That we slept together. It's a lie!" And in the presence of the two stern-faced men she lost all dignity and control. The words poured forth with the tears she could not control. "Oh God, he's such a dirty rotten liar, Mr. Mansour! A liar who's trying to ruin me. And my husband. If he says these awful things about me...these filthy lies....I don't know what will happen. I don't know what to do. I need your help. Oh God, please, will you help me?"

The younger man sat ramrod straight with his arms crossed. She dared to look at the father as he eased himself forward, taking some of his weight on the arm rests. He could not hide his discomfort. He spoke in a soft voice whose eloquence seemed at contrast with Charlotte's pleading.

"Mrs. Brant. Please. Compose yourself. You are right. Horace Brant was my oldest and dearest friend. We enjoyed a friendship over many years." He raised his tumbler in silent tribute, brought the glass to his lips but did not drink. "Your father-in-law was an educated man, a man of culture. And me, I am a simple man. The fine doctor and the scrap man." He permitted himself a smile. "My daughter lives because of this fine man. Our association, this long, long friendship....I am rambling, I'm afraid, but I want you to see, to understand...the doctor and I shared certain beliefs. Like the doctor, I value family. Above all else. The doctor knew, and I do too, that family is the source of true happiness. When you know this simple truth, Mrs. Brant, you are able to see through shallow people, through lies, through 'shady deals', as you call them...."

170

Charlotte was sure her frailty must be emblazoned on her burning cheeks. She longed to flee. She could not speak, could not disclose any more of her failings to this stern judge. She turned imploringly to the son. His expression had not changed: he was indifferent. She drew a deep shuddering breath and spoke in a whisper.

"I've come to you, Sir, because I am frightened.....terrified. I'm afraid I may lose everything...my husband...my home. My husband told me once that you were the man who...who got things done...who could get things done." She knew she was repeating herself, but she felt as if her mind and tongue were out of sync. "He said his father had told him you could arrange things....." The words were like weights picked up and set awkwardly on the table between them. Miserable, knowing the man was judging and measuring and finding little of worth, she struggled on. "It's true, what Ebbs says. We did talk about getting that piece of land. It was wrong. And I almost went along with it. But in the end, I didn't. I didn't sign anything...and now he says I did agree, and–."

"You signed nothing?"

"No! No! But he'll lie, and–."

"Mrs. Brant. You've come here to ask for my help in disposing of a problem. Let me be as clear as possible. We deal in the truth here. Now. There's nothing signed? No paper?" His eyes were probing and relentless.

She dropped her head into her hands. "There's more. I slept with him. Once. It was when we met to work out the land deal. Just once. And now he says he'll tell my husband, and–."

"Mrs. Brant, I wonder if you'd excuse us for a few moments. Perhaps you could walk out in the yard. Or you might prefer to wait in your car? If it were easier for me, I'd walk outside with my son while we discuss your.... problem. I hope you don't mind."

"No...no...not at all. I understand. I just want to say I really do need your help, gentlemen. And of course, I'm willing to pay..any amount...." She reached down for her purse, but stopped, aware that the mention of payment seemed inappropriate, even dirty. "I'll be happy to wait outside," And she went to wait outside, leaving her fate to the two dark-suited men.

Frank watched her get into her while Continental, and waited for his father to speak.

"This woman, what do you think of her?"

"I do not like her. There are such women....slick. Women like her, they have to look good. It's important to them. They pay a lot to look good. A lot of flash, but nothing else. I do not like her."

"Hmmm...'slick'...that's good." He chuckled mirthlessly at his son's description. "Yes, they know how to look good. But what do they lack? What is missing? I'll tell you. It's character. They have no character. Now, this one. No fool, this one. She and this man, Ebbs, they had a plan, all right. And they might have succeeded with it. They came close. That mountain land is worth a lot of money."

"So, why is she here, seeking our help?"

"The will did not favor her husband as she and Ebbs had anticipated." And Eli told his son about Horace's plans. "She backed the wrong horse, as they say. And now our slick woman has re-discovered her love for her husband. You see what I mean about character?"

"Cut her loose. You owe her nothing."

"I would like to agree. She is not a virtuous woman. But I must tell you...." Again he shifted painfully, seeking relief he could not find. "I cannot simply send her away. You must know why I say this."

"She's trouble, Father. She asks too much. You owe her nothing!"

"I cannot support her actions. They are vile and repugnant. But you must realize, her husband's father was my dear friend. We were like brothers. I know how he felt about his children...I cannot allow this man Ebbs to bring pain into the life of my friend's son."

"But –."

"No....Son, I am sorry, but I must overrule you. I have no stomach for the matter, nor for the woman. But I cannot turn my back on her...on her and her husband. Go. Call her in. Please."

The old man's lower back was afire with pain, and now his legs began to throb. He could find no position to ease the knife thrusts between his shoulder blades. His son ushered Charlotte into the office. She'd wiped away the streaks of teary mascara, run fingers through her hair, and reapplied lipstick. She was almost presentable again.

"Please sit down, Mrs. Brant. I remain seated, you must excuse me. My old bones are troubling me today."

She lowered herself tentatively to the edge of the chair, and the old man continued, "I will not keep you long. You are no doubt in a hurry to get back." He leaned forward. "I must be honest with you. My son and I find grounds to disagree, I regret this. We prefer to be in agreement. Nevertheless, we have discussed your request, and we have come to a decision. Because of your association with my old friend, we will help you." He waved off her response. "Let me finish. We provide this service only because your father-in-law meant so much to me. That is the only justification. I do not lecture you, but you must understand that in helping you, this one time, we do not approve or defend your actions. It was wrong. You were wrong."

172

Charlotte paled, but forced herself to meet the rebuke head on, "You're right, Sir, it was unforgivable. I don't –."

He cut her off. "My son would have let you face the consequences of your actions. But I have prevailed in our discussion. Go home, now, Mrs. Brant. You will have your chance to enjoy this life, with your loving husband. The hindrance you spoke of will be removed. Go home now."

"But, how will –."

"Goodbye, Mrs. Brant. I doubt we'll have the chance to talk again."

Frank showed her to her car, and stood back as she turned and drove out of the yard. He had not spoken to her the whole time. He heard the crash of glass and splintering wood as he mounted the office steps. He rushed through the door to see his father sprawling spasmodically across a broken upturned chair and still in the act of trying to right himself as he crashed face forward, the whiskey bottle spilling its remains from somewhere under his collapsing body. He tried to speak, but no words came from his contorted lips, rather a gurgling retch as his eyes, unseeing, rolled back in his head.

Frantically, when nothing he could do would revive the old man, Frank dialed 9-1-1. The paramedics arrived ten minutes later, and worked on him for another five minutes before loading him into the ambulance to speed him to the Wyoming General. He was pronounced dead at 5:20 p.m. It was just about the time a smiling Charlotte Brant climbed out of her white Continental to join her husband for dinner preparations at their Saddlebrook home. The Haimes were expected at 6:30.

CPSIA information can be obtained at www.ICGtesting.com
Printed in the USA
LVOW102038150812

294335LV00004B/16/P